PRAISE FOR

Pearls and Poison

"Readers are sure to be immersed in this outrageously entertaining and hilarious mystery. This third in the series con-
tinues to highlight sharp dialogue, eccentric characters, and
expand on the mystery that is Walker Boone."
—*Kings River Life Magazine*

"The diverse cast of characters . . . are hilarious and completely endearing. Given the book's (very) Southern setting,
Brown manages to keep things exciting and colorful enough
to please all cozy mystery lovers—and not just those who
can relate to living in the South. The mystery aside (which
is incredibly enjoyable and not easily predictable), the
mounting tension between Reagan and Walker make reading
this charming mystery novel worthwhile. . . . Brown's Consignment Shop series is now my favorite go-to cozy mystery
series."
—*Dreamworld Book Reviews*

"What a fun ride this series is! It will keep you laughing
and cheering for Reagan and her cohorts through the entire
book. Duffy Brown keeps her readers on their toes with so
many twists and turns, your head will spin. The author has
a true flair for writing snappy dialogue and bringing the
reader right into her story . . . Duffy Brown splashes Southern charm and coziness throughout the entire book. Nobody
does it better than she does."
—*Socrates' Book Review*

continued . . .

Killer in Crinolines

"Brown deftly spins the tale of Reagan's many misadventures while sleuthing, fills her story with Southern eccentrics, and offers up a magnolia-laced munificence of Savannah color."
—*Richmond Times-Dispatch*

"A fast-paced cozy with lots of twists and turns. Brown has a knack for writing dialogue, and readers will find themselves so engrossed in the story, it's hard to concentrate on anything else."
—*Debbie's Book Bag*

"Great characters, funny dialogue, twists and turns, and a little romance. What more could you want in a cozy mystery? If Agatha Christie lived in Savannah, she would have written this novel. Charming, clever, and sometimes creepy, a really good read."
—*Sweet Mystery Books*

"So, click martini glasses or frosty bottles or iced-tea cups, and swig back the high times as Reagan and her Auntie TCB in one of the most fun and Southern-flavorful mystery series on the market."
—*Book Reviews by David Marshall James*

"Southern coziness at its finest! A most enjoyable read—mystery fans will love this one. It's the kind of book that makes a bad day good!"
—*Socrates' Book Reviews*

"If you have read *Iced Chiffon*, then you'll absolutely LOVE *Killer in Crinolines*. In fact, if you weren't hooked on the series after reading *Iced Chiffon*, you bet your derriere you'll be hooked after reading this one. Its compelling mystery and engaging plot will have you staying up countless hours into the night . . . If you're a fan of Southern mysteries and just cozy mysteries in general, I HIGHLY recommend checking out this new series by Duffy Brown! You won't regret it, I promise."
—*Dreamworld Book Reviews*

Iced Chiffon

"A Southern comfort cozy with Yankee tension . . . A treat. Not to be missed."

—Annette Blair, *New York Times* bestselling author of *Tulle Death Do Us Part*

"An amazing mystery debut . . . Riveting."

—Mary Kennedy, author of the Talk Radio Mysteries

"A hilarious romp through a consignment shop where customers may end up with more than they bargained for."

—Janet Bolin, author of the Threadville Mysteries

"A delightful world filled with charm and humor."

—*New York Journal of Books*

"This amusing, thoroughly entertaining mystery . . . has perfect accomplices, plenty of suspects, and humorous situations."

—*RT Book Reviews*

"Besides a fabulous look at Savannah, especially the haunts of high society, Duffy Brown provides a lighthearted, jocular amateur sleuth."

—*Gumshoe Review*

"Delightful . . . If I could give it six stars, I would."

—Examiner.com

"A pleasant beginning to a new series . . . A light tone, a quick pace, [and] good old Southern hospitality . . . all come together for a charming read."

—*The Mystery Reader*

"A strong story; fantastic, well-developed characters; and a great mystery . . . *Iced Chiffon* was a stellar read and I can't wait to see where Duffy Brown takes these characters next."

—*Cozy Mystery Book Reviews*

Demise in Denim

DUFFY BROWN

BERKLEY PRIME CRIME, NEW YORK

THE BERKLEY PUBLISHING GROUP
Published by the Penguin Group
Penguin Group (USA) LLC
375 Hudson Street, New York, New York 10014

USA • Canada • UK • Ireland • Australia • New Zealand • India • South Africa • China

penguin.com

A Penguin Random House Company

DEMISE IN DENIM

A Berkley Prime Crime Book / published by arrangement with the author

Berkley Prime Crime Books are published by The Berkley Publishing Group.
BERKLEY® PRIME CRIME and the PRIME CRIME logo are trademarks of
Penguin Group (USA) LLC.

For information, address: The Berkley Publishing Group,
a division of Penguin Group (USA) LLC,
375 Hudson Street, New York, New York 10014.

ISBN: 978-0-425-27470-5

PUBLISHING HISTORY
Berkley Prime Crime mass-market edition / April 2015

PRINTED IN THE UNITED STATES OF AMERICA

10 9 8 7 6 5 4 3 2 1

Cover illustration by Julia Green.
Cover design by Diana Kolsky.
Interior text design by Kristin del Rosario.

Chapter One

THE convertible top was down, a crescent moon hung low over the marshlands, and the night sky was filled with a bazillion stars as I drove Walker Boone's precious red '57 Chevy toward Tybee Post. It was a perfect spring night except that my palms were sweating, my heart was rocketing around in my chest, I shook so bad it was hard to keep the car on the road, and there were one, two, make that four police cars on my bumper, their red and blue lights flashing in my rearview mirror.

Of course I wouldn't be in this fix if Conway Adkins hadn't been found dead in his very own bathtub and Boone hadn't gotten himself accused of the murder. Taking Boone's Chevy and heading off in one direction to get the cops off his tail while he took my new cute-as-a-button pink scooter and escaped in the other direction seemed like a really good idea . . . till now.

Figuring I'd pushed the *surely you can't be after little ol' me* routine as far as I could, I pulled to the side of the road, careful not to drown Boone's car in the swamp and wind up gator food. As the string of cruisers lined up behind me, illuminating the dark like fireworks on the Fourth of July, and traffic slowed to snap iPhone pics that would make me an instant Savannah celebrity of the wrong kind, the gator-food option looked pretty darn good.

"Get out with your hands raised" blared from the cop's bullhorn. Teeth chattering and knees knocking, I finally wrenched the car door open and stood, arms up. Immediately they were handcuffed behind me. Okay, I'd expected this to happen, but the real deal was downright terrifying. *Breathe*, I ordered myself. *Think calm and cool and try not to babble like you always do when scared spitless.*

"You're not Boone," a cop growled as he spun me around. "Where is he?"

A loaded question if ever there was one. I gave Officer Deckard—least that was what his name tag said—the innocent-and-clueless arched-eyebrow expression. "Why now, I have no idea where Walker Boone is and can we make this quick, I got to get home to let my dog out to pee."

Deckard's lips thinned, the little capillaries in his eyes ready to pop. He yanked the collar of Boone's much-too-large-on-me leather jacket and whipped the Atlanta Braves ball cap off my head and tossed it into the cattails. "You know where he is. You wanted us to think you're Walker Boone."

"Me? I run the Prissy Fox consignment shop in Savannah." Was that squeaky voice really mine?

"And I've heard about you. You're a total pain in the ass, always sticking your nose in where it doesn't belong."

"There is that."

Deckard picked me up by the collar, my frightened gaze now level with his really-pissed-off one. "We both know Boone's wanted for murdering Conway Adkins. We have Boone's gun, we know he did the deed, and here you are helping him get away by driving his car and wearing his jacket and hat, and leading us on a wild-goose chase."

"Would I do that?"

That got me the *how'd you like to rot in jail for the rest of your natural life* cop glare. "If you're not helping him, how'd you get the keys to his car?"

"They were in the ignition."

"You stole his car?"

"He took Princess."

"Kidnapping?"

"A scooter. It's new and pink and the helmet smells like cotton candy on the inside, I had to pay extra for that, and that's the truth, the whole truth, and nothing but—" That got me tossed in the back of a cruiser. I think the cotton-candy part pushed Decker over the edge, and twenty minutes later I was sitting across from Detective Aldeen Ross in the Dumpster-green police interrogation room back in Savannah. This night was not improving.

I knew enough not to touch under the table, avoid anything wet on top of the table, and step around slick spots on the floor. The reason I possessed this valuable information was that this was not my first time in the police interrogation room on Habersham Street or my first time meeting up with Ross. Fact is, Aldeen Ross and I were sort of buds depending on which side of the law I happened to be standing on at the moment and whether one of us was willing to share a six-pack of sprinkle doughnuts from Cakery Bakery.

"Boone can't hide forever, you know," Ross said to me in a flat matter-of-fact voice even though the look in her eyes suggested that Boone probably had enough street smarts to hide forever if he wanted to.

"He didn't kill Conway," I said. "He isn't a bullet-between-the-eyes kind of guy. He's an attorney, upholds the law, I doubt if he cheats on his taxes, and there's the little fact that Conway was Boone's daddy. He's not about to kill his own father, for Pete's sake, even if the piece of crud deserved it."

Ross sat back in the chair, her navy poly jacket pulled tight across her pastry-enhanced girth. "The way we see it," she said, "is that Conway the elder walked out on Walker when he was a baby, married money, had nothing to do with Walker all his life even when he was living on the streets, and never claimed him as his own. Conway the elder had nightmares of burning in hell for all eternity for his sins so he told Walker who he was, left him the Old Harbor Inn in his will to make up for being a first-class ass, and then Walker did Conway in before he could change the will back. Plus Walker had thirty-four years of ticked-off under his belt to egg him on. Sounds like motive for murder to me."

"Except you and I both know that Boone doesn't egg, and if he did Conway in no one would ever find the gun or the body, and what about everybody else who hated

Conway? They aren't going to be erecting statues in his honor anytime soon around here."

Ross stood and leaned across the table toward me, her voice low and her brown eyes intense. She put her hand over the little microphone that recorded the conversations in this room. "Keep in mind Boone's got his share of enemies, and they're tickled pink he's on the run, and they'll be even happier once he's rotting behind bars. Somebody framed him, and if they think you're out to rectify the situation you'll be the next one in their crosshairs. The best way to find out what's what is to act like you hate the guy, and that's going to be real tough with that dopey look on your face when you mention his name."

"He kissed me."

"Forget the kiss."

"It curled my toes." I rolled my eyes up. "Singed my brows."

Ross pointed a stiff finger at the door. "A cold shower and a bad memory is your only hope. Now get yourself out of here; I'm late for my midnight doughnut and if you find out where Boone is you better tell me."

"You bet."

"You're lying.

"Only when necessary." I hurried out the door before Ross changed her mind about setting me free. Personally I didn't think there was enough cold water in the Arctic to kill the aftereffects of a Walker Boone kiss, but unless I wanted to go the lobotomy route it was worth a shot.

It was late and I was tired to the bone as I stepped out into the police parking lot. I hated that Boone was on the lam, I really did, but the upside was it gave me some time to think about what that kiss meant. Another upside was that I had myself a car, a really sweet car. No one had reported the Chevy stolen, so the police gave me back the keys and here it was parked right in front of me. It was all nice and red and shiny as if waiting for me to take it home and tuck it into my garage, which had been carless since I'd divorced Hollis the Horrible, who drove off with the Lexus I paid for.

I lovingly stroked the ragtop, unlocked it, and sat behind the wheel, inhaling the scent of fine leather and a hint of residual exhaust that graced sublime vintage cars. I cranked the engine over, listening to the low rumble, feeling the vibrations up my spine and across my neck. I eased the gear into drive, inching forward so as not to hit the cars or either side or nick the Chevy.

Then I put the car in reverse and put the Chevy back to where I found it. That one of the Chevy's fins took out the front light of an old tan pickup parked next to me was testimony to just how little I knew about being the captain of a vintage boat. I killed the engine, got out of the car, and left my contact info on the truck.

Here's the thing: If I drove out of the police station in Boone's car, the reporters hanging around would see it and follow me and ask a bunch of questions about Boone that I didn't want to answer. They'd probably hunt me down later, but if I snuck out of here now that would give me time to figure out what to say. Wouldn't you know it, after two years of schlepping myself on and off buses and hoofing it from one end of this city to the other, I finally get a car to tool around in and I couldn't even use it.

A cruiser pulled into the lot and parked by the rear entrance to the police station. Two uniforms wrestled one of Savannah's drunk and disorderlies from the backseat, and I used the distraction to slip out of view of the reporters, slink across Hall Street, and fade into the shadows. I headed down Habersham, flanked on each side by restaurants and bars closed for the night. It was a darn shame they weren't open, as a Reuben from the Firefly would taste really terrific right now.

I cut across Troup Square, one of the twenty-three parks in Savannah. This one had a doggie fountain where Bruce Willis, my four-legged BFF, loved to socialize with the other canines and— Holy cow! BW! He hadn't had a potty break in hours. I could picture him howling by the door with his back legs crossed. I took off in a run, cut through Whitfield Square with moonlight filtering through the big oaks draped in Spanish moss, and darted around the gazebo that every bride in the city used as a backdrop for wedding pics.

Hanging a left onto Gwinnett, I caught sight of the light in the front display window of the Prissy Fox, my consignment shop on the ground floor of my less-than-pristine Victorian. Someone was sitting on the decomposing front porch steps. Either it was a green alien with round things poking out of its head or it was my Auntie KiKi dolled up in night rollers and face cream.

"Lord have mercy," she said in a stage whisper so as not to disturb the residential quiet around us. "I thought Ross done locked you up and swallowed the key." Auntie KiKi hiccupped and saluted my presence with her martini.

KiKi was my only auntie, my next-door neighbor, and

more often than not my partner in crime solving. She was also the local dance instructor for such things as cotillions, weddings, anniversaries, and coming-out parties of any variety. KiKi was a nondiscriminatory kind of dance teacher.

"What are you doing up at his hour? Uncle Putter's got to be wondering where the heck you are."

KiKi patted BW, who was sprawled out beside her and snoring like a hibernating bear. "Poor thing was cutting up such a ruckus over here with his barking and whining I had to see what the problem was. He peed like a racehorse once I got him out by the bushes. Putter's asleep with his headphones and *Dreaming Your Way to Long Drives and Short Putts* blaring into his brain."

"Martinis?" I looked from KiKi's glass to the silver shaker. "It's after two." I wedged myself between KiKi and BW, and KiKi handed me a glass. "And three olives?"

"Honey, from what I've seen it's a three-olive night." KiKi pulled her iPhone from the pocket of her yellow terry robe that matched her yellow terry slippers. She tapped on the little blue birdie app and pulled up a video with me surrounded by the police and flashing lights, my hands behind my back and getting hauled off toward a cruiser.

KiKi slid the phone back into her pocket. "You need to be keeping yourself up if you're going to be starring in social media like this. Your mamma is a judge, after all, and the Summersides got a family reputation to protect." She took a long drink. "So, I'm thinking this has something to do with Conway deader than a mackerel in his own bathtub with a bullet between his beady little eyes and Walker getting the blame. Twitter knows all."

This time I took a sip of martini, the cool alcohol sliding down my throat and taking the edge off a hair-raising night. "Here's what's going on," I said to catch KiKi up on what happened. "The police found Walker's .38 revolver and it was the same gun used to do in Conway Adkins, who we now know is Boone's daddy. Best I can tell, Detective Ross doesn't think Walker killed Conway, because earlier tonight she called Mamma to let her know what was going on and Mamma called me. Judge Gloria Summerside couldn't very well get involved in this herself now could she, so contacting Boone got passed on to me. Anyway, I showed up on Boone's doorstep to tell him the cops were on their way to arrest him and we came up with the *I take his car and he takes my scooter* plan to give him time to get away."

"Did he kiss you?"

"How'd you know?"

"You say his name and get a dopey look. Got any idea who did in Conway?"

Here's the thing with Auntie KiKi . . . She was family. Getting her involved in dangerous situations was something I really tried to avoid, but I seldom succeeded. Still, I had to try. "Uncle Putter's not going to be happy if you get mixed up in this. It's bound to be risky. He'll have a hissy."

KiKi took a sip of martini and gave me her devil smile. I knew I was going to lose the argument before she opened her mouth. "This is Walker Boone we're talking about. He caught me when I fell off that there fire escape some months back, your own mamma put him through law school, and he showed Putter how to birdie the sixth hole out at Sweet Marsh Country Club, for which my dear husband will be forever grateful. I wouldn't be one bit surprised if Walker Boone was hiding under our bed this very minute with Putter's blessing."

"Uncle Putter would harbor a fugitive?"

"In the name of golf, all things are possible." KiKi winked and poured a refill martini from the shaker. "While keeping BW company and waiting for you to get home, I've been making a list of who could have done in Conway. I didn't know the man all that well, personally, but I got it firsthand that he was into doing the horizontal hula with the marrieds. Maybe a jealous husband did the deed. Then again, there was no love lost between Conway and his other son, Tucker. Tucker got raised in the big house with all the money and private school and the like, but maybe Tucker had enough of Daddy Dear driving him crazy for thirty-something years and pulled the trigger. Best I can tell from the kudzu vine is that Tucker and Conway never got along, and lately things had gotten even worse."

"Murder's a lot of not getting along."

Something crashed inside the house, shattering the night quiet. I jumped, KiKi sloshed her martini, and BW didn't flinch a muscle. KiKi's eyes rounded, the white circles against the green facial goop giving the appearance of a hard-boiled egg in a salad. Sensible women would scream, call 911, grab the martinis and dog, and run like the dickens. Auntie KiKi and I were many things, but I don't remember *sensible* being on the list.

I set my glass beside KiKi's and grabbed Old Yeller, my indestructible yellow pleather purse that had saved my behind on more than one occasion. KiKi snapped up the silver cocktail shaker for either whacking or drinking; with Auntie KiKi it was hard to tell which. We stepped over the sweetest pet but worst watchdog on the planet and opened the door to the entrance hall and once-upon-a-time dining room just beyond.

Moonlight spilled in through the rear windows, silhouetting the racks of dresses to the left; blouses, pants, and jackets to the right; and the table in the center with jewelry and evening purses. I flipped on the switch for the chandelier.

"Who's there?" I called out.

Footsteps skittered across the floor over our heads. I had either a big rodent problem or a break-in. Beady eyes? Whiskers? Skinny tail? Yikes! Truth be told, I was hoping for the break-in. I tore up the steps, with KiKi right behind me. We turned the corner at the top and faced a big guy with alcohol-infused breath and wild-looking bloodshot eyes that I could make out even in the dark. I had a break-in *and* a rodent problem. The guy took a swing at me and missed. KiKi threw the rest of the martini in his face and I added an Old Yeller uppercut to his jaw.

"I give up! I give up!" The guy stumbled back against the wall and slithered down to the floor as I switched on the hall lights.

"Tucker Adkins?" KiKi said as the guy swiped at his eyes. "What in the world are you doing in this here house uninvited? You should be home taking care of your family and your daddy's funeral arrangements."

"What I'm doing is taking care of my daddy's killer." Tucker staggered to his feet. "I'm here looking for Walker Boone. Why else would somebody like me be in a second-hand clothing store?"

DUFFY BROWN

I hadn't seen Conway Adkins very often, but from what I remembered Tucker had his daddy's rounded chubby face and receding hairline. Tucker pointed in my direction. "You were driving Boone's car; you were wearing his jacket and helping him get away. I saw the whole thing on Twitter. I figured the cops would have you locked up for doing such a thing, and since you and Boone are obviously an item he'd be in your house hiding out. I saw green-curler girl here out on the porch with the mangy mutt so I got in through the back; it was a piece of cake. You really need a better hiding place for your key."

"You're here looking for Boone?" I asked.

"He killed my father, my own daddy, and he needs to pay for it and I'm going to find him."

Drat! This was just what Ross said would happen. Because I was driving Boone's car, everyone would think I was helping him escape the long arm of the law no matter what. On the other hand, if it seemed like Boone and I were enemies and I made up some spiel as to why I didn't like him, others who had it in for Boone might confide in me and I could find out who had it in for him. Heck, it was worth a try.

"Are you kidding? Boone means nothing to me," I blurted. "Fact is, we're enemies. Yeah, big-time enemies." I parked my hands on my hips and went for the ticked-off wounded-victim look. "Boone took me to the cleaners in my divorce a couple years ago, and this is my chance to see him knocked down a peg or two. That guy thinks he's so special, that he's hot stuff, a real know-it-all if ever there was one, and good-looking. Actually he really is good looking with dark eyes and he has a terrific butt and—"

KiKi kicked my ankle, snapping me back to the situation at hand, which was *not* fixating on Boone's butt. "Look," I continued, "I took Boone's car because he owes me, and with him on the run this was my chance to even the score a little. I lost everything in that divorce, including my own car that I paid for. Do you believe that? I want Walker Boone behind bars as much as you. If he were here in my house I'd call the police myself and applaud as they hauled his very nice-looking butt out of here."

Tucker leaned in a little closer. "You got kind of a dopey look on your face."

"That's revenge," KiKi chimed in.

"Sure doesn't look like revenge."

KiKi dropped the shaker on my foot.

"Ouch!" I yelped, an expression of pain and agony now replacing the dopey look—least I hoped so.

"Boone's hiding somewhere in this city," Tucker said. "I'd bet my last dollar on it. He's going to try his best to pin Daddy's murder on someone else, and I'm going to make sure he's the one who goes to jail like he deserves."

"And I'll help you," I said, lying my little heart out as Tucker started for the steps. "I'm sorry about your father," I called after him. "Even if you two didn't get along, it's mighty hard to lose a parent," I added, doing a little digging of my own.

Tucker stopped and trudged back up the steps, his eyes trying to focus. "What are you talking about? My daddy and I got along fine. We were best of pals."

"Except he left the Old Harbor Inn to Walker Boone and not you," I said, remembering what Ross told me earlier at the police station. "There had to be a good reason why he did such a thing."

"Yeah, there is." Conway's eyes got even angrier than before. "Boone talked my daddy into changing his will is what happened. Boone threatened him, and Daddy had to do what he said because Daddy was afraid of Boone. He was a gang member, for crying out loud. You don't mess with the gang, everyone knows that."

"If Boone was into extortion, why not just demand money? Why the inn?"

Tucker's face reddened, his eyes blazing mad. "How the heck should I know? Ask Boone, he's the guilty one." Tucker stumbled down the stairs and out the back door, as KiKi and I stared after him.

"I really do need to find a better hiding place for my spare key," I said to myself as much as KiKi. "Do you think Tucker was poking around here looking for Walker because he's so distraught over his daddy on a slab over at House of Eternal Slumber?"

KiKi picked up the shaker. "I don't know about the distraught part, but there's no doubt that Tucker wants Walker in jail and the sooner the better."

I grabbed a towel from the hall closet to mop up the martini. "What if he's the one who set Walker up to take the rap for the murder Tucker committed? I bet Tucker didn't much like that Daddy left the inn to Walker. That had to tick him off."

"Except Tucker's mamma was from money and left him the bulk of the estate when she died four years ago. It's hard to imagine Tucker Adkins giving a hoot about fluffing pillows and room service. Maybe he truly is distraught over losing Conway."

KiKi and I exchanged a *yeah, when pigs fly* look and KiKi added, "There's some reason the old boy's got a bee in his bonnet, and it's more about finding Walker and putting him away than revenging poor dead Daddy. I wonder what Tucker Adkins is up to."

"And how did Boone wind up in the middle of it?" I looked around the upstairs. "He's out there, somewhere close."

KiKi yawned and headed for the stairs. "You never know about Walker; he could be right under your nose and you'd never see him unless he wanted you to."

Chapter Two

EARLY-MORNING sun peeked through my bedroom window and a loud banging came from the front door. Prying open one sleep-deprived eye, I focused on the clock flashing six. My higher-math skills said that made for three and a half hours of sleep. That wasn't sleep, that was a long nap, and nothing good came from door banging at six A.M.

BW stared at me from the hallway, his tail wagging and a *yippee, it's company* look in his eyes. Usually BW and I shared the bed, but the hall was cooler and spring cool was fast becoming summer heat. More banging came from below, and BW and I poked our heads out the bedroom window to see cars pulling to the curb and people with cameras hustling up my sidewalk. The press had obviously realized I wasn't being held at the police station, and to add to the joy of the morning a guy in a camo jacket was standing on the roof of my porch and coming my way.

"Say cheese." He snapped my picture and petted BW.

"What the . . . You can't do this. I'm a mess. I have on a Hello Kitty nightshirt with SpaghettiO stains." *And I didn't have on a bra!*

I hunched over to hide the obvious and the guy gave me a toothy grin and a thumbs-up sign and snapped more pictures as another photographer scrambled onto the roof, elbowing camo guy out of the way.

"You all are trespassing," I said, as BW wagged his tail.

"So what are you going to do about it, chickie?" camo guy sneered.

I heard a soft creaking and some cracking, and then both photographers dropped straight through the roof butt-first, landing on the porch below. Four wide eyes stared up at me, the two prone bodies surrounded by shards of rotting lumber and old shingles. For sure I hated having a hole in my roof, but deep down inside a little voice said, *See, jackass, that's what I'm going to do about it.* I added a thumbs-up gesture and toothy grin and that was good except for the reporters below snapping more pictures. This was clearly one of those *always wear clean underwear* moments that your mother warned you about. You put on something crappy with stains and you're going to get caught . . . I was now living proof.

More pounding came from my front door as BW and I ducked back inside. I could call the police, except for the little fact that the police and I weren't exactly on the best of terms at the moment and I didn't have a phone. I pulled on a T-shirt and jeans, ran a comb through my hair and a toothbrush around my mouth, and then flew downstairs with BW trotting right behind me. "Are you ready for your fifteen minutes of fame?" I warned BW.

He wagged his tail harder and added a bark that I took as a yes, so I tore open the door to cameras snapping and videos whirling.

"Where's Walker Boone?" one reporter asked, followed by, "Why did you help him escape?" Another added, "Why did he kill Conway Adkins?"

Oh yeah, this was the way I wanted to start the day . . . except maybe it *was* . . . sort of. "Look," I said, holding up my hands surrender-style. "I don't know where Walker Boone is." Least that part was true enough. "I just want to see that no-good scalawag behind bars. He represented my ex in our divorce, and all I got out of the deal was this run-down house." I pointed to the hole in the roof. "Now it's my turn to see Boone sweat, and I'm loving it."

"Don't hand me that line of bull," camo guy grunted, favoring his left leg. "You and Walker Boone have worked on the same cases; I've seen you around."

"He's an attorney; our paths cross and he gets in my way a lot and I usually have to end up saving his sorry miserable behind." Hey, if I'm going to lie I should make it a hum-dinger, right? "I have no use for Boone other than to see him behind bars and end up being on the short end of the stick for a change. That's why I took his car when I realized he was on the run. It's my turn to be the winner. What's he going to do about it, report the car stolen to the cops? That jerk owes me."

"I think you're lying," the second guy who fell through

the roof said, a lump forming over his right eye. "You two are an item and you're sleeping together."

"You're kidding, right? You saw my Hello Kitty night-shirt. Not exactly *come and get it, big boy* lingerie."

The guys nodded in agreement and I added, "I'm doing all that I can to find Boone and get him convicted for murdering Conway Adkins. In fact, if you all hear where he is or anything about the murder I'd appreciate you letting me know. I'd like to go laugh in his face." Then I slammed the door shut and hoped to heck my big old lies took root.

I peeked out the front display window, which at present featured a blue pencil skirt and tan blouse with a cute cross-body bag. The cars and vans pulled away from the curb— yay for that—as Auntie KiKi scurried across her lovely front lawn that butted up to my front weed patch. Her hair was still done up in rollers, but the green face goop was gone.

"What in the world is going on now?" she asked as she shuffled up the steps in fluffy slippers. "I heard cars and a crash. How can I get my beauty rest with this racket around here?"

I nodded at the roof and pointed to the debris of the porch. "New skylight. The press was here." I pointed to the roof. "And they were even up there. I fed them the same baloney about Boone that I dished out to Tucker."

"The press? Sweet mother, you think they bought it?"

"I'm not exactly living in the lap of luxury here, so the part about the rotten divorce and getting taken to the cleaners rings true enough."

KiKi sat down on the top step and we watched BW do his morning ritual of sniff and water the lawn. KiKi plopped her chin in her palm, closing her eyes. "I need a martini," she mumbled.

"It's six in the morning, not at night!"

"Well, I'll be." KiKi's eyes shot wide open. "See, this is what happens when I go to bed late and wake up early; my internal clock is on the fritz. Maybe Cakery Bakery has a martini-flavored doughnut and that'll take care of both of the sixes at once. Be ready in ten, we're on a mission."

Not waiting for an answer, KiKi headed for her house, and a few minutes later, sans bathrobe, she backed the Beemer down the drive. BW took the rear seat and I claimed shotgun. Leaving BW home during a doughnut run was never going to happen. Some dogs could sniff drugs, some found missing people, and some even sensed heart attacks. BW's special gift was a doughnut run. He could feel the vibes in the air when fried chunks of yummy pastry were just around the corner.

KiKi hung a right onto Abercorn as the sun was just peeking through the live oaks. We watched Savannah come to life with the usual morning rituals of getting the paper, walking the dog, catching the bus, drinking Starbucks, and putting on makeup while driving. KiKi found a parking space a block away from the bakery, and we followed BW, his doggie nose hot on the doughnut scent.

"Mercy me, there's a line?" KiKi gasped when we got to the green storefront with a cupcake etched on the glass double doors. We walked past the little white tables littering the sidewalk for al fresco carb indulging, then went inside.

"What in the world is everyone doing up at this hour?" KiKi huffed as we passed the customers sitting in wire-frame sweetheart chairs with matching marble-top tables. A ceiling light decorated with gingerbread cookies added to the delicious ambiance of the bakery, and a cupcake clock on the far wall ticked off the minutes. I swear I gained two pounds just surveying the décor. KiKi beelined for the display cases in the back, and her dismay over the crowd quickly gave way to the lure of things round, fried, and filled. She pressed her nose to the glass. "So many doughnuts," she murmured, a bit dreamy. "So little time."

"You! Reagan Summerside! Get out of my shop," a voice called from behind me.

I spun around to face GracieAnn Harlow, the new owner of the Cakery Bakery. GracieAnn had gone pleasantly to plump as all bakery owners should, least in my opinion. She had on a pink dress, the Cakery Bakery uniform, and a white apron with an order pad and pencil stuck in the front pocket. GracieAnn was such a kidder these days, always poking fun and having a laugh . . . least that was what I thought till I got hit in the forehead with a raspberry truffle doughnut covered in a chocolate drizzle.

"Get out!" GracieAnn pointed to the door as drips of raspberry trailed down my nose.

"Excuse me?"

"Out!"

"But . . . but we're friends," I said. "We're buds. I rescued you, remember. And I'm one of your best customers." I stuck out my tongue and captured a drizzle. "What's this all about?"

GracieAnn pursed her mouth tight, her green eyes little slits. "For the record, it was Walker Boone, that darling hunka-hunka man, who rescued me, and you're nothing but a traitor, a Judas, a double-crossing hypocrite. I saw the morning news on TV." She pointed to a TV in the corner, as everyone in the shop nodded in agreement. "We all heard what you said. You want Boone behind bars!" A bear claw filled with vanilla custard went splat across my chest.

"You got this all wrong. I can explain."

"We heard what we heard," GracieAnn added, and the ticked-off looks on the other customers' faces suggested that if I didn't leave on my own they'd help me along.

I leaned across the counter and hooked my finger at GracieAnn to do the same. "I just said what I did to get Boone's enemies to talk to me so I can find the real killer," I whispered, our noses inches apart.

GracieAnn's eyes got beady. "You'd say anything for a doughnut."

"Okay, I can't argue that, but I'm not lying." I did the cross-over-my-heart routine.

"Hit the bricks."

"Not even one glazed to see me on my way?"

"Out!" GracieAnn's breath smelled of vanilla and cinnamon. I inhaled the scent of secondhand doughnut as GracieAnn glared at Auntie KiKi. "And what about you?"

KiKi studied the full display case and smacked her lips. BW fused himself to her leg and KiKi pointed to me. "I never saw that woman in my life and neither did this dog and that's our story and we're sticking to it and we'll take two crullers, four sprinkles, and a coffee and a water to go, thank you very much."

When it came to doughnuts and family loyalty, doughnuts

won every time. Picking chunks of bear claw off my shirt, I plopped them into my mouth and headed for the door. I sat at one of the shaded little white tables on the sidewalk and waited for KiKi to come out. One of those sprinkle doughnuts she ordered better have my name on it.

"Lord have mercy, girl, what do you think you're doing?" Mercedes said as she hustled up to the table and wedged herself into the tiny wrought-iron chair across from me. Mercedes was housekeeper extraordinaire by day and mortician beautician by night, meaning not much happened in this city without her getting wind of it. She drove a pink Caddy and dressed right out of Nordstrom's catalog. Sprucing things up living or dead paid a heck of a lot better than running a consignment shop.

"Honey," she said to me. "Are you trying to get yourself killed, and if you are you need to be touching up your roots for when they find your sorry carcass. What's it going to be? Blonde? Brunette? Make a choice, 'cause right now you look skunk and you need better clothes. You run a nice consignment shop, for Pete's sake."

"I can't afford my consignment shop."

"I declare, girl, how do you keep getting into these messes?"

"So are we talking about that fire out at the lumberyard a few months ago, or when that house exploded and I sort of lost my eyebrows, or when I drove into the marsh with the alligators, or—"

"I'm talking about today, this very morning. You were on the news, big as you please. That's how I knew you were here having doughnuts at the Cakery Bakery . . . where else would you go at this hour?"

"So, besides the roots and nightshirt, did I look all that bad?"

"You looked like we should be measuring you for a coffin." Mercedes let out a long-suffering sigh. "You know Mr. Boone has friends, mighty good friends like me, who won't be taking kindly to that crack about wanting to put the man behind bars."

"I got a plan."

"We'll be sure to put that in your obituary."

"Detective Ross said I had to act like I was anti-Boone so the suspects wouldn't clam up when I started snooping around. If they suspected I was out to find the real killer I'd get nowhere fast."

"Did you ever stop to consider the little fact that you're not going to get any help from the pro Boone camp, and that includes Big Joey, Pillsbury, and the Seventeenth Street boys? My guess is that particular group's hunting you down this very minute. You need to straighten them out before you're on the receiving end of more than flying doughnuts." Mercedes swiped a glob of custard from my chin just as Auntie KiKi and BW pranced out of the bakery with a piled-high tray of goodies, having obviously seen Mercedes out here with me.

Without saying a word we set out the coffee and split the doughnut collection, and I put BW's portion on the tray on the sidewalk. Simultaneously we all selected a portion of the sprinkle variety and savored the moment. It was the good-friends-plus-pup way of doing things around here.

Mercedes licked icing off her thumb and looked at me. "Okay, now that we're sugared and caffeinated, we need to be thinking about who did in Conway and we need to be doing it quick before the cops find Mr. Boone. The man won't go peaceful, we all know that, and it would be a crying shame if something happened to his fine self. He sure does offer up some nice eye candy around here."

KiKi added another packet of sugar to the coffee just in case three packets weren't enough. "If you want my opinion, Tucker Adkins gets top billing after breaking into Reagan's house last night."

Mercedes dropped her doughnut in her coffee. "Sweet mother. Why would he do such a thing?"

KiKi took a nibble of her cinnamon twist. "He says he's looking to avenge his daddy dearest and put Boone in jail, but he's more interested in the jail part than the daddy part, I can promise you that."

Mercedes spooned her doughnut out of her coffee. "I know the maid over there at Lillibridge House. I help her clean on occasion when she gets overworked or they got a party going on. She told me that Tucker and his daddy were never close. Fact is, she said Conway got along better with Steffy Lou than he ever did with his own son. Tucker was a mamma's boy, never worked a day in his life and walked off with a nice chunk of change when his mamma died. The thing is, after she died Conway told Tucker about Walker being his other son and he didn't take it well at all."

I stopped a sprinkle doughnut halfway to my mouth. "'Didn't take it well' in that he'd kill him?"

Mercedes fed a chunk of doughnut to BW, his head in her lap. BW knew how to play a crowd. "Tucker Adkins likes nothing more than easy money and the good life. I can't see the man risking jail over a half-brother he never knew he had. He might go ballistic and pitch a fit, but murder's not his style, best I can tell."

She hunched across the table, drawing us all close. "But I got another idea. I've been thinking maybe those gold-digger sisters did in Conway. Anna and Bella had me on the phone last night making sure I put both their names on my clean and casket list. I only got so many openings, and they know if they get me to do their houses now I'll take special care of their husbands when they get over to Eternal Slumber, which those two are hoping occurs right soon. It's what happens when feisty twenty-somethings marry rich eighty-somethings. Seems like a mighty big coincidence that with Conway dead and Boone on the run, two spots came available with neither of the octogenarian boys in the best of health, from what I hear."

KiKi sipped her coffee and nodded. "And we all know that this being Savannah, there's nothing more important than a proper funeral no matter who's doing the dying, planned or otherwise."

"Waitaminute," I said. "You really think Anna and Bella would knock off Conway and frame Walker to get Mercedes to clean for them?"

"And bury their husbands proper when the time came so they wouldn't get talked about," Mercedes said. "Their grandma Annabelle was married three times, all to rich old men who wound up out at Bonaventure within two years of saying *I do*. Anna and Bella are legacy gold-diggers."

"And maybe killers," KiKi chimed in. "I'd say those two are worth a look-see. Besides, and I hate to say it, we have

no one else on our who-killed-Conway list." KiKi let out a
deep sigh, polished off her coffee, snagged a napkin and
flicked glaze off her peach blouse, and then checked her
watch. "I got a cha-cha lesson with Bernard Thayer at nine.
Mr. Savannah Weather is determined to get on *Dancing
with the Stars* this year or bust a gut trying. Least he pays
double, and I got my eye on a Gucci purse on eBay."

"And I have a Tuesday house to clean," Mercedes offered.
"Then I'm heading over to the Slumber and take care of
Conway as soon as the police release the body, and get him
gussied up for the layout tomorrow. I owe him since I
cleaned his place all these years. It's going to take a moun-
tain of putty to fill in that there hole between his beady little
eyes. Getting shot with a .38 is nasty business, goes in like
a BB and comes out like a potato. You should attend the
funeral," Mercedes said to me as KiKi and I stopped eating
our last doughnut thanks to the potato comment.

"Odds are good the killer will be there," Mercedes went
on. "He'll want to be checking out his handiwork and it's a
fine time to step up your anti-Walker campaign if you really
think it'll work. You best be letting Big Joey and the boys
in on your plan, and the sooner the better for your own good
health, if you get my drift."

Mercedes headed off in one direction and KiKi in the other
to collect the Beemer. I hitched Old Yeller onto my shoulder,
and BW and I started across Broughton toward Seventeenth
Street. We crossed MLK and the large perfectly restored
Savannah houses gave way to smaller ones with faded paint
and AC units perched in front windows, where few residents
had the need to lay out and tan as theirs was hereditary.

This was Big Joey territory, with Pillsbury the doughboy who managed the corporate money as second in command. The Seventeenth Street gang took care of their own and a few others along the way. They had a nice investment portfolio and a terrific health care plan that I could attest to, as they had graciously folded me into their system. I was tolerated in the land of not belonging mostly because I knew Boone and my crime-solving skills bordered on amusement and curiosity. None of that counted for squat today, proven by the fact that I had three of the boys following me, and from the looks on their faces this was not a welcoming committee.

I stepped up my pace, and the boys did the same. I spotted the two pink myrtle trees that any Savannah gardener worth his blooms would salivate over, trotted up the steps, and knocked on the screen door.

"I hear you be looking for trouble," Big Joey said when he answered the door. He started to close it, but BW wiggled his way inside, looking for his usual treat as if all were normal.

"It's not what you think," I blurted to Big Joey and the boys. "I'm trying to find Conway's killer by acting like I want to get even with Boone for messing me in over my divorce. Here's my plan: If I give the impression I'm anti-Boone, I'll find others who have it in for him and maybe I'll find out who set him up. Got any ideas?"

Big Joey stepped out onto the porch as my escorts closed in from the back. I felt like an Oreo cookie.

"You took his car," Big Joey growled.

"Hey, he took my new pink scooter."

This brought smiles all around, and the ominous atmosphere shattered. Guess pink-scooter topics of conversation didn't come up all that often in the hood. Big Joey folded his muscled ebony arms across his chest and leaned against the porch post. "Sorry I missed that. Any idea where he be?" Big Joey asked, as my escorts ambled off.

"My guess is Boone will steer clear of friends in case he gets caught. He wouldn't want to drag us into any trouble with the police," I said. "Maybe he'll look me up once my *I hate Walker Boone* campaign gets going."

"That idea's never going to happen with that dopey look on your face, babe."

"I'm trying for revenge mixed with loathing."

"Try harder."

"So I've heard."

"You chill, the boys and I got this."

"Except you really don't," I tried to reason. "Look, we have to work together. You can get into places I can't, and I can get to places you can't. Besides, I got another interest in this. I need the money. Conway Adkins was right in the middle of redecorating and he promised to consign his furniture with me. I had buyers lined up for his cherry dining room set and living room couch, cash in hand, ready to go, and then Conway goes and gets himself polished off."

"Thoughtless."

"I want to solve this case to get the crime scene tape off Conway's house so I can get my furniture and buy a car of my very own."

Big Joey let out a deep sigh.

"Hey, I'm a terrific driver."

This brought a smile, confirming my entertainment status. "Bus be good."

"I like cup holders."

"Later, babe."

BW and I headed for home: the Prissy Fox, a far trot from the land of brotherly love. Depending on the bus driver and if I happened to have a sandwich bribe from Zunzi's, I could sometimes pass BW off as a furry child with leash and hitch a ride. Most of the time puppo was a big no-no. See, this was exactly why I needed a car, a nondiscriminatory mode of transportation.

Duh, I had a car! I had Boone's car! I didn't take it last night because the press would follow in hot pursuit. But now that that particular ship had sailed, there was no reason to hide. I might have a hole in my porch roof, but I also had a '57 Chevy convertible at my disposal. Seemed like a pretty fair trade since Boone had my scooter.

Chapter Three

"THIS was a really good idea," I said to BW as I pulled the Chevy to a stop, letting a band of tourists cross State Street to get to Oglethorpe Square. Adam Levine sang to me from the radio and a hot twenty-something guy gave me a wink. A sassy poodle on a pink leash shook her pompom tail at BW and added a *hey, big boy* yap. "You got to admit," I said to BW. "This kind of stuff never happened to us on a bus."

Tail wagging, BW sat up a little straighter, not taking his eyes off the poodle. "Don't get any ideas, big boy."

BW leaned farther over the edge of the door, tongue hanging out, salivating, lust in his eyes. Men—two-legged or four, they were all the same when it came to shaking pompoms. I continued down Abercorn and tossed my head, letting my hair float out into the breeze, followed by wolf whistles from the two guys overhead working on the phone lines. All this was because I had the right car? It sure wasn't from my two-toned roots.

I pulled my last Snickers from my purse—one that I'd been saving for a special occasion—and very carefully, so as not to get any chocolate on the white upholstery, split it with BW. I guided the Chevy around back of Cherry House and bid the lovely Adam farewell till next time. Keeping the car idling, I opened the garage door, lugged a ladder off to the side, and dragged an old grill out of the way to make room for the newest occupant.

I unsnapped the boot used to cover the convertible top when it was down, then carefully raised it and locked it in place. I slowly maneuvered my—least for a bit it was mine—sexmobile inside and killed the engine.

My last car of two-plus years ago was a cute little used hatchback named Blueberry. Hollis got the Lexus because he sold real estate and he insisted he had to look successful to be successful. Blueberry got great gas mileage and was cheap to insure and a breeze to park even in the tightest of places, but in the ten minutes that it took me to drive from the police station to my house the Chevy got more attention than little ol' Blueberry ever did. I locked the garage, and BW and I strutted ourselves inside to get the Prissy Fox ready for the day.

I pulled on my usual shop garb of black capris and a white blouse, clipped my hair back, and swiped on some mascara and lip gloss as BW watched me from his new favorite spot out in the hall. We went downstairs and I got the cash from the safe, also known as the rocky road ice cream container in the freezer. I transferred the money to the cash register—also known as the Godiva chocolate box sans chocolate, but it still smelled great when I made a sale.

I flipped the lights on and turned on my little radio to WRHQWR105, the quality rock station, hoping to hear more Adam Levine. I kept the volume low as background music and then opened the front door.

"'Bout time," a blonde gal in Saks' finest huffed as she and her clone bustled inside the shop. "You know how long I've been waiting out there on that miserable porch with the hole in the roof? Ten whole minutes. What kind of shop is this?"

One that doesn't open till ten and right now it's nine thirty, I thought to myself. Not that I said that out loud, as the customer is always right . . . even if they can't tell time or read the hours posted on the door. "Are you shopping for something in particular that I can help with?" I asked in my sweet-shop-owner voice.

Four eyes rounded and clone one gasped, "You think *we* shop at a secondhand store?" They exchanged looks, sighs, and shoulder rolls all at the same time, as if rehearsed. Clone two thrust a list at me. "We're here on business. There are a lot of men's clothes here, nice ones. How much will I get for them, and I'll need them sold right quick."

"These are good brands, but men's clothes don't move as fast as women's. It will take a month, maybe two."

"See, Anna," clone two said to clone one as she hitched her Prada bag up onto her shoulder. "I told you so. This isn't going to work. You need something else to tide you over till the lawyers settle the estate and you get the money free and clear."

Clone one tapped her foot. "That means I'll just have to live off the credit cards? But a girl needs cash; it's not proper for her not to have cash in hand. What will people think if I have to fork over a credit card all the time? This is a disgrace, Bella. What am I going to do?"

Anna? Bella? The gold-digger sisters?

"I'm so sorry about your husband's passing," I offered.

"Oh, honey," Bella huffed. "He's not dead . . . yet. But a girl's got to be prepared for these things if they should come her way unexpected-like. I'm just getting affairs in order for when the time comes sooner or later."

"And we are so hoping and praying for the sooner part," Anna added.

"Fact is, we're off to see Odilia right now on how we can hurry the situation along a bit," Bella said.

"He's critical and you don't want him to suffer?"

"Things are critical all right, and I'm doing the suffering." Anna tsked, her face pulling into a frown. "I cannot believe that Walker Boone person tried to convince our husbands to change their wills like he did and make our inheritance proportional to years married. Of all the nerve! What if they go and do such a thing? How dare that man stick his nose into our business? He so deserves to be behind bars."

Two customers came in to shop and Anna added in a low voice, "That's why we came here to talk to you. We saw you on the morning news and realized you dislike that no-good, low-rent, middle-Georgia Boone person as much as we do. I could cut the man's heart out with a spoon, I could, and it's a darn shame too with him being so fine and delicious to look at. One glance at that man and a girl wants to sink her teeth into his tight little butt. So you can take the clothes, right?"

I was still back at Boone's butt.

"I'll bring the clothes over when dear Clive passes on so you can get them right out on the floor fast and sold quick-like."

The sisters trotted out the front door and down the side-walk as Mercedes came in the back door. Her hair was always soft and sleek and her makeup perfect, and the peach pashmina draped around her shoulders accented her dark skin perfectly. I wanted to be Mercedes when I grew up.

"What in the world were the gold-digger sisters doing here?" she asked. "Those two gals are not exactly the consignment-shop type."

"They're inquiring about selling men's clothes."

Mercedes stopped dead. "Holy Mary in heaven. Well, there you go. Those two got plans and it's not where to spend their next anniversary. Think we should warn the poor unfortunates married to them? It only seems fitting that we do something."

"'Your wife's planning to knock you off' may not go over too well, but they are paying a visit to Odilia right now to speed things up." We both made the sign of the cross at the mention of the local voodoo priestess, who knew how to get the job done. Nine months ago Wanda Fleming went to Odilia because her daughter wasn't getting pregnant. Last week she delivered triplets.

"I knew it," Mercedes said, slapping her palm on my checkout counter, which was actually an old green paint-chipped door I had found in the attic and laid across the backs of two chairs. "It's like I figured all along. Anna and Bella are prime suspects in this mess with Conway, and if they're planning on their very own husbands' demise, doing in Conway and framing Walker for the deed is a piece of cake, don't you think? It's a perfect fit."

"They did mention Boone and it wasn't to sing his praises, except for his butt. But how would they get hold of Boone's .38?"

"Honey, every woman in Savannah praises that man's fine behind, and the fact that Mr. Walker keeps a .38 in his desk drawer is legendary. Word has it that someone used it to put a bullet right into his wood-paneled office, of all things. Do you believe that?"

I did the big swallow. Actually I did believe it 'cause I sort of did the shooting.

"But the reason I came over is I got news," Mercedes said. She came around to the back of the counter and whispered, "I was fixing up Conway to 'Stayin' Alive,' that being my favorite fix-up music and all. I was taking my time, making him look real good, and lo and behold if some guy didn't barge right into the room big as you please. He pulled out a carving knife and stabbed Conway right in the heart. I mean, the man's already dead as a post, for Pete's sake. How much deader can he get and now I got another hole to fill in, like I didn't have enough work from the .38 and it messed up the embalming something fierce. Some people have no consideration."

"'Stayin' Alive'?"

"The Bee Gees."

"Did you call the police?"

"Folk are already croaked when we get 'em, nothing much more can happen to them, right? The Slumber is not exactly a flashing-lights-and-sirens sort of establishment. We're more into lilies and ferns and hankies and tea and cookies and 'Doesn't he look good for a dead guy.' I have no idea who the man was, but I thought you needed to know we got ourselves another suspect. I mean, if the guy's ready to kill Conway when he's dead, I figure he could have done the deed when Conway was up and kicking. There's pissed off, and then there's really and truly pissed off, and stabber guy fits the second category, wanting to make sure the deed is done for real."

Mercedes did the impatient shuffle as I rang up a sale for the strappy sandals I'd had my eye on and the cute cross-body bag out of the display window. She waited for the woman to leave, then said to me, "I bet dollars to doughnuts that the stabbing guy will be at Conway's funeral. You truly do need to get there and bring Miss KiKi with you; she knows everyone."

"I hate funerals."

"Honey"—Mercedes put her arm around me—"the only ones who like funerals are those who inherit the loot, the florists, and the funeral director. But the way I see it, at least we got ourselves another suspect."

Mercedes hustled herself off to putty Conway back together, and three customers brought clothes in to consign. I went through the stacks, selected which items worked for the store, and then tagged and priced them and put them on the racks. By one o'clock I'd sold three skirts, two jackets, four pairs of shoes, and a really ugly coat that I thought I'd never get rid of. I also sold three black dresses thanks to Conway's funeral. Maybe I needed to rethink my view on funerals; they weren't so bad after all.

I really could do with a mannequin, I decided as I assembled a new window display of skinny jeans, white sweater, and straw hat. A mannequin would look better than the hangers in the window, that's for sure. I hung the clothes, adding a cute chair and table to complete the display look as BW ambled out the door to greet Chantilly hurrying up the walk.

Chantilly was a true friend and once-upon-a-time UPS driver. She was now chief cook and bottle washer over at Cuisine by Rachelle, she made the best mac and cheese on earth, and she was engaged to Pillsbury, the Seventeenth Street gang doughboy. That meant she had someone to cuddle up to at night and to invest her hard-earned money, and there was always good food in the house. Chantilly was one fine cook.

"Here's that mac and cheese you ordered for lunch," Chantilly said to me, setting a white paper bag on the counter. She shuffled back to the door, cutting her eyes in one direction, then the other.

"Ordered?"

"Just open the blasted bag."

"But I didn't—"

"Eat!"

When it came to mac and cheese I didn't have to be coaxed, like with broccoli and carrots. "Looking for someone?" I asked, since Chantilly was still standing at the door.

The cops, she mouthed. Okay, this was getting curiouser

and curiouser. I opened the bag, pulled out a spork and cup, pried off the lid, and dug into the best three-cheese combo in the city. It even had those little toasted breadcrumbs sprinkled on top and—

"Napkin!" Chantilly yelped, pointing to the bag. "You need a napkin. Your mamma would have a hissy if she saw you not using your napkin!"

Three customers and I stared at Chantilly as if she'd clearly lost her ever-loving mind over a napkin. The South was all about manners, but this was over-the-top etiquette even for Savannah. I put down the container and carefully plucked the napkin from the bag. I did a little shake to fluff it open, and right there in the middle was writing. *Stay away from Dixon, stay out of my house, no eating in the car.*

"A mutual mac-and-cheese lover," Chantilly offered, still gazing out the door.

"And you're worried that someone might be onto your message service?"

"Crossed my mind. I think you're supposed to take the napkin seriously."

I jabbed my spork at a big empty space in the hallway. "Right over there is where Conway's dining room set and living room furniture belong. I have customers waiting to see that furniture, money in hand, and I have a big fat hole in my roof. I'm not staying out of anything. I'll try not to eat in the car, but if I happen to drive past Sisters and BW feels a fried chicken urge coming on, I can't deny BW, now can I?"

"You take the bones out of the chicken?" Chantilly gave me a concerned frown.

"Of course I take out the bones. How'd our mutual mac-and-cheese lover look?"

"I'm just the delivery person. Pillsbury says if you get involved in this they're going to lock you in a closet and throw away the key, and you should know you got a really dopey look on your face."

A customer left without buying anything as two more entered, looking at the sale rack in the front by the counter. Chantilly pulled me over to the jewelry display table and picked up a pearl brooch. "Who's Dixon?" she asked, holding up the brooch as if to admire it.

"You're going to rat me out?"

"You saved my behind when everyone thought I knocked off Simon . . . not that the jerk didn't have it coming. So now I'm going to help you. If Pillsbury finds out what we're up to, we'll both be locked up in that closet." She put down the brooch and picked up some black beaded earrings. "So who do you think pulled the trigger on Conway?"

I picked up a matching bracelet to the earrings. "There's a guy who knifed him after he was already dead, two sisters who don't like him or Boone, and Boone's brother who's a complete jerk, though knocking off his own father seems a bit of a stretch."

Chantilly rolled her eyes, shook her head, and tried on a string of faux pearls that looked pretty decent considering they only cost ten bucks. "A lunatic, two women, and a ticked-off brother, is it? Walker is so screwed. Who's Dixon?"

"Mason Dixon, VP over at the Plantation Club. Conway was the president, and Dixon wanted the position and he owed Conway money. I know what you're thinking, that doing in Conway gets rid of the debt and he gets the presidency. The thing is there's no tie to Boone, and Boone was framed for a reason."

"Walker must have found something important about this Dixon guy or he wouldn't have told you to steer clear. I say we need to talk to Dixon." Chantilly took a yellow scarf to the checkout counter and I started to write up the sale. "What do you think about me going to the Plantation Club and asking about a membership?"

I snapped my pencil. "I think we're headed for that closet."

"Pillsbury's at an accounting seminar in Atlanta; he won't find out. The club doesn't allow many of my particular skin tone in as members, and I have to be recommended. I dated the cook a few years back, but I don't think that's what they have in mind. While Dixon and everyone else is doing their best to be politically correct, that will give you a chance to poke around in his office."

"Boone and I tried that, and Dixon barged in on us. But it is a good idea. If I can find an IOU or something that proves Dixon owed Conway money, that might give the cops someone else to consider besides Boone."

"You're right, it is a mighty good idea." A devilish smile tripped across Chantilly's lips. "I'll get off for an hour tomorrow afternoon. I'll be obnoxious and irritating. I'll wear something slutty."

"I wonder how big that closet is?"

At six I closed up the Prissy Fox. I fed BW his daily hot dog, which was now low-fat so he'd keep his manly physique. I put two scoops of Canine Cuisine in his bowl, then straightened the shop for tomorrow. I hung up clothes left in the cute little dressing room that used to be my pantry until I painted it yellow and hung a curtain in front of it. Since I'd only ever used it to house a few cans of Spaghet-tiOs and maybe green beans for when I had a health food attack, I really didn't miss the space that much.

I opened the door to let BW do his evening sniff-and-sprinkle routine. He bolted out the door like getting shot from a cannon and tore across the street. Dang! Every once in a while this happened, usually when I least expected it. What did he see: a rabbit, a squirrel, a cat? BW was on the hunt and now I had to find him, and the fact that I'd had less than four hours of sleep didn't matter to BW one little bit.

"Why are you staring at the street?" Auntie KiKi wanted to know as she came out the front door of Rose Gate, her lovely white-and-blue Victorian that had been in the Vander-pool family since Sherman and his buddies showed up. It was Tuesday night, canasta night, and KiKi had on her lucky tiara. KiKi killed at canasta, so I guessed the tiara worked.

"BW is on a run after some critter."

"Please, Lord, do not let it be a skunk," KiKi lamented. We exchanged looks, both remembering last month and that skunk encounter and the twenty cans of tomato juice to get rid of the odor.

"My guess is one way or the other he'll wind up at Boone's house looking for a snack," I said.

"I'll take Drayton and you take Lincoln and we'll meet up at Boone's."

"What about the Tuesday night canasta girls?" I pointed to the tiara.

"We decided to call it off. Steffy Lou Adkins plays with us, and it didn't seem right to be swilling pink margaritas and eating red velvet cake without her there and considering Conway's wake is tomorrow night and all. Steffy Lou is such a sweet girl, and Conway's passing hit her real hard. I was taking the tiara out for a spin so as not to break the lucky streak it seems to have going. Now we best get a move on before the dogcatcher snags BW and it costs you a pretty penny to get him out of jail."

KiKi backed the Beemer out of the drive and slowly motored down Gwinnett calling, "*Here, doggie, doggie, doggie.*" I got BW's leash from inside along with Old Yeller and snatched up two hot dogs to bribe BW away from whatever got his attention in the first place. A soft warm glow settled over the city as streetlights blinked on and office lights faded to black. I searched alleys, front yards, and a few Dumpsters, but there was no sign of BW.

I cut through Troup Square, checking the doggie fountain there, one of BW's fave watering holes. A lot of canines were out for an evening stroll but no BW. I cut across Charlton. The big oaks shaded the street by day and filtered moonlight at night. With the cobblestones and perfectly restored old homes, the street was pretty much as it was a hundred years ago, and right there on Boone's porch that happened to be connected to one of those lovely old homes was Auntie KiKi with BW. Guess that tiara really did have lucky powers.

"You know," KiKi called to me as I climbed the wrought-iron steps to the porch, "if you had a cell phone I could have told you we were here."

"You are a bad dog," I said to BW, shaking my finger at

him. In response he wagged his tail, sniffed at my pocket, sat, and gave me his paw. I gave him a hot dog. What can I say? I'm a puppy pushover. I clipped the leash to BW's collar as KiKi peered into Boone's window.

"There's not much to see," I said to KiKi, knowing exactly what was inside since I'd sort of finagled my way in a few months ago. "Boone's house is all *Southern Living* on the outside and college dorm on the inside. I don't think he realizes he has a dining room." I scooped up the junk mail overflowing from the mailbox and stuffed it in Old Yeller. "It's like advertising to the world, *No one's home, come rob me.*"

"Somebody already got the message," KiKi said in a sharp whisper. "I saw a flashlight moving around on the floor inside."

"Maybe it's a reflection off the streetlight."

I got the *get your behind over here* auntie scowl.

"I'm coming, I'm coming." I crept over to the window. "Boone?"

"He'd never chance it, too risky. Whoever it is, they're up to no good or they'd have the lights lit like a normal person. I got an idea." And before I could stop her KiKi cleared her throat and said in a loud voice, "Now that we found our doggie all safe and sound, we should be going home and have some nice hot chocolate." KiKi stomped down the steps, motioning for me to follow her.

"Hot chocolate?" I said in a low voice as I trailed behind. "Where'd that come from?"

"Seemed to go with finding a lost dog." When we got to the bottom we continued on down Charlton.

"What are we doing now, oh great cocoa lover?" I asked KiKi as we moseyed along.

"We'll pretend we're leaving all nice and peaceful-like, then we'll sneak around to the back alley. With someone in the house I'm betting the door is already unlocked. Since Boone got his gun stolen and it was used to frame him, maybe it's the same person planning more trouble."

"Do you really think there's a need for more? And think about this: If it *is* the killer, he knows how to use a gun."

KiKi gave a wicked little laugh and patted her Prada purse as she hitched it up on her shoulder. "Oh, honey, he's not the only one you can count on for that."

Chapter Four

THE three of us—Auntie KiKi, BW, and I—turned for the alley. Keeping to the shadows, we doubled back to Boone's house and slunk up to the rear door, and KiKi turned the knob. It opened with a little click and KiKi gave me an *I told you so* look. Inside the only sound was BW panting and pawing and my heart pounding at the thought of KiKi packing God knows what in her purse.

I pulled my flashlight from Old Yeller; the beam landed on the stove, refrigerator, and Formica table and matching vinyl chairs. In another house they could pass for vintage chic décor, but I knew Boone. These were hand-me-downs from Pillsbury or Big Joey. I followed KiKi into the hallway and past the dining room as my light picked out what had to be the ugliest table east of the Mississippi.

"Previous owners left it," I whispered to KiKi.

"Good idea."

The only things in the living room were Boone's chair and desk piled with papers, a leather couch worn to comfortable, and a small TV sitting on a bar stool. KiKi faced me, palms out in an *I don't know where our burglar went* gesture.

The floor creaked behind us and before I could turn around KiKi got shoved hard into me. I stumbled backward, tripped over the desk chair, and fell on my butt, with KiKi landing on top of me. Old Yeller skittered across the floor in one direction and the flashlight in the other, outlining a pair of terrific purple heels running off, their clack-clack-clack fading down the hallway toward the back door. Any woman who could run in heels like that deserved my undying respect. BW in his wonderful watchdog way lay down beside us and licked KiKi's face.

"BW!" I screeched. "Bad guy. Get him . . . her." Yeah, like that was going to happen.

KiKi rolled off to the side and pointed to the hall. "Go."

I scrambled to my feet and tore for the back door till I tripped over BW running beside me. In the world of dog, all was play and games and *is it dinnertime yet*. I landed flat out like a squashed bug, and BW yelped and added a puppy whine for good measure because I probably stepped on his paw.

"Oh my stars and garters, this is terrible, are you okay?" KiKi wailed. With flashlight in hand she darted right by me, stopping at BW. She knelt down, raised his adorable little puppy paw, and patted his head. "Oh, you poor little sweetie. Did you get a boo-boo?"

"What about poor niece?" I whimpered in a burst of self-pity, my hands and elbows skinned and raw.

"If you're bleeding, try not to stain Walker's hardwood floors, dear," KiKi said, still looking at BW's paw. "I think they're original pine."

"God forbid I stain the floors! Did you happen to see who pushed you?" I levered myself to a sitting position, rubbing my knees.

"Maybe we should get BW to the vet and get him checked out. He's holding his leg up and looking downright pitiful. You went and broke your poor doggie's foot, of all things."

I limped over to KiKi and BW. He jumped up on me, paws to shoulders, and licked my face. He looked back to KiKi, dropped back on all fours, and held up his paw and whined. "I think we're being conned." I caved and gave BW the other hot dog that he knew I had, and then we all trooped back to the living room.

"I wonder what our burglar was after? This place isn't exactly the Telfair Museum."

I retrieved Old Yeller by the couch, and KiKi stood in a patch of moonbeams slicing through the front windows. "Well, there's sure not much to burgle here, I can tell you that," she said, gazing around the room. "The TV might bring five bucks on a good day, and the desk might be an antique but it would take two men and a crane and not a woman in heels to get the thing out of here. We were standing right by the desk when we got pushed," KiKi said, coming my way. "See if there's anything worth stealing there."

I flipped on the desk light and we both stopped dead, staring at Boone's business card impaled on a white satin stiletto. "The man sure does lead an interesting life," KiKi said with a laugh.

"Looks like a wedding shoe. I wonder what Boone did to deserve this?" I rifled through the papers in a folder on top, and KiKi pulled open the side drawer.

"Boone's got a dentist appointment on Friday," I added. "His water bill is due and his gym membership is due but they'll give him a discount if he renews by his birthday next month. I didn't know Boone belonged to the gym." And I didn't know his birthday till now.

"Honey, a man doesn't get a body like that pushing a pencil across a legal pad, and I say we pay the bill on behalf of every female in the city who . . ." KiKi stopped midsentence and held up a photo. "And what do we have here?"

"It's a young guy in jeans and wearing one of those monogram sweaters in style back in the day," I said. "The girl's around maybe nineteen. I'm guessing they're a family since she has a baby in her arms."

KiKi pointed to the gazebo in the background. "This is Wright Square and there's a 'CA' on the sweater. Conway?" KiKi and I exchanged looks. "I think it's Conway with more hair and less muffin top. He was darn good-looking." KiKi flipped over the photo and we both sucked in a quick breath as we read, *Conway, MaryEllen, and baby Walker.*

"Lord have mercy," KiKi said in a hushed voice. "It's Walker's mamma and daddy. Oh, honey, if Walker had this here photo he knew all along that Conway was his dad."

KiKi plopped down hard in the desk chair. "This is terrible bad news. I wish we'd never found it. It goes to motive of Walker coercing Conway into changing his will and leaving him the Old Harbor Inn, then killing him before he could change it back. It's just as Tucker said."

"First of all, I wouldn't believe anything Tucker Adkins said if he swore to it on a stack of Bibles." I snapped up the picture, my brain racing. "And I'm sure Boone didn't know Conway was his dad till last night when I came to warn him that the cops were on their way to arrest him. He was a total mess trying to make sense of the idea. No way he knew before that."

KiKi waved the photo in the air. "But he's got this picture right here. We knew right off this guy was Conway, so Walker had to know, too. It's not just some random picture."

"That's just it, I don't think he did have the picture. I doubt if he's ever seen it. I think someone left it in the desk to make Boone look guilty. Bridezilla with the satin shoe didn't have any trouble getting in here, and neither did we. These old houses aren't exactly Fort Knox. The picture wasn't buried under any papers or stashed out of the way, it was right here on top and easy to find. Someone left it."

"Bridezilla?"

"She's ticked off that she didn't walk down the aisle. This picture is personal against Boone, wanting to frame him for murder. The cops haven't been here to look around yet or they'd have that yellow crime tape across the door, but it stands to reason they'll come snooping soon, and someone wanted to make sure they find this picture."

"I'm guessing Conway had it in his house and whoever killed him went through his things and found it to plant here and, and . . . oh, Lordy, Reagan, honey, we got ourselves another little problem."

"We should put that on T-shirts," I said, searching the desk in case there were more pictures.

"The cops are here."

My head snapped up to strobing lights bouncing off the interior walls. "That's why no yellow crime tape on the doors. Create a false sense of security? The cops were hoping Boone would show up. How dumb do they think he is?"

"They're desperate to find him, is all. You should hide and take the picture with you." KiKi shoved it into my hand along with the shoe. She snagged BW's leash.

"What about you?" I asked.

"I'm not the TV celebrity wanting to get even with Boone. The cops will think you're here stealing stuff. Besides, I've got my trump card to play. Go hide in the pantry."

"What pantry?"

"Old house, big kitchen, there's a pantry." KiKi clipped her tiara in my hair, and I snagged the flashlight and scurried down the hall. I said a quick prayer to anyone listening and pulled on the first door I found.

"Police!" came the muffled voice from the living room. "Hands up and stay where you are."

Boone clamped one hand over my mouth and yanked me inside to what was obviously the pantry. Carefully he closed the door and turned off the flashlight, casting the crunched space of shelves and food products into total darkness. "You're stepping on my toe," I whispered. "You smell like peanut butter."

"You're stepping on my toe and I'm hungry." Boone shimmied one way as I did the same, our legs now twining together. My chest was now fused to his, my hand on his arm, his on my butt. My heart did the slow heavy thud, my mouth went totally dry, and I could hardly breathe. It had nothing to do with the cramped space of the pantry and everything to do with Boone being in it. I should have taken my chances with the cops.

"Oh, I'm so glad to see you, officer," KiKi said in the lovely exaggerated Georgia lilt she brought out for special occasions as the conversation drifted in from the living room. "I do believe I'm about to have myself a little spell right here on the spot."

Boone shifted again to get more room, with my forehead now pressed to his scruffed chin and his arm sandwiched between my boobs. My heart kicked up a notch; actually it kicked up three notches, and my insides were on fire. *Think of something else besides Boone*, I ordered myself.

"What are you doing here?" the officer said. I recognized that voice, and it didn't conjure up happy memories. Deckard! It was the cop who pulled me over when I was driving Boone's car. See, I could think of something else besides Boone . . . until he scooted left and I realized I wasn't the only one affected by our present close situation.

"I'm rescuing my poor little puppy here," KiKi said. "We were walking along like we do every night about this time, and lo and behold if he didn't pull away from me, the little rascal."

Holy cow. If KiKi said the back door was open, Deckard and his merry men would search the house and find Boone and me and the peanut butter crackers. *Think, KiKi, think*, I sent out in mental telepathy.

"He pushed on the back door and he ran in," KiKi said. "Mr. Boone lives here, you see, and gives my dear doggie treats, and now that the poor man is on the run, I figure puppy just misses him something terrible and came in anyway." KiKi's voice warbled and she added some sniffing for good measure. Auntie KiKi, the queen of bull.

"The dog pushed on the door?" Deckard asked in a not-convinced tone.

"He's a strong pup, and I'm betting the back door was ajar all along. You know how nothing fits quite right in these old houses," KiKi said. My guess was she was gearing up to play her trump card that could get her out of any and all sticky situations, especially with the fifty-somethings born and raised on Savannah cuisine.

"Well, I best be going now," KiKi added. "I've got to get back home to my wonderful dear husband. Maybe you know him? Dr. Vanderpool, but we all call him Putter."

"Doc Putter? The cardiologist? Yes, indeed, I sure do know the man," Deckard said, his voice now sweet as Auntie KiKi's peach cobbler. "He carries that putter with him everywhere. Fact is, he did a triple bypass on my mamma last year. She's better than new, I tell you. Lord be praised and alleluia. You go on home, Mrs. Vanderpool, and the boys and I will lock up. Tell the doc that Deckard sends his best now, you hear? Sure is a cute little puppy you have here."

There was a scurrying of footsteps that drowned out the rest of the talk, followed by doors closing, and then more doors closing, and then dead silence. It was best to wait to make sure no one was in the house and that no one came back, but I'd been divorced for two years and not had the pleasure of male companionship for longer than that, and here I was front to front with Walker Boone, hands down the most handsome guy in Savannah, who had kissed me senseless one day ago.

I opened the pantry door and jumped out with Boone right behind me. I took one look at him, moonlight in his hair, broad shouldered, narrow hipped, and silhouetted in the patch of white. A girl could stand just so much temptation. I threw my arms around his neck and dove in for a kiss till Boone took my arms and set me back.

"Did you read the note I sent over with Chantilly?" he asked. "What happened to *stay out of my house*? Have you been eating in the car?"

"All you can think about is your car?" I pointed the heel of the satin shoe at myself. "What about me?" I twitched my hips, jutted my boobs, and held out my arms. "What about *this*? I got pretty good *this*, you know."

Boone swallowed and looked pained. "You ate chocolate in the car, didn't you?"

"Maybe a little, and it was before I got the note." I took a step toward him, and he took a step back and ate another cracker. "We can't do this, Reagan," he said in a ragged voice.

"Oh yes we can," I said, my voice equally ragged. I felt devil horns sprouting on my head. "It'll be fun. I'm a little rusty, but I'm thinking it's like riding a bike and it'll come back to me really quick and—"

"No hanky-panky." Boone took another step back.

I stepped toward him. "I'll settle for the hanky."

"And then you'll get that dopey look on your face worse than ever, and the cops and everyone else will know that we've been together. Listen, someone wants me out of the picture and if they have to go through you to get to me, they'll do it and not think twice. I don't want you involved in this mess; stay out of it. That's why I wrote the note."

"Hey, you're not the only one with something to lose, you know."

"Lord save me, it's the furniture speech."

"I'm a businesswoman with a dog to support."

"Unless you want to be buried in that furniture, forget about it."

I parked my hands on my hips. "So why the heck are you here?"

"A friend of a friend saw lights inside and I got the message. I figured someone was up to no good. I should have known it was you causing mayhem. Go home and run your shop and butt out, period, blondie."

"You know, you say that every time things get a little crazy because you're afraid something will happen to me."

"Something always does happen to you."

I pulled the picture from my pocket and held the flashlight to it. "KiKi and I weren't the only ones in here tonight. We were out with BW and we saw the lights too and thought you were being burgled. Then we found this on your desk." I held up the shoe. "And we found this in your desk." I pulled out the picture. "We figure a really pissed-off bride left the shoe and the killer planted the picture. I'd say it's another piece of the *let's frame Walker for murder* puzzle."

Boone stared at the picture for a long moment, not moving, barely breathing. "The happy family," he said, his voice dripping with sarcasm.

"You know, at this particular time it probably was. Then Conway married for money and your mamma took off and left you with Grandma Hilly."

"It could be worse," Boone said, still looking at the picture.

Truth be told, I wasn't sure how it could be much worse, since Boone's Grandma Hilly died when he was around fifteen and he took to living on the streets.

"I could be Tucker, a wealthy boozed-up wart on society's backside," Boone added, the twinkle back in his eyes. "I'd say the killer's someone who has it in for me and for Conway and wanted to get rid of us both."

"And the shoe?" I held it up. "Tick anyone off lately?"

"She wanted me to sue her ex-fiancé and I graciously declined."

"Not graciously enough."

Boone shoved the picture in his jean pockets. They were baggy, torn denim, life-in-the-projects quality. His black hoodie was ripped and frayed at the neck. "We got to get out of here," he said. "The cops are going to keep an eye on this place from here on out. There's a loose board in the back fence that the kids use to cut through the alleys. Give it a yank and slide through. Stay off the streets for a few blocks in case the cops are on patrol."

He opened the fridge and stuffed two apples in his pocket and a half loaf of bread under his sweatshirt along with the jar of peanut butter and the crackers. For sure Boone knew people who would hide him, but he was staying away from friends so they wouldn't get caught up in his ordeal. I couldn't even imagine the hovel he was holed up in. I grabbed all the cash I had from Old Yeller, two tens and a five, and shoved them at Boone. "Take it, it's rent for the car."

He stuffed the money back in my purse, then opened the freezer and pulled a wad of bills from a mint chocolate chip ice cream container. "A little something I picked up from a friend." He winked, then headed for the back door, turned, and came back and kissed me hard.

"What about the dopey look?" I gasped, totally surprised I wasn't a puddle on the floor.

"You've got a satin shoe and are wearing a tiara. Some things are worth the gamble." He fiddled with the tiara, a warm sultry look in his dark eyes.

"It's KiKi's. It's for luck."

"We definitely need luck."

Boone kissed me again, this time slow and soft on the forehead. "Watch your back, blondie," he said, his lips forming the words against my skin. "There's some mean people out there and they're playing for keeps. I don't want you hurt over this."

"I don't want you hurt either," I said in a choked voice, barely able to get the words out. He looked at me for moment, his eyes dark and unfathomable. Then he walked out the door. The house was lonely and quiet except for the hum of the fridge and the slow heavy thud of my heart.

I refused to cry. Things would get better, I promised myself. They had to. I'd make sure they did. Boone didn't come all this way from being a half-starved street kid to living in a gorgeous house on Madison Square to wind up in jail for something he didn't do. And besides, BW would never forgive me if I let that happen to his doggie daddy. I waited a few beats, checked the back alley for stray cops, and then darted for the fence.

I cut across Drayton to Pinky Masters, the home of

Tabasco popcorn, hands down the very best late-night snack on the planet. Pinky's was a dive bar with the jukebox presently blaring Beyoncé, the perfect cure for me feeling down in the dumps. The place was frequented by everyone from teachers at SCAD—Savannah College of Art and Design— to local store clerks to the garbage pickup guys who kept Savannah neat and tidy. It was truly Savannah's melting pot, and right there in the back corner was Mercedes. She was eating popcorn, swilling something tall and cool, and intently checking her iPhone messages.

I snaked my way through the standing-room-only crowd to the back table. "More dead people waiting for your expertise?" I said as I sat down.

Mercedes looked up, a grin tripping across her face. "Girl, what are you doing in here?"

"Eating your popcorn." I dug a handful of spicy yumminess out of the little blue plastic basket on the table. "I didn't take you for a Pinky girl." I looked at Mercedes's lilac jacket with matching scarf. "I figured you were more of the Old Pink House variety or maybe the Bay Street Blues Club."

"Those places are right fine for sure, but at the moment I'm hiding out and taking a load off. Fixing up Conway was a lot of work and I'm beat to the bone. Besides, the Pink House doesn't have Tabasco popcorn, now does it?" She leaned across the table. "Any chance you've run into Mr. Boone? I sure hope he's doing okay. I'm truly worried. I sort of got him into this mess."

"Best I can tell, this all started years ago and you sure aren't to blame." Using every ounce of self-control I possessed, I kept my face blank. Boone was right about there being a killer out there, and I didn't want Mercedes in the line of fire if I could help it.

Mercedes's eyes rounded. "Well I do declare, you have seen the man."

"Okay, this is so not fair. How did you know? I didn't squish up my eyes or wrinkle my nose or get all dreamy and slobber."

"Oh, honey, that is sure true enough, but you did squash your handful of popcorn to nothing but a bunch of crumbs." She nodded at the table, which had bits of popcorn scattered across the top. "So, does he have any idea who did in Conway?"

"He's not talking if he does, but I got a few names that fit and—"

"And sweet mother above, there goes one already on the list," Mercedes said in a rush and jumped up, pointing across the crowd. "It's the guy who did the jab-and-stab on Conway at the Slumber." Mercedes snagged my hand and zigzagged through the crowd, elbowing patrons out of the way till we stumbled out onto the sidewalk.

"Do you see him?" I asked Mercedes.

"There." She pointed to a newer white pickup passing right in front of us. "Brown hair, short dude, cowboy hat, that's him all right. He must have spotted me and took off." She pursed her lips. "So I ask you, what kind of man goes after a dead guy? It's the craziest thing I ever saw since I started over at the Slumber. Conway's layout is tomorrow; you got to come, you know this nut-job is bound to show up. He's sure enough got something against Conway."

I slapped my hand against my forehead. "Did you happen to get his license plate?"

Mercedes gave me a *duh* look.

"Think you'd recognize the guy without the hat?"

"I'm counting on him recognizing me at the funeral and making a run for it again, just like he did. You need to be around to give chase if it happens." Mercedes posed a hip and rolled her shoulders. "My womanly roundness isn't as agile as your skinny self for that kind of thing."

"Hey, you outdid me just now."

"And I used it all up in one big swoop. Now it's your turn."

We headed for Mercedes's pink Caddy, and I gave her the lecture on there being a killer playing for keeps and that she needed to be careful. She dropped me off at Cherry House and I promised to get to the funeral. The upstairs light in Auntie KiKi's bedroom was on, meaning she and Putter were settled in for the night. I opened the back door to the Bruce Willis welcoming committee of puppy whines and tail wagging. That's the thing with dogs; no matter how crappy the day went and even if your hair had roots and you'd been hiding in a pantry and looked like death warmed over, your doggie was glad to see you.

We trotted upstairs and I did my minimal night prep, and then we collapsed into bed, with my feet dangling over the edge and BW sprawled out in the hall, his new favorite place for catching the breeze coming up the steps. My body wanted sleep, but my brain was on overdrive. Who was at Boone's house and left the picture? Who was Mercedes's blade man, and if Boone didn't do more than kiss me soon, I was joining the nunnery.

Chapter Five

"WHY in the world did it take you so long to get home last night?" KiKi wanted to know the next morning as she watched me dump the debris from the hole in the porch roof into the garbage can. "I did my part and got rid of the cops for you; what more was there?"

"There was Boone hiding in the pantry." I tossed in the rotting shingles.

"Sweet Jesus in heaven, what was the man doing in there?"

"Eating crackers and peanut butter. He said the neighbors are keeping an eye on the place and saw our intruder. Guess they called Big Joey or something. Anyway, I showed him the picture and we were right, he'd never seen it before. Best I can tell, he doesn't have any idea who's setting him up, though he probably wouldn't tell me if he did. Like always he wants me to stay out of it."

"And if he has an ounce of sense he knows you're not." KiKi sat down on the little wooden stool I had behind the counter. "Did he happen to let slip the names of any suspects?"

"No, but Mercedes has someone in mind." I swept up the last of the roof shrapnel and tossed it in the can. "When she was getting Conway spiffed up for his last big fling, some guy barged in and stabbed Conway right there on the table in front of her. Scared her to death." I rolled my eyes. "Sorry, the death thing just slipped out. Anyway, she figures it's someone who wants Conway real dead, and the chances are good he'll show up at Conway's wake tonight. She thinks we need to be there and chat him up, find out who he is." I lugged the garbage can to the side of the house.

"We?" KiKi asked, following me back into the shop. "Remember the last funeral *we* attended at the Slumber? The wigs, the upside-down fern, the fire department, and we had to hide in the bushes. I hate hiding in bushes; it's downright undignified for a woman my age. Think I'll pass this time around."

"You're going to make me go all alone?" I folded my arms and gave my dear auntie a hard look. "Something's up. No way would you miss the social event of the month, and you belong to the Plantation Club so you and Uncle Putter have to go because Conway was president. Fact is, not going would be a sacrilege. The only reason you're holding out is that you need a favor, a big one. Let me guess, you got another single doctor who needs a date."

KiKi fiddled with a display of earrings I had on the

checkout counter. "Not that." She bit her bottom lip, then threw her arms wide open and looked skyward. "I can't take it anymore. It's the Shakin' Seniors. One more dance lesson with Melvin Pettigrew and I'm tossing myself in the river. His hands are everywhere they have no business being. If Putter sees him in action there's going to be a duel out at Forsyth Park, and unless it involves golf clubs Putter will lose."

"Melvin's eighty-something, you can take him."

"Melvin's an octopus with bad breath. I need a break. I'm starting to get hives." KiKi held out her arms with red welts.

"Tell him to back off."

"Tell BW to be a watchdog."

"I get your point. All right, all right, I'll teach the class. Just one."

"Two, since I got two arms with hives."

"Fine. Besides, nothing can be worse than teaching the fox-trot to the teens." I looked at KiKi. "Did you just say 'wanna bet' under your breath?"

"I'll meet you at the Slumber at seven-ish by the big fern next to the tea table. Don't touch the fern, don't let Uncle Putter chip fallen rose petals into the casket, and most important of all, save me some windmill cookies."

KiKi headed off for a mambo lesson with the Dunlaps at eleven. They planned a Caribbean cruise and wanted to do it up in style. Two customers brought in clothes that I had to pass on, being as they were more Goodwill than prissy. At twelve sharp AnnieFritz and Elsie Abbott trotted up the front walk, with a big wicker basket slung over Elsie's arm.

I'd asked them to watch the shop while Chantilly and I stirred things up over at the Plantation Club.

The Abbott sisters lived next to me on the other side in a small Greek Revival–style house. They were left the place by Cousin Willie, who proclaimed sausage gravy and biscuits the fifth food group and was now chowing down at the great fat farm in the sky. Elsie and AnnieFritz were retired teachers and supplemented their income by renting themselves out as professional mourners. No one got the grieving attendees at a wake sobbing louder and longer than the sisters. They were top billing for all the major funerals, and for a 30 percent discount on funeral wear at the Prissy Fox they were happy to fill in when needed.

"I suppose you'll be attending Conway's funeral tonight?" I said to the sisters as they came inside.

Elsie pulled a lovely pink doily from the basket and fluffed it open across the desk as AnnieFritz unpacked a flowered teapot and matching china cups. "Oh, honey, you know we are. We're pulling out all the stops. Sister and I've been practicing like crazy to make sure we can hit the anguished high notes. We brought along our special lemon tea to keep our vocal cords warmed up. It's our duty to give Mr. Adkins a proper send-off now. Botching this would be mighty bad for business, mighty bad indeed."

AnnieFritz cleared her throat, squared her shoulders, and let out with a sorrowful howl that nearly had me breaking into a fit of tears for no reason at all. BW stood beside her, licking her hand in sympathy, and Elsie passed around the box of tissues to the others in the store, who were now sobbing.

"I think you nailed it." My breath caught; a tear slid down my cheek and I had no idea why.

"They don't pay us the big bucks for nothing." Elsie went over to the round table in what was once the dining room. She picked up a black lacy hat with a wide brim and simple black rose. "And I do believe this will be a nice addition to my ensemble, don't you agree, sister dear? We always need to be updating our attire and looking our best. Steffy Lou is even having us at the burial out at Bonaventure tomorrow morning to give her loving father-in-law a final tearful good-bye. Isn't that the sweetest thing ever? We can't be wearing the same thing to the wake and the burial, now can we, it just wouldn't be proper at all."

AnnieFritz poured out the lemon tea, added drops of honey, and took the cups to the ladies shopping. Not doing so would be the epitome of bad manners and not like the sisters at all. I started in on my tea as Chantilly strutted her stuff into the shop.

"So, girlfriend, what do you think?" Chantilly smoothed her hand over her dress and jutted one blue sequin-clad hip. She batted her long fake eyelashes. Everyone stopped what they were doing and stared openmouthed. Least it brought the crying to an end.

I led Chantilly out onto the porch and whispered, "Are you trying to get into the Plantation Club or just *do* everyone in the club?"

Chantilly harrumphed. "You said you wanted a diversion. I figure this here is a diversion. I said I was going slutty."

"Asking the time of day is a diversion, and I was thinking

tight jeans and sweater. Remember the closet Pillsbury mentioned? This is one way to get there quick."

Chantilly fluffed her sprayed and shellacked hair. "Here's the thing: I figured if I just showed up in something marginally offensive the receptionist at the club would tell me to make an appointment and put us off for another day and then another and so on. If I show up in this little number that I wore at a Tina Turner costume party last year and if I threaten to hang around the club till I see Dixon, they'll get him right quick. I'll ask a bunch of stupid questions about the club, drive him crazy, and you can look around while I keep him busy and everyone else looking on."

"What if he calls the cops?"

"For what? Wearing sequins in the middle of the day? My guess is he'll be polite and give me the 411. I'll tell him I'll think about it and leave." Chantilly turned serious. "Walker is Pillsbury's best friend, and Walker helped me when I had problems with Simon. I owe him. Let's see what falls out of the plantation tree when we give it a little shake."

"This is more hurricane than shake, but I get your point. Fifteen minutes should do it. We get in and we get out and if things blow up the way they sometimes do, you get out of there and take care of yourself." I grabbed Old Yeller from under the counter, and Chantilly and I moseyed to the car.

"You'll have to drive the Jeep." Chantilly heaved a deep sigh and reluctantly passed over the keys as we crossed the street. "I'm having a devil of a time driving a stick shift in six-inch heels, and if I take these things off I'm never getting them back on. They give a whole new meaning to *tight*."

I took the keys, but she didn't let go. "Be careful, okay? I love this car."

"I'm a good driver."

"Uh-huh."

I slid behind the wheel and Chantilly levered herself, her heels, and her hairdo into the passenger side. Cherry House and Rose Gate were in the Victorian district of Savannah, and we headed for the historic district and the Plantation Club. Deciding a Jeep was not in sync with Chantilly's outfit, I parked a block away and we hoofed it to the club, causing two accidents along the way.

"My friend here would like to talk to Mr. Dixon about membership in the Plantation Club," I said to the gal behind the reception desk. "Think he can spare a little time to explain things to her?"

"He's busy." The receptionist, in a navy suit and white blouse, gave Chantilly a disapproving stare. "You'll have to make an appointment, and he's really busy for the month, maybe the next two months or even three."

Chantilly waved her hand in the air. "Why, I just bet he's tied up with all sorts of important things that go on around here, so I'll just wait out front of this fine establishment till he can squeeze me in."

"Out front?" The receptionist jumped out of her chair. "Like on the sidewalk out front? Sweet Jesus save us, you can't be doing a thing like that."

"Well now, don't you worry your pretty little head about me." Chantilly tsked. "Of course I can wait by the door. It's a fine day, not a cloud in the sky."

The receptionist shagged Chantilly by the elbow. "No need to go outside, you can wait in the Robert E. Lee room and I'll find Mr. Dixon right quick." Chantilly teetered on her spike heels and gave me a little finger wave over her shoulder as she followed the receptionist down the hall. Since the club watchdog was now preoccupied with Chantilly and her sequins and had forgotten all about little ol' me, I headed off in the other direction and made for the back service stairway, which I knew about from when Boone and I were trying to get information.

"Hey," a waiter called to me as I ran up the steps. "What are you doing back here? This isn't for guests."

"I'm . . . a new hire," I said, flashing a bright smile. "And . . . and I'm looking for Mr. Dixon because . . . some floozy wants to talk to him about being a member. She's threatening to wait outside till he finds time to meet with her. We can't have that now, can we? What will people think is going on around here? The receptionist told me to check Mr. Dixon's office, and maybe you can look for him in the bar area? He's not picking up his cell."

"Gate crashers is what we call them around here," the waiter said with a big smile. "I'll get on it." He hurried off and I panted my way up to the third floor, making a solemn promise that if I didn't have a heart attack I'd take up a morning activity other than eating doughnuts.

Peeking around the corner, I spotted Dixon getting into the small elevator, and as the door slid closed I made for his office. I let myself in and gently closed the door behind me. If Dixon owed Conway money he'd have a record of it, something signed and dated. He could keep the information at his house, but more than likely any money transactions between Conway and Dixon happened here. From what I'd heard, Conway and Dixon didn't have a *let's do lunch* kind of relationship. It was more likely that the reason Conway lent Dixon money was to lord it over him. Those two deserved each other.

Dixon was a neatnik with things all nice and tidy. A calendar of events for June sat next to a stack of invitations for the annual summer ball, and next to that was a club member application from some guy named Grayden Russell. His residence was the Old Harbor Inn. I stared at the application. Boone had mentioned Grayden Russell's name the night we switched modes of transportation—something about Russell being out to get him? I had no idea who this guy was or why he was after Boone.

The side drawer held club stationery; the other side drawer was packed with power bars and M&Ms. The middle drawer was stuck. I didn't have time for stuck. Chantilly was downstairs playing for time, and I didn't trust Mason Dixon any further than I could throw him. I pulled harder; something was still holding it in place till I gave one more yank. The drawer gave way, sending me stumbling backward as it sailed out of the slot, hit the floor, and flipped over, and a .38 duct-taped to the underside slid off.

Whoa! Guess the Plantation Club wasn't all jasmine and sweet tea; the boys knew how to play rough. Carefully, I picked up the gun and the tape to reattach it, and there stuck to the tape was a picture. Holy Moses, it was another happy-family photo. Not exactly like the one at Boone's house, but close. I almost dropped the blasted gun.

I sat on the floor, because my legs were jelly, and tried to make sense of what was going on in front of me. If Dixon had this photo, he knew Conway was Boone's father. Conway Adkins didn't lend Dixon money—he *gave* it to him? The money was a bribe to Dixon to keep his mouth shut? Conway might have told Tucker that he had a brother, but only after Mrs. Adkins died. Having Walker as part of the Adkins family had been a deal-breaker since the get-go. My guess was Conway had been paying Dixon off for years.

A piercing screech filled the club. Fire alarm? I crawled over to the window. No smoke billowing out the front, but whatever was going on, the fire department would arrive in minutes and here I was in Dixon's office with a gun in my lap and my best friend downstairs in all her slutty glory. If we made the papers, Pillsbury and Boone would be in lecture mode—*What were you thinking?*—for months, and of course Chantilly and I would be sharing that closet.

With the alarm blaring, sirens approaching, and my hands shaking, I taped the picture and gun to the underside of the drawer, then scooped up the pens, pencils, Tic Tacs, and other office paraphernalia and slid the drawer back in. I peeked out into the hall to make sure the coast was clear and that no one saw me leaving the office. I tore down the steps as firefighters galloped up. I put my hands over my face and did some faked coughing and gagging, even though there wasn't any smoke. I pointed upstairs. "Dogs, cats, kids."

Any firefighter worth his hose would go after a dog, cat, and kid. Then I bolted out the open rear door into the back alley and smashed flat into a blue pinstriped suit with a red carnation. Dixon! Eye-to-eye, we both stared at each other for a split second as Dixon tried to remember who I was. I took the opportunity to dash for the Dumpster, then on to the next alley, coming out on Barnard. The street was clogged with fire trucks, EMS units, and cops, but no Chantilly and no smoke.

"Psst" came from a Jeep double-parked next to a police cruiser. Chantilly's eyes peered at me just above the window line; her once-bouffant hair now tumbled around her head and her makeup was smeared. I ran for the Jeep and jumped in, and Chantilly laid rubber before I had the door shut.

"You're a mess," I said, taking in her hair and clothes. "Did you get caught in the fire?"

"The old goat chased me around that Robert E. Lee room, and he's a fast little devil. Had me sweating like a pig."

"You're kidding!"

Chantilly cut her eyes my way and snarled. "This is not the look of frivolity. I dodged that no-good louse as long as I could to give you time in his office, but when he pinched my butt I hit him with my shoe and then the fire alarm went off, thank heavens. I figured you saw what was going on and pulled the alarm to save me."

"Must have been one of the employees with a conscience who saw what was going on. Why would Dixon do such a thing and not think you'd go to the cops or at least tell someone what the jerk's like?"

"He said no one would believe the likes of trampy me over the sophisticated likes of him, but at least I'm okay now. I lost my shoe in the chaos and worked up an appetite, but as soon as I get a meat loaf sandwich from Parkers with extra provolone I'll be fit as a fiddle. An apple a day may keep the doctor away, but we all know that meat loaf from Parkers is good for the Southern soul."

I added an amen because it seemed fitting, and then we headed down Drayton. We pulled into Parkers, where a body can fill up their car and themselves all at one stop. Chantilly kept the Jeep running and I knew the deli squad well enough to ask for asap service; five minutes later Chantilly and I were at Emmet Park under the massive oaks in front of the Old Harbor Inn munching meat loaf and slurping Diet Coke to offset the calories from the extra provolone.

"So tell me this wasn't all for nothing," Chantilly said around a mouthful. "Did you find Dixon's IOU to Conway? If Dixon killed Conway he wouldn't have to pay it off, and that sounds like motive to me."

"Things are little more complicated." I slurped up a chunk of meat loaf. "I found a picture of Conway with Boone's mom, and she was holding him as a baby. The photo was taped under Dixon's desk along with a .38 Special. That means Dixon knew Conway was Boone's dad long before two nights ago, and my guess was Dixon was blackmailing Conway. The money wasn't a loan from Conway; it was a payoff. As much as Dixon is a creep and a letch and basically loathsome in every way, this kind of kicks him out as murdering Conway. I mean, why would he kill the goose that lays the golden egg?" I took another bite of my sandwich, and Chantilly dropped hers in her lap.

"Holy freaking tomatoes and I'll be a monkey's uncle," she said on a long exhale. "I never saw that one coming. I wonder how Dixon found out about Conway and Walker, and how did he get the picture?"

"Conway and Dixon had offices next to each other; maybe he overheard something. Maybe he snooped."

Chantilly licked a glob of provolone off her thumb and picked up her sandwich. "Maybe Conway got tired of Dixon's threats and refused to pay, and Dixon killed him. That guy is no Southern gentleman, I can tell you that. I'm mighty glad someone pulled that fire alarm. Not that I couldn't have gotten out on my own, but with the added commotion I didn't cause a scene."

Chantilly polished off her sandwich. "I've got to get back to Rachelle; she's cooking up a storm at the shop and I've had the pulled pork simmering since last night. We're catering a light dinner for the Adkins family and close friends tonight after the wake. Business is really good."

"If you got caught in this dress at the Plantation Club, it might not be so good."

Chantilly batted her eyes. "Honey, you're forgetting this is Savannah; everyone around here loves a touch of scandal now and then, and our business would probably double. Besides, no one can resist my pulled pork and mac and cheese."

Chantilly dropped me at Cherry House, and the Abbott sisters headed for home to rest up and gargle in preparation for the evening activities. I hung up the latest clothes brought in, then locked up the Fox at five and fed and watered BW. Going with the idea that anything was better than my two-toned hair that everyone saw fit to tell me about, I decided to go blonde, mostly because I found a bottle of Summer Sunshine dye back in the closet. I dumped on the goop, wrapped my head like a fortune-teller, and spent the thirty-minute wait time doing laundry since I was down to my last pair of panties.

I headed for the shower and by six thirty I was dressed in basic black and the pearl earrings and bracelet Mamma gave me for my sixteenth birthday, and carefully backing the Chevy out of the garage. That I'd gotten two wolf whistles and a hubba-hubba on my way to the Slumber gave me an ounce of confidence that I didn't look too bad. That the attention was all for the Chevy was a possibility I refused to consider.

I berthed the sexmobile in a pay lot where I had plenty of room so as not to ding it, then teetered off toward the Slumber in my three-inch heels. Okay, three wasn't all that many inches for heels, I'll give you that, but when you're used to flip-flops it presented a real challenge.

The House of Eternal Slumber was a pristine white frame dating back to eighteen-something-or-other with an original wrought-iron widow's walk and multiple add-ons that had been built as it went from family to family to deadly business.

I joined the somber procession up the main brick walk lined with tulips and daffodils. I avoided the long reception line of *I'm so sorry* and *doesn't he look great* and *did they catch Walker Boone yet* and headed for the tea table, better known as ground zero for the latest news from the kudzu vine. The scent of flowers, mints, and bourbon hung in the air, the Abbott sisters did an award-winning job of wailing over by the sleeping Conway, and the horde of guests sniffed and sobbed into starched white hankies. There was even a piano player softly playing music to die by. It was indeed a perfect Savannah funeral.

I snagged a windmill cookie, looked for KiKi, and spotted Tucker Adkins ducking out of the reception line and heading straight for me.

Chapter Six

"**W**ELL, did you find Boone?" Tucker asked in a low voice, his whiskey breath washing over me as he backed me into a corner. He pulled up next to a gargantuan flower arrangement with a white "Conway" sash across the front, just in case someone forgot who was in the big wooden box across the room.

"I have no idea where Boone is," I said, hoping I was convincing. "We can talk later. Right now you have guests to attend to and—"

"Forget them. I just want that guy found and the sooner the better, and you want the same thing, right?" Tucker plucked a lily from a display sent with deepest sympathy from Mason Dixon, probably bought with Conway's very own bribe money. Tucker squashed the flower in his hand

and ground his teeth. He looked around as if Boone would pop out from behind a fern. "Where the devil is that guy?"

"I'm guessing you loved your dad more than you thought you did?"

"Yeah, right. It must be because every time we were alone since Mother died, he'd throw Walker up to me. *Why can't you be self-sufficient like Walker? He's successful, respected, and what happened to you? You're not half the man he is and you've had every advantage.* Yeah, like the advantage of being hounded. Do you know what it's like to have your brother who you didn't even know you had tossed in your face day after day?"

"I'm an only child."

"Yeah, well, that's my plan, too. I want to see Boone rot in jail, and it needs to happen quick."

Tucker stormed off, the quick statement echoing in my ears. This brotherly hatred thing ran a little deeper than I expected, and if Conway did constantly toss Boone in Tucker's face I could understand why. But why was time an issue? Why go after Boone now?

Auntie KiKi handed me a cup of tea. She lowered her head and the brim of her big black hat covered the fact that she pulled out her little silver flask and discreetly poured a splash or maybe three splashes into the china cup. "Now you know why Southern ladies wear big hats to funerals."

"Alleluia," I said, taking a sip and letting the contents burn a path to my stomach.

"I figured you needed it after having a friendly chat with the local resident sociopath. I heard the conversation. The man takes jealousy to a whole new level, and frankly I sort of understand. But why does he need to find Walker so quick? His daddy's dead, he can't get any deader."

"Good question." I took another gulp of tea; my head was starting to swim, but overall I was mellowing out till I spotted Mason Dixon coming in the door. "Give me the hat, I'm desperate," I said to KiKi.

KiKi took out the flask and I stuffed it back in her purse. "Not that."

"I thought you were talking code for 'more, please.'"

I snagged KiKi's hat off her head and jammed it on mine, pulling the brim down in front. "Mason Dixon's over there in the receiving line. I don't need him to connect me to Conway, and if he sees me here he'll know something's up."

"And he would do that because . . ."

"Chantilly and I sort of paid him a visit this afternoon, and I sort of rifled through his office upstairs as he chased her around a conference room downstairs. I collided with him while exiting when the fire trucks came. He had a picture of *the* happy family taped to the bottom of a drawer, so I'm guessing he was blackmailing our present man of honor."

"Sweet mother, where in blazes was I when all this was going on?"

"Dancing." I gave KiKi a little push. "Go find out if he knows it was me in his office. You're a member of the Plantation Club; ask him about the fire department and the blue sequins and see how he reacts."

KiKi's jaw dropped. "*That* was you? There were sequins and the fire department and I wasn't invited?"

"The fire part wasn't planned."

KiKi harrumphed and trotted off as Mercedes came up beside me. "Did you see him? He's right over there."

"I know, honey, and you did a mighty fine job. The make-up's perfect, only a slight indent where that bullet went in between his eyes." Not that I'd looked, but it was one of those little white lies to be nice to Mercedes and save me face time with the dead.

"Not Conway," she hissed. "Stabber guy. I told you he'd show up." Mercedes scooted behind me and crouched lower. "He's in a blue sports coat and spotty mustache and standing by himself and looking pissed." She nodded across the room. "Go talk to him, find out who he is."

"I know nothing about him, and *why do you hate Conway?* isn't a great conversation starter."

Mercedes pursed her lips. "Just how long has it been since you did a little flirting?"

"I can't count that high, and you really expect me to hit on a guy at a funeral? Isn't there a law or something?"

"Are you kidding? Weddings and funerals are where all the action happens. Most everyone here is over fifty and graying, so you got a better-than-average chance of getting chummy with the guy, or at least you would if you didn't have that purse. Yellow? Really? Say something subtle like *nice jacket, great stache, how do you know the deceased?*" She gave me a quick once-over. "But the hat's got to go."

Before I could stop her, Mercedes whipped off the hat. I grabbed for it and tripped, and my tea poured down the front of my dress, drawing everyone's attention. Stabber guy's gaze landed on Mercedes, his eyes widening in recognition. He hustled for the front door as Mason Dixon headed for me. Guess that answered the question of him connecting the dots of me being at the club this afternoon and in his office, which was probably not quite the way he left it.

"Go out the back and catch him there." Mercedes pointed to the hallway.

It was either hang around here and face Dixon and his questions about me being in his office or catch up with Mercedes's mystery man. Maybe this time I'd get the license plate. I ran for the door.

Outside the traffic on Price Street was light but the Slumber parking lot was jammed. I stopped to see which car lights blinked on, and as I turned around, the white pickup barreled toward me; I stumbled back and somehow got propelled into the bushes far enough so as to not get squashed flat on the pavement.

"Are you okay?" Mercedes wanted to know as she bustled out the door and the pickup merged into the traffic. "Did you get the plates?"

"*JT* is all I saw." I looked around. "I have no idea how I didn't get run over."

"You must have jumped. An adrenaline rush. These things happen. So now we got a white pickup, Georgia plates, and the two letters. It's more than we had before. We could get Ross to help us."

I gave Mercedes an *are you out of your mind* look.

"Right, no cops. They wouldn't be happy that we're sticking our noses in this. I better go back inside to make sure no one's dropped something on Conway or is giving him a hard time."

"Honey, the man's dead. The hard times have passed."

"You'd be plumb amazed how many people feel a need to touch and poke the dead guy. Guess they think they can wake him up or something." Mercedes gritted her teeth. "You need to wipe yourself off before getting back in Mr. Boone's fine car. Tea stains on white upholstery would be downright criminal. You can use the bathroom in the composition wing." Mercedes nodded to the addition. "First door to the left."

"Composition wing?"

"Don't ask." Mercedes went back inside and I ducked into the next door down; the hallway was eerily quiet except for a few creaks and maybe a moan or two, but that was strictly an old house settling, and the fact that this happened to be a newer addition was beside the point. I pushed open the bathroom, done up nicely in mauve and gray with a little love seat and Steffy Lou Adkins sitting there smoking a cigarette. She froze midpuff, eyes huge, and she dropped the cigarette. "I . . . I . . ."

I picked up the cigarette and handed it back to her. "You don't have to explain to me. This is a most difficult time. I'm truly sorry for your loss."

The local consignment shop gal and the owner of stately Lillibridge House didn't exactly travel in the same social circles, so I knew Steffy Lou Adkins only via tales of the kudzu vine and Auntie KiKi.

"Why, I thank you kindly for that." Steffy Lou took another long draw off the cigarette, the red tip glowing bright and the nicotine relaxing her a bit. She eyed Old Yeller for a second and, doing the Southern-lady thing, tried her best not to shudder.

"I gave up this completely disgusting habit years ago," she said, studying her cigarette. "It's terrible bad for my singing voice and all, but sometimes . . . Well, this has all been so overwhelming with losing Daddy Conway. No one is ever prepared for such a tragedy in their life, and to think that Walker Boone is suspected of doing the deed is devastating indeed. The doctor even gave me some pills to try to calm me down, but nothing's working." She took another puff of the cigarette. "This is all so dreadful."

She looked at me with a critical eye, her cigarette poised midair. "I know you, you're that girl who was on TV. You said you were trying to get even with Walker because he did you an injustice."

Steffy Lou shook her head and puffed, the soft curls of smoke fading into air. "Everyone is indeed entitled to their own opinion in this here world, but I must say that you've got it all wrong with Walker. I'm sorry about your divorce, I truly am, but he's one of the good guys. I don't care what the evidence says; Walker Boone didn't kill Conway. He'd never do such a terrible thing. It's just not like Walker at all." Her voice wobbled and she dabbed her eyes with a handkerchief.

Okay, this did not reflect her husband Tucker's view on the situation at all. I wetted a towel and swiped at my tea stains, but I was more interested in Steffy Lou's take on what was going on than my dress. "You know Boone?"

"Oh my, yes. We're on the Tybee Post Theater committee to save it from the wrecking ball and now from the greedy developers who want to buy it outright. It's such a lovely theater out there on Tybee Island, and I planned this dinner and talent show coming up to make money to help save the place. Walker did all the legal work for free, bless his heart. We worked together morning, noon, and night to get the papers filled out just right. The committee's trying mighty hard to get the theater on the National Registry to save it; we're even having those special car license plates issued to draw interest. The very night Walker was charged with murder and had so much on his mind, he came to warn me that this Grayden Russell person wanted to buy the theater and that I might be in danger if I didn't go along with it. Now I ask you, does that sound like a cold-blooded killer? He was worried about me more than himself."

I dropped the towel. "Who *is* this Grayden Russell guy? He's new in town?"

"From Charleston. Up there they all think they're better than we are down here in Savannah, but the way I see it they are the ones closer to those Yankees. Seems Russell came here with his sights set on buying the theater to turn it into a resort of some nature that's bound to be dreadful. Walker felt that Russell intended to get rid of the two of us as a warning to the theater committee to sell."

Steffy Lou sat up straight and raised her chin. "Well, let me tell you, that tactic might work up North where he comes from, but it doesn't stand a chance here in Savannah."

She snuffed out her cigarette in a little silver compact she obviously kept for smoking lapses and snapped the evidence closed up neatly inside. She stood, shoulders back, head high, eyes set. "That man will never, and I do mean never, get his hands on the Tybee Theater if it takes my last dying breath." She poked herself in the chest. "I am of the theater, a patron of the arts. A performer. As God is my witness, the theater will be saved."

I waited for a band to strike up "Dixie," but when that didn't happen I offered, "My auntie took me to see *Peter Pan* there when I was little. It was fantastic."

Steffy Lou smiled, her eyes sparking. "Oh my goodness, I played one of the Lost Boys." She cleared her voice and let out a pretty decent rendition of "I Won't Grow Up" right there in the composition addition bathroom.

I applauded and Steffy Lou bowed. The whole thing seemed a little odd, but Steffy Lou deserved a smile. She'd just lost her father-in-law, who'd seemed to treat her well, and the poor woman had married Tucker Adkins, God help her.

"I best get back," she said, tossing a mint in her mouth and adding a spritz of something vanilla from a little atomizer to kill all evidence of smoker gone wild. She obviously had this experience down to a science.

"Everyone will be wondering where I am." She opened the door and glanced back to me. "I sure do hope you change your mind about Walker Boone being guilty. He's a fine man, he truly is. He deserves better than he's getting, I can tell you that, but things seem to be stacking up against him and I don't rightly know how to turn it all around. I'm truly afraid for him."

Steffy Lou floated out the door in a wave of black taffeta, Southern sophistication, and sweet vanilla. She headed down the hall and I hoisted Old Yeller onto my shoulder, opened the back door, and slipped into the night, my brain fixated on Grayden Russell, whoever he was. The parking lot seemed to be Mason Dixon free, so I headed for the car but changed my mind. Figuring KiKi would be hungry after a night of twenty questions with Mason Dixon and the fact that I'd skipped dinner to catch up on laundry, I suffered the pain of walking in heels and hoofed up Price to York in a quest for food. I could drive the sexy Chevy, but it was easier to leave it moored safely at its present location and walk.

Inhaling deeply, I caught the spicy scent of Walls' BBQ a block before I spied the little red bench on the covered porch. Walls' was a hidden-away hole-in-the-wall kind of place, surrounded by small day shops and frequented by locals and tourists lucky enough to find it with the help of Yelp and Google Maps. My mouth started to water in anticipation of tender ribs with a side of collard greens. I'd get the small portions for a change, as pigging down at this hour probably wasn't a great idea for my waistline or my digestive system, but . . . but someone was following me?

During the day York had its share of foot traffic, but at night I walked alone. The shadows were dark and deep, with lamplight tucked behind oak leaves and layers of Spanish moss. Usually those things offered ambiance with a touch of Southern romance; right now not so much.

I could feel eyes boring into my back, and I did what any woman would do in my situation. I hugged Old Yeller tight like a security blanket and ran like the devil to get my ribs! I ordered quarter portions, then tore back to the Chevy, my feet not touching the ground and basic primal fear spurring me on. By the time I garaged the Chevy I had blisters the size of peach stones and I was walking barefoot.

I took the moonlit path around the side of Cherry House,

feeling calmer with Southern cuisine tucked under my arm and BW and KiKi waiting on the front porch with a shaker of martinis. For some, home was supper on the table at five, cookies in the oven, or a fire in the hearth. For KiKi and me it seemed to be a martini shaker and a dog on the porch, and a few of those cookies were okay, too. Home sweet home indeed, even if it did have a hole in the roof.

"So that's where you hightailed it off to," KiKi said to me as she eyed the white bag in my arms and inhaled deeply. She had on the blue floral housecoat I'd given her for her birthday and matching rollers already curled into her hair. She handed me a frosted martini glass, with a toothpick speared through a tiny gherkin pickle.

"Out of olives?"

"We don't want to be boring."

"It's been a day of sequins, fire trucks, and funerals." *And stalkers*, but KiKi didn't need to fret over every little detail of my life, now did she? "I think we're at a ten on the nonboring scale."

I put the bag from Walls' between us, and the heavenly aroma surrounded us as KiKi smacked her lips. "Find anything out from Dixon?" I asked, handing her a take-out container. I took the other and pulled out a plain hot dog for BW that Walls' threw in for free. BW parked between us and I broke the hot dog into nice bite-size pieces, and then we all three dug in.

"Dixon is not a happy camper, I can tell you that," KiKi said, slurping sauce off her fingertips. "My guess is it has to do with you in his office and suspecting him of blackmail. I'd watch myself with that one, dear."

She patted my knee, then took another bite of rib, her eyes glazing over in ecstasy. "You got to realize that the Plantation Club might be all proper decorum on the outside, but underneath it's pretty much the Wild West show and last-man-standing mentality." She expertly caught a drip of sauce with her tongue. "Did you happen to find Mercedes's mystery man?"

"He was that guy at the funeral in the cowboy hat. He nearly ran me over in the parking lot with his white pickup."

KiKi stopped the rib bone halfway to her mouth. "Built like a fireplug? Mustache? Crazy eyes?"

"One of your dance students?"

"Angie Gilbert's husband. She's my canasta partner and she's a nurse. She used to visit Conway at his house and give him B-12 shots and a little personal attention to rev up his heart, if you get my drift."

I licked sauce off my pinky. "Well, the old boy saw fit to kill Conway a second time; do you think he has it in him to do the deed the first time?"

KiKi shook her head. "He was out of town, a flight to New York. He goes every other week like clockwork. Angie timed her B-12 visits that way."

"He could have doubled back."

"It's a 747, honey, not a Honda."

The stalker event killed my appetite. It was a rotten ending to a rotten day when even Walls' didn't look good to me. I packed up the greens and ribs for later.

"Are you okay?" KiKi asked with a hint of concern.

"Too many windmill cookies, is all. So," I added fast, to keep KiKi from asking more questions, "that takes Angie's husband off the table for killing Conway, and Mason Dixon doesn't fit either. Why would Dixon kill the guy who was paying him off? The gold-digger sisters were angry with Conway and Boone, but murder's a big leap. Tucker hated his dad, but why kill him? Just don't return his phone calls and don't invite him for Thanksgiving dinner. Any other gossip floating around?"

Auntie KiKi slurped her martini, the perfect accompaniment to ribs or in KiKi's opinion anything else. "Some guy is trying to buy the Tybee Post Theater, and no one's much liking the idea."

"That's Grayden Russell; he's staying at the Old Harbor Inn. I met up with Steffy Lou Adkins in the little girls' room at the Slumber, and she said Russell was after Boone."

"Steffy Lou and you chatting it up?"

"She liked my purse."

KiKi snagged a napkin, mopped herself up, and then finished off her martini. "You know, I haven't been to the Old Harbor Inn in years, and this Russell person seems to be sittin' right in the middle of all this mess."

"That's a stretch."

"Honey, all we got is stretch. I hear tell the inn serves up a mighty fine breakfast."

"Breakfast there is only if you bed there."

"We'll improvise. Mess up your hair, wear your bunny slippers, and dream up a room number. I'll have the Batmobile fueled up and ready to fly at eight sharp."

Chapter Seven

"WHAT do you mean, KiKi can't make it?" I said to Chantilly, both of us not quite awake, which was proven by the fact that we were staring blankly into my empty refrigerator at seven thirty in the morning.

"That's why I'm here," Chantilly said. "KiKi is having an attack of tummyitis and wants me to fill in even though I didn't get to bed till after two from catering the Adkins wake, and why don't you ever have food in this house?"

"I have SpaghettiOs and hot dogs."

Chantilly stifled a burp. "KiKi said something about breakfast at the Old Harbor Inn. I thought you had to bed at the inn to breakfast there."

"You do; KiKi and I were going to breakfast-crash." I gave Chantilly a hard look, as what she had just said about KiKi started to sink in. "A tummy problem? Well, that explains why I can't find my leftovers of ribs and greens from Walls' in here. It was right there." I pointed to the second shelf. "She knows where I keep my spare key and helped herself."

"Girl, everyone knows where you keep your spare key."

"Hey, I moved it."

"Where this time? The second flowerpot instead of the first?"

"Maybe. That thieving auntie snuck over here in the middle of the night in a barbecue frenzy and ate my food and didn't even leave me the bag." I sucked in a breath. "Wow, that was a lot of leftovers on top of what she already scarfed down; the woman deserves to have a jelly belly."

Chantilly closed the fridge door. "The ribs and greens aren't going to magically appear just because you want them to. Frankly, ribs at this hour isn't my thing anyway, and if we're going to crash breakfast let's get a move on. How are we going to do this?"

"No idea. I don't do ideas at seven thirty."

"So is there some special reason for all this?" Chantilly added as I kissed BW good-bye on the snout and watched as he dragged his favorite chew toy to the top of the steps.

"We're going to see a man about a murder . . . I think," I said, closing the back door and heading for the garage.

"Oh goody, the perfect follow-up to yesterday. Some people start the morning with the newspaper and Frosted Flakes, you know."

I backed the Chevy out of the garage and powered down the convertible top. "We got to put on the boot."

"It's summer; I don't do boots in summer."

"It's the thing that covers the convertible top when it's down."

"That's a lot of trouble."

"You'll thank me."

Grumping and grousing, Chantilly got out and together we performed the time-honored tradition of snapping on the leather boot, and then we took off.

"This is simply amazing," Chantilly said, her face to the sky, as sunlight peeked through the low-hanging branches of the live oaks forming a canopy overhead. Two hard hats offered wolf whistles and a wave, and Chantilly and I smiled and waved back. Some women would find this offensive, but in my book a little male appreciation was just what I needed to keep my hormones pumping.

"Thank you." Chantilly grinned.

"You're welcome, but we need to be thanking Boone."

"You know, everyone in this city should have a convertible. It should be some kind of city law," she purred.

"Until it's August, one hundred in the shade, and mosquitoes are the size of a bus." Having a car was really nice; the more I drove Boone's, the more I wanted one. No bus to wait on, no walking in the rain unless I wanted to, I could pick up Fox supplies and consignment items, and I could make midnight runs to Parkers in my jammies if BW and I felt the need.

I took East Broad heading toward the Savannah River; the tourist traffic picked up the closer we got to the historic district. I crossed Bay Street, eased around Emmet Park, and dropped down onto the stone street below Factor's Walk, where back in the day factors called out bids from above for the cotton wagons passing below. The lower level of the Old Harbor Inn was to the right; the hotel was sandwiched neatly between Factors Walk and River Street. Prime real estate indeed.

"Look out!" Chantilly braced herself and I slammed on the brakes as a gray sports car gunned up the short lane lined with river rocks, cars, people, and us. It squealed around the corner as pedestrians dived for safety and offered the one-finger salute in reply.

Chantilly stared at me wide-eyed. "What the—"

"Are you okay, Miss Chantilly?" the valet from the Old Harbor Inn asked, rushing our way.

"I . . . I think so." Chantilly flipped back her mussed hair, and I felt my heart settle back into my chest. Chantilly did a double take at the valet. "We've met?"

"Lamar Jones." The valet smoothed his smart maroon vest, which was the same color as the Old Harbor Inn's awnings. "I've seen you with Mr. Pillsbury. He got me this here gig and a place to stay. Righteous dude." Lamar's lips pulled into a hard line and he gazed toward the corner. "And Grayden Russell's a jerk."

"You know him?" I asked.

"He's staying here and probably taking his car around to River Street on the other side to drop off that heavy surveying equipment he lugs around. He and some other guy get out at the docks early, taking measurements and whatever before it's congested with tourists waiting for ferries and deep-sea fishing boats. Maybe today someone will push Russell in; he treats the staff and everyone here like dirt." Lamar's gaze fixed on Chantilly. "Please don't be telling Pillsbury I said that. He'll be pissed I was being disrespectful."

Chantilly did the lock-the-lips thing, and I passed Lamar twenty bucks and a business card that I had made up for the Fox. "If you could let me know what Russell is up to, I'd appreciate it, and do you mind if we park here for a few minutes?"

Lamar passed back the twenty and added a smile. "There's a spot behind you for this sweet ride, and be my pleasure keeping you up to date."

Lamar welcomed another guest to the inn as I parked the Chevy and killed the engine. I turned sideways in my seat and faced Chantilly. "Okay, we need an excuse to talk to Russell. Something friendly and casual."

"So how does this guy fit into a murder?"

"Russell was after Walker and Steffy Lou Adkins because they wouldn't get behind his plan to buy the Tybee Post Theater; they're trying to save the place as a theater for the performing arts. Now Steffy Lou's father-in-law is dead and Walker is framed for the murder. KiKi thinks there might be a connection of some sort."

Chantilly stared at me for a beat. "Really? That's all you got?"

"Right now it's the best I got of anything."

"Lord have mercy, Walker's gonna fry." Chantilly got out of the car and hooked her finger in a *follow me* gesture. "Since we're here, we'll talk to the guy."

"Breakfast-crashing?"

"Still got that twenty? I'm starving, aren't you starving? I just bet Russell feels the same way and I bet he's a man who likes to be catered to. I'm a caterer, I know about these things."

I had no idea what Chantilly was talking about, but she

seemed to have a plan and that beat the nothing going on in my brain. We opened the door to the Old Harbor Inn and I followed Chantilly inside. The reception desk was on the upper level, and we trooped to the main floor, avoided the desk, and headed toward the clatter of china and chitchat from guests in the back. I took in the yellow-and-white breakfast room overlooking the Savannah River with sightseeing boats, tenders, and ferries at the docks. Chantilly talked shop with the headwaiter. She slipped him the twenty and came back with two white Old Harbor Inn towels and a tray laden with pastries, plates and napkins, and a coffee carafe and mugs. "How do you feel about being a waitress?"

"Depends on the tips."

Chantilly stuffed the towel into her waistband across her front to look waitresslike and I followed suit. She snagged the tray, I took the carafe, and we headed out the back entrance onto River Street.

Sure enough, our man Russell was standing on the dock. He had on a red Atlanta Braves baseball cap, and there was another guy with him in khakis and a green polo. Some sort of surveying camera/telescope thing was set up on a tripod, drawings were laid out on a little table, and a toolbox sat open with tape measures and the like spilling out onto the wood plank flooring. It was just like Lamar said.

"Yoo-hoo, Mr. Russell," Chantilly called in a friendly voice, adding a big toothy grin. "We have some nice refreshments here for you and your guest, compliments of the hotel. We like to take special care of our important clients."

Russell stopped staring through the telescope thing. He gave us a lurid once-over, making my skin crawl. Wolf whistles and waves were fine; Russell was plain creepy. He eyed the coffee. "Sure, why not."

I poured out two mugs and Chantilly offered the pastries, saying, "You gentlemen are sure hard at work out here in the morning sun. Don't you think our Savannah docks are safe enough?"

"Just checking things, is all. Don't you worry your pretty little heads about it," khakis guy said in a smart-man-to-dumb-woman voice. Munching a slice of pound cake, he gazed out at the river and said to Russell, "This is going to work. We'll get the divers here to check the water depth. Savannah's a deep-river port; we're good to go. How's that guy you're working with?"

Russell hunched. "Not the sharpest knife in the box. You'll meet him at the game." He held out his mug to me for a refill and stopped, eyes focusing. "I know you."

Drat. Everybody knew me. I needed one of those big-round-glasses-with-plastic-nose disguises. It couldn't be any more obvious than my present face.

"Thought you were a waitress over at the Plantation Club," Russell continued.

"I freelance a lot."

"And you were on TV, something to do with Walker Boone." Russell glanced over to Chantilly. "Get out of here, both of you."

"More Danish?" Chantilly offered the tray.

"Buzz off and stay out of my business." Russell's eyes hardened to bits of gray steel, and he picked up a hammer from the toolbox. "You don't want to mess with me, girl. Whatever you heard, you didn't hear. Got it?"

Normally I was a get-out-of-here kind of person, especially if there was a hammer involved, but I had zilch on finding Conway's killer, getting Boone off the hook, getting the crime scene tape off Conway's house, and finally getting my blasted furniture and a car.

"Why are you so interested in the docks?" I pressed on. "What property are you buying and why are you going after the Tybee Post Theater?"

Something flickered in Russell's eyes. Bingo, I'd hit a nerve. "I like river property and I like show tunes, wanna make something of it?" He took a step closer and I didn't back up. "You have no idea who you're messing with," he hissed.

"Maybe I do." My insides shook so bad I thought I might fall apart, but I still didn't budge. It wasn't that I was heroic but more the fear that if I did move I'd collapse.

"We got a problem over here?" a policeman on horseback said as he trotted on over.

"We're just having morning coffee," Russell beamed, holding up the mug, and Chantilly offered the policeman a Danish. "And taking a few dock measurements. The Savannah River is a beautiful sight."

Mr. Policeman bent down and snagged the pastry. "Hey," he said to me. "Don't I know you?"

Glasses with nose for sure. "Just a waitress." I nodded at the inn.

Chantilly grabbed my towel and tugged me along. "And we have to get back inside right now. This is our busy time. Yep, busy little bees."

We dodged an orange tourist trolley motoring down

River Street, its auto-play warbling on about the exploits of James Oglethorpe and his peeps, and we ducked into the back entrance of the inn. Chantilly stopped me inside the hallway and closed the door. "What in the name of all that's holy are you doing? Did you see that dock out there? You're going to wind up facedown in the water right beside it."

"Yeah, but we poked the bear."

"Ya think?"

I dropped my voice. "Now we know why Russell is here, and it's not just to buy the Tybee Post Theater. He's after the Old Harbor Inn, too. I saw it on the plans spread out on that table."

Chantilly started to say something, and I shook my head. "We can't talk here."

A maid hustled by, then stopped, eyeing the tray and giving us a curious look. "Who are you?"

Chantilly and I simultaneously slapped on bright cheery smiles, the Southern woman's answer to any and all unpleasant situations that might arise.

"Why, we're with Mr. Russell, who's staying here at the inn with you all." Chantilly handed her the tray as I passed over the carafe, and then we added our aprons. "We're just returning these, and Mr. Russell said to tell you that the pastries were divine and to add the charge to his room. And if it's not too much of a bother, to tack on a nice fifty-dollar tip for the valet out front who is always so helpful and polite beyond words."

The waitress gave us one of those *what the heck are you talking about* looks. "Mr. Russell said that? Just between us, the man's not much of a tipper."

"See there, he's mending his ways." Chantilly smiled and we took off down the hallway. We cut through the inn and came out onto the back lane where we'd parked the Chevy. "So let me get this straight," Chantilly said as I powered up the car. "Russell really wants to buy the Old Harbor Inn?"

"That's what it looks like to me." We waved to Lamar, who was busy with other guests, and headed for the land of Victorian houses and fewer tourists.

"Jiminy Christmas, can things get any worse?" Chantilly ran her fingers though her long curly hair in frustration. "We got to keep this to ourselves. Boone's for sure going to fry if it gets out."

"I don't get it. Why does this matter so much?" I asked, stopping for a red light.

"Because if Boone knew about the sale of the inn and he knew Conway left the inn to him, it looks like Boone knocked off Conway before he could sell and cheat him out of the inheritance."

"Holy freaking—" The car behind honked, jarring me back to the moment. I hit the gas and motored on. "But Boone didn't know about the inheritance till after Conway was dead."

"There's no way of proving that. The Russell deal is another nail in Boone's coffin."

"Mind if I make a McDonald's stop?"

"Boone is going to skin you alive for eating in this car, I can tell you that . . . except I could do with a McMuffin right now. And about a gallon of coffee to get my brain cells activated. Things are not improving here, kemosabe."

Chantilly cracked her knuckles as we motored into the

drive-through and ordered up. I headed for home and pulled the Chevy around back to the garage and killed the engine as we polished off breakfast from a bag. "We can talk later," I said, downing my last bit of apple pie. "I've got to open the shop, and you need to get to work, too. If you think of something, send it over in another order of mac and cheese."

"We just polished off a bazillion calories. We shouldn't be hungry till next week."

"Except for your mac and cheese." I added a smile so she'd know I meant it. "Thanks for going with me this morning."

We climbed out of the car; both of us had a lot more questions than answers and no idea how to turn things around.

"I'm not telling Pillsbury what we found out about Russell," Chantilly finally said. "If the Seventeenth Street guys get involved in this, it will make Boone look more guilty—if that's possible—with ties to the gang. And you know Pillsbury will tell Boone about the inn and how it makes things even worse, and the guy's got to be lower than a snake's belly as it is."

Chantilly gave me a hug, her voice cracking. "What are we going to do, Reagan?"

I couldn't talk, with a lump the size of Georgia in my throat, the apple pie like a brick in my stomach. I hugged Chantilly tighter. "We'll figure it out. We figured out what happened with you and Simon, and we'll get this right, too." Then I offered up a quick prayer that I was right.

"We're just missing something," I added. "I can feel it. It's like a big old mosquito out there buzzing around in the dark driving me nuts."

Chantilly let me go and swiped away a tear. "Well, when you smack it down flat, honey, you let me know." She trotted off for her Jeep, added a little wave, and then headed for Cuisine by Rachelle over on Jefferson. I headed inside.

My brain was mush, but somehow by ten I was open for business as usual. With new customers bringing in clothes to consign, I didn't have a minute to think more about Russell buying the inn and Boone rotting in jail. Change of season was always good for the Fox. People cleaned out closets and brought their gently worn items to me. With a little luck they would find a few things here at a bargain to fill that spot they'd just cleaned out. Recycling at its finest . . . and Reagan Summerside made money.

"Business sure is brisk," Anna said to Bella as the sisters pranced in the front door during a momentary lull.

"See, it's just like I told you." Bella smiled. "This here shop is a great idea." I started to offer a greeting, but they strutted right past me as if I didn't exist. Guess I wasn't worth the effort, since I hadn't planned on dying and leaving them money.

By noon I'd taken in two full racks of clothes to sell that needed to be priced, and I had people standing in line to check out. BW took to sleeping behind the counter so as not to get stepped on, and the sisters were still hanging around the shop looking at the clothes. My guess was they intended to bring in some of their own to consign, and that was fine by me. For sure they were complete snobs with questionable morals, but they had great fashion sense.

I closed the shop at six sharp. If I hadn't had KiKi's Shakin' Seniors and Melvin the octopus to contend with, I would have stayed open longer to let a few more people shop, and I could have cleaned up the place since it was trashed. It would also have given me time to think about the Russell/Old Harbor Inn situation. But I did have the dance lesson at seven, and I wanted to look in on KiKi. She hadn't been over all day to get the skinny on Russell, and that was so un-KiKi-like. Either dear Auntie was in a terrible state or she was wallowing in her soaps.

I didn't see Uncle Putter's car in the drive, so he wasn't on hand to offer sympathy. It also meant KiKi was well enough to be left on her own and the *terrible state* possibility was off the table. I made up a pot of mint tummy-soothing tea, then begged some blackberry scones from the Abbott sisters, who were recouping from the Conway Adkins wake with a pitcher of margaritas. I picked flowers from KiKi's lovely garden and put together a cheery get-well-soon tray.

"Teatime," I sang out as I knocked and opened KiKi's bedroom door. Princess the cat—who morphed into a snarling, hissing, biting Hellion the cat when KiKi wasn't looking—sat perched on a satin pillow. The TV warbled on from the other side of the room and Auntie KiKi sobbed uncontrollably into a white hankie. Her eyes were red and blotchy, her nose was running, and tissues were strewn across the covers like little puffs of fluffy snow.

"Sweet mother in heaven, who died?" I asked, figuring it had to be that to warrant so much anguish. I set the tray on the nightstand and gathered KiKi in my arms. BW jumped up on the bed, gave Hellion a wide berth, and offered whiny sounds of sympathy.

"Alfonzo," KiKi managed between choking back sobs. "He's truly gone!"

"Oh, honey, that's terrible." I held KiKi tighter. "Did you know him well?"

"Oh my, yes. Eleven years now. He went to Brazil to rescue Arielle and got captured by the pygmy headhunters and they ate him for dinner."

Ewww! And I thought I'd had a tough day. "Oh my God! Oh my God! I am so sorry," I soothed, patting KiKi, who was now blubbering on my shoulder. "How did you find out? Are the authorities sure that's what happened and he's just not missing in the jungle and . . . Waitaminute, there aren't pygmies in Brazil, and they don't eat people."

"Of course there are, and yes they do." KiKi sobbed louder still. "*The Years of Our Splendor* would not make up such things. And Alfonzo was such a biscuit, he was just starting to get that touch of gray at the temples that men do." She let out a deep sigh. "He's so romantic."

"Honey, trust me, Alfonzo will show up next week as a twin, a ghost, father, uncle, cousin, or maybe he'll crawl out from under a rock. He's coming back, I promise."

"You really think so?" KiKi sniveled, looking at me now and swiping at her eyes.

"I truly do." I grabbed a tissue and blew KiKi's nose. "And you can make sure if you check online to see if Alfonzo renewed his contract."

"That seems a bit like cheating."

"So is having man-eating pygmies in Brazil." I fluffed KiKi's pillows, except the one Hellion occupied, and then I poured out the tea. "How's your stomach?"

"Getting itself up and running. I think Putter brought home a bug from the hospital, is all. I tell you, that man's immune to everything; he's got the constitution of a rhinoceros, but this ailment sure had me down for the count." KiKi sipped her tea and broke off a crumb of scone. "I was perking up right fine this afternoon till the Alfonzo situation. Sent me right into a relapse, it did."

"I think what got to you was sneaking over to my house and devouring my leftovers from Walls'."

"Whatever are you talking about?" KiKi sipped tea and ate more of the scone between feeding bits to the resident pets.

"The ribs? The greens? Eating too much of that stuff will really get you late at night. No wonder you got an attack of jelly belly."

KiKi scrunched her nose and wagged her head. "Reagan, dear, I was in this here bed all night and I have no idea what on earth you're talking about."

"Of course you don't, and that's just fine as long as you're feeling better." Heck, I wouldn't be too anxious to own up to an overindulgence of that magnitude either. I stood and smiled and kissed KiKi on the head and smoothed back her curly red hair, thankful that an upset stomach and Alfonzo were the only things upsetting KiKi.

"Guess I better get myself downstairs; the Shakin' Seniors will be arriving. Any words of advice for Melvin?"

"The .38's in the desk drawer and the .22's in the closet. Feel free to help yourself."

Chapter Eight

BY eight the Swingin' Seniors were smiling and waving and trooping out the front door, the last strands of something country-western thumping in the background. I ran the dust mop around Auntie KiKi's dance studio, which had once been the dining room and parlor.

Back in the day of the horse and buggy and when folks came a-callin' in their top hats and hoop skirts, a fifteen-room Victorian house was all the rage. But when Auntie KiKi came along she figured that thirteen rooms were as good as fifteen, she and Uncle Putter needed money for medical school, and setting up her very own dance studio was a dream come true. Plus it paid the bills.

I punched up KiKi's iTunes playlist of music to tidy up by, and the Beach Boys came to life telling me that "God Only Knows." Amen to that.

"You are such a cheater, cheater, pumpkin eater," Auntie KiKi said as she came down the stairs in a peach robe that went to her toes. She parked herself on the bottom step with BW sitting beside her, his head in her lap. "I could hear the thump of that music all the way upstairs, you know. I'm guessing you did a little cha-cha, threw in the electric slide, and ended up with the Texas two-step."

"Those are dances; we danced."

"And not a touchy-feely dance in the lot. You chickened out."

"I improvised a little and it worked; everyone was happy. How are you feeling?"

"I seem to be doing a bit better." KiKi yawned, then patted BW and stood. "Putter should be home soon. He gave one of those *olive oil for butter* and *applesauce for sugar* talks to the Scrumptious Savannah cooking club tonight. If they don't tar and feather the dear man and run him out of town, he should be home by nine. Lock up on your way out."

KiKi started up the steps, then stopped, her face pulled into a frown. "How did you and Chantilly do with that Grayden Russell person over there at the inn? Did you find out anything that can help Walker?"

KiKi was already feeling poorly, and I saw no reason to add to it. "We've got a few leads."

"Oh, boy. That bad?" KiKi wagged her head and continued on. "We'll figure it out; we're just missing something, is all. Something that ties this all together."

I knew KiKi was right, even said the same thing when I was with Chantilly, but we were running out of time. Detective Ross might not believe Boone knocked off Conway, but it was her job and every other Savannah cop's to bring him in. Boone was a wanted man and Savannah wasn't that big. Sooner or later their paths would cross. Boone hadn't left the city, I was sure of that. I could almost feel him watching everything, everybody. I could feel him watching me.

I turned off the lights, letting one burn in the living room for Uncle Putter, the soft glow filtering into the dance studio of cream stucco walls and high ceilings. Frank Sinatra sang "I'll Be Seeing You" and I hoped there wouldn't be big black bars between Boone and me when that happened. I closed my eyes for a moment, the music washing over me, and I let my mind wander, searching for answers.

Why kill Conway? Why frame Boone? Why had all this happened now, and where was Boone? Was he okay? I slowly opened my eyes, and there he was right in front of me. It was dark and I was tired and I wanted him to be here, so maybe he was. He took me in his arms and we danced to Frank and seeing old familiar places. I could feel Walker's breath tease my hair, his heart beating slow and steady against mine, his warm hand at the small of my back pressing me close, his thigh brushing . . . my thigh brushing, his hand holding my hand.

We glided across the floor, the room dappled in soft shadows and moonlight. He tipped me back in a long slow dip, his mouth on mine, the heat of his lips setting me on fire as we stood there, the song fading away. I blinked my eyes open and . . . and Boone was gone. Or, was he never really here? I looked at BW. He yawned and smiled, winked, and then went back to sleep. Again, worst watchdog on the planet.

Still in a daze, I checked all the doors to make sure KiKi was locked up safe and sound. I glanced back to the dance floor one last time to see if Boone would somehow reappear. Was it a dream? Was it real? Did I need therapy? I missed him more than I thought possible.

With the help of an oatmeal cookie from KiKi's golf ball cookie jar, I finally convinced BW that we had to return to the land of no AC. I had a window unit on the first floor to keep customers happy—nothing worse than wiggling into tight jeans with sweat slithering down your legs—but the second floor was open-windows territory and a breeze if I was lucky. The very top floor was more attic than finished house. In the dead of summer the top two floors were like an oven, but in spring it was the scent of flowers and ocean and new-cut grass.

"I have a prezzie for you," I singsonged to BW, who was now wagging his tail as we crossed KiKi's front yard, which butted up to mine. I opened the back door of Cherry House, went to the fridge and pulled out a little white box, and headed for the front porch, with BW's nails tapping across the hardwood floor as he followed me. We sat together on the top step and I opened the box.

"Do you remember what today is?" I took a Chicken McNugget from the box and split it in two. I popped half in my mouth and fed the other to BW.

"One year ago you and I became BFFs. I was in a bad way and you weren't any better. We'd both been abandoned. You were hiding under this very porch, though then there wasn't a hole in the roof. I shared my McNuggets with you." I broke another one in half. "I'd just opened the Prissy Fox. I needed money to keep Cherry House going and I had a closet full of designer clothes I didn't need since Hollis the now-ex had kicked me to the curb for Cupcake the now-dead."

BW seemed only marginally interested in my sentimental walk down memory lane. I kissed him on the snout and he gobbled a McNugget right from the box. "So here we are, just the two of us, one year later. Any chance you'll start doing the laundry anytime soon?"

I got an eye roll, I swear I really did.

"Vacuum?"

BW chomped two nuggets right out of the box.

"Are you happy?"

This time I got a burp and a doggie head in my lap. I took that as a yes.

MORNING BUSINESS WAS BRISK AGAIN, THANK YOU, Jesus. Actually it was crazy busy with everyone in an *I need a new spring wardrobe* frame of mind. I had to break up a fight over a pair of blue strappy Kate Spade shoes and convince a customer that, yes, the Prada bag was real and, no, I did not sell knockoffs. I signed up two new consigners who brought in terrific clothes as a girl in her late twenties, wearing denim short-shorts, heels, and a halter top flipped a really nice wedding dress onto the counter. "I don't want to be seeing this here thing ever again. Sell it quick and mail me the check. Harper Norton, 126 West Harris."

"It looks brand new." I unzipped the dress from the long plastic bag.

She flipped back her long straight hair, which had to be

DUFFY BROWN

the very devil to keep in Savannah humidity. "It *is* brand
new. Never been used; I'm still single." Harper held up her
hands and wiggled her fingers. "See, no ring. I couldn't get
my money back on the flowers, the cake, or the reception at
the Madison. That no-count Walker Boone is their attorney,
said I signed a one-week cancellation agreement and that I
should just be glad I didn't marry the creep who broke up
with me at our rehearsal dinner.

"Let me tell you," Harper went on. "All that's easy for
Boone to say. He's not the one out all the money. Do you
have any idea what a sit-down dinner with open bar costs
these days, especially at a nice hotel here in town? I maxed
out my credit cards and it'll take me years to pay them off
and I'm still not married!"

"I know you," I said, giving her a long look and thankful
for once I wasn't hearing that statement. "You played the
piano at Conway's wake the other night. You're really good,
especially considering the occasion and that you were in
competition with the sobbing Abbott sisters."

"Yep, that was me all right. I play funerals, weddings,
anniversaries, bar mitzvahs, happy engagements, happy
divorces. Steffy Lou and I went to school together, so she
hired me, bless her heart. Credit card debt is a scary thing,
especially if it's for nothing but a broken heart. Actually,
the broken bank accounts bother me more."

Harper puffed out a long breath and pulled a satin shoe
from a bag. "I lost the other one or you could sell these, too.
They were expensive. Maybe someone will buy this one that
I have left and use it as a planter or candy dish."

Reaching under the counter, I found the satin shoe KiKi

and I got at Walker's house and plopped it on the counter. Harper's eyes nearly popped out of her head. She looked from the shoe to BW and back to me. "Holy catfish, that was you I pushed out of the way when I dropped off the shoe at Walker Boone's house? You know, I just planned to leave the thing on the back stoop because I was ticked and felt the need to vent. But then the door was wide open so I thought what the heck, I'll see how the other half lives. To tell you the truth, that was a mighty disappointing experience. So, what were you doing in Boone's house?"

"Looking for a runaway dog. Did you see anyone hanging around?" I wanted to know, hoping maybe Harper got a look at the person who dropped off the happy-family pictures.

"Nope, it was just me nosing around the place; the man doesn't even have a decent TV and that couch is a disgrace. Anyway, when you showed up I freaked out and ran." She turned back to the dress. "So, can you sell this blasted thing for me or what?"

"Oh my, I bet I could sell this dress in a heartbeat," Bella said, wandering over to the counter and picking up a corner of the wedding dress. "This is lovely indeed. Vera Wang? Everyone just loves Vera. Designer items are a big sell these days. Anything with a logo or tag gets top money even in consignment shops."

Anna faced Harper and turned her back to me. "You could get a lot more for this dress in a more upscale shop than this one. You need to take it somewhere else."

"Hey," I butted in. "This *is* an upscale shop and I *do* get top dollar."

"Like where should I take the dress?" Harper asked, totally ignoring me. "I need money."

"Well now, you best keep your eyes open," Anna added. "You just never know what shops are going to be popping up around here in this city. Things can change when you least expect them to."

Harper snapped the dress off the counter and said to Bella, "Thanks for the tip, I appreciate it." She floated off in a cloud of white chiffon, with Bella and Anna right behind her, and I saw a nice profit from the sale of a terrific wedding dress float out the door. *What was that all about?* I wondered.

"What was that all about?" Mamma asked, walking in and plopping a big box of food on my checkout counter.

"A lost sale that would have been really nice, and what's with the box?"

"Lunch." Mamma smiled and waved her hand over the contents. "A nice nutritious lunch."

"And dinner and breakfast for a month," I said, peeking inside. Mamma had on a new black *I am the judge* suit. She also had a navy scarf with tiny orange polka dots looped around her neck.

"There's nothing but hot dogs in your fridge," she went on. "BW is going to look like a sumo wrestler in no time if you keep it up."

"Sumo might stand a chance, but a wrestler, never. He's a lover, not a fighter, and those hot dogs have no nitrates and they are low fat," I said while exchanging Mamma's navy scarf for a cream one I had on display. Mamma was a fantastic judge, no doubt about it, sharp as they come. But she didn't have one drop of fashion sense in her whole body.

KiKi and I shared the opinion that it was indeed divine intervention from the powers above that made Mamma a judge, where black was the color of choice.

"And that's not all BW eats," I added, feeling like a bad dog mommy. "I feed him really expensive high-protein dog food that comes in those little silver and blue bags and it has no by-products, whatever that is."

"And he eats it?" Mamma asked, one brow cocked in doubt.

"Of course. Sometimes." Maybe. I rummaged through the box of apples, bananas, grapes, and avocados. Packages of ham and turkey, cheese and bread. I finally hit pay dirt; the Fig Newtons were buried in the bottom.

"You don't have the whole story, you know," I said with a full mouth and getting a *this is my cross to bear* glare from Mamma. "KiKi steals my leftovers, sees my empty fridge, then tattles to you. Think of it this way: If KiKi didn't filch my ribs and greens in the first place, I'd have more food in the fridge than hot dogs."

Mamma tsked. "KiKi knew you'd say that and maintains her innocence, and for your information you're starting to sound just like a lawyer." Mamma leaned closer. "So, have you seen one certain lawyer lately?"

If I told her that Boone had suddenly materialized at KiKi's and we'd danced in the dark, Mamma would think I was drunk or crazy or both. "He's close, I can feel it."

Mamma did a little shuffle and glanced around the room as if Walker would pop out between the dresses. "You always did have good instincts, except when it came to marrying Hollis, of course. I chalk that one up to your daddy's side of the family. A few of them have the lights on but nobody's home, if you know what I mean. But I didn't come here to just drop off food and discuss genetic flaws; I have inside information."

Two customers strolled in and Mamma came around to the back of the checkout counter and faked being busy by adding the navy scarf I just took off her to a black sweater. There was no hope. "Mr. TA is contesting his daddy's will," she said in a hushed voice. "I heard it straight from the estate lawyer this morning over breakfast at Clary's. TA is going for diminished capacity. That means he's saying Daddy Dear was off his nut when he drew up the will. Can you imagine saying such a thing about your own father? And in case you doubted just how much he hates his brother, he told everyone at the grave site yesterday that he'd rot in hell before he'd let his daddy's killer get the Old Harbor Inn."

"Clary's? You went to Clary's for breakfast? I just bet you got The Elvis and how could you not bring me some? I love The Elvis."

Mamma nudged the box. "I brought you good food."

"Sourdough toast stuffed with peanut butter and bananas is good food." I let out a forlorn sigh. "So, do you think TA just said all that stuff to show off in front of a crowd? I mean, he does like being front and center, even standing by an open grave with a hearse in the background."

Mamma added an orange scarf to a red sweater, and I felt my eyes cross and heard a customer suck in a sharp breath clear across the room. "Shooting off his mouth could be part of it," Mamma said. "Personally I'd go with good-old-fashioned greed since the inn's a fine piece of property.

The thing is everyone knows that TA inherited family money, a lot of it from what I hear. Maybe he just wants the inn because he can't have it. The man's like a two-year-old with a bank account and driver's license."

"Okay," I said, trying to put some pieces together. "We know who gets the inn, we've known that for a while now. But I wonder who inherits the money? Here's the thing, if TA is going after that person too, this isn't just about brotherly un-love. Maybe TA's not as well off as we all think he is? We really need to see the will, find this other person who gets the money and see if TA has been rattling their cage as well as hating our favorite lawyer. When is there a reading of the will?"

"That only happens on bad TV reruns, dear. These days the attorney files the will in probate court, then sends copies to each of the beneficiaries."

I snagged Old Yeller from under the counter and dumped the contents onto the counter. Mamma watched in grim fascination as purse flotsam of pens, half-eaten mints, dog biscuits, three combs, a wallet, a flashlight, some rope, and three Snickers wrappers bounced across the top along with the assortment of Boone's mail. Mamma picked up a flyer that gave five dollars off at Vinnie Van Go-Go's pizza. She wagged her head. "Is nothing sacred?"

"Don't know if I'd jump right to sacred, but Vinnie's calzones are pretty freaking awesome."

"I mean messing with someone else's mail." Mamma waved the flyer in the air.

"Think of it as a public service. Boone's mailbox was stuffed full and spilling out all over his porch, and we collected it so the place didn't look unoccupied like no one was home for days, but actually we were too late because someone was already there and—"

Mamma eyes widened. "We?"

"Let's go with me and BW taking a night walk and winding up at Boone's house. But this mail isn't really mail—I mean look at it, it's nothing but ads," I said, hurrying on to avoid more questions. "There's nothing like a bill or bank statement, and there's no big thick *here is the will* envelope. Where the heck could it be?"

"Let's see," Mamma said, pairing green earrings with a purple necklace so it looked like we were doing work. "The funeral was yesterday, so out of respect I'm guessing the lawyers waited till this morning to file the will over at the courthouse. Copies of it will probably be sent out to the beneficiaries by courier this afternoon."

"But the courier won't go to Boone's house," I said, looking at the pile in front of me. "Where do you think Boone's real mail is? Where does he have that delivered?"

"His office," Mamma and I said together. "Dinky can sign for the envelope," I added. "Then we can get it from her. Dinky and I are friends."

Mamma shook her head. "Doesn't matter if you two are joined at the hip, dear. Dinky can't sign for the envelope; she's not Walker, and as we know he's MIA at the moment. No Walker, no will; the courier will simply take it back to the estate attorney and try again at a later date. The law is pretty specific on how wills are handled."

"Or maybe Boone's not really MIA after all," I said, feeling a lightbulb moment coming on. "Maybe Boone's right in his office and just a little shorter now and doesn't have facial hair and he's blond."

"Blond?"

"I bet Boone would look great blond, and maybe he's wearing a hat. A hat would help. What do you think? It worked pretty good last time I tried it." I scooped everything back into Old Yeller. "Quick, call KiKi and tell her to watch the shop."

"What if she has a dance lesson?"

"Tell her to teach it over here. Everyone will love it, a little hip-hop while they shop; it even rhymes and there's enough room right here in the hallway."

Mamma rubbed her forehead. "Are you doing what I think you're doing?"

I grabbed a men's suit off the rack, along with a shirt, a tie, and a brown straw fedora I'd just taken in. "Put your hands over your eyes, Mamma, you don't want to get involved in this. You are a judge, after all."

Mamma took my hand. She tucked a strand of hair behind my ear, her eyes softening. "Grandma Hilly cleaned offices down at the courthouse for years; we were friends. If our roles were reversed I'd like to think she'd keep an eye on you and lend a hand. We'll meet up tonight at Jen's and Friends and you can tell me how things go. Try not to get arrested and if you do, dear, don't admit to anything. That diminished-capacity idea might not work for Conway, but you trying to pass yourself off as Walker Boone fits the bill pretty well."

Chapter Nine

I PARKED the Chevy, snagged the suit, shirt, and fedora out of the backseat, and locked the car. I took off in a dead run for Boone's office, the suit streaming behind me like a kite. It was already after noon and the envelope with Conway's last will and testament might be delivered any-time now.

Boone's office was a white-stone two-story. It was over a hundred years old with an elevated entrance designed for the horse-and-dirt-street days and keeping dust and grime at bay. The office faced Columbia Square and was next to the Kehoe House, now a terrific bed-and-breakfast and haunted for the last century by the Kehoe twins. Some kids can't wait to leave home; others you just can't get rid of.

I took the stone steps and pushed open the frosted glass door with "Walker H. Boone, Attorney at Law" stenciled on the front. Dinky sat behind her big mahogany desk littered with yellow legal pads, a laptop, a cell phone, an array of baby pictures, and a bouquet of plastic flowers that was really a stapler. She had a box of tissues in front of her and was crying her eyes out.

"Sweet mother, what's wrong?" I asked, rushing over. "Look, if this is about Alfonzo and the pygmies, I think he signed the contract, so all's well."

She looked up at me and sniffed. "What are you talking about?"

"What are you crying about?" Dinky and I were about the same age and friends since my divorce from Hollis, with Boone being his attorney. Dinky had held my hand during some tough times, tried to convince me things would get better and that I really shouldn't strangle her boss because she needed the job. We bonded over lattes and gossip, and I ended up being a bridesmaid in her wedding.

"Everything's wrong," Dinky wailed, getting up and pacing across the blue Oriental rug in her office. "Mr. Boone is accused of murder and an Officer Deckard was just here asking me a million questions. Does he really think I know where Mr. Boone is or that I'd tell him if I did? Then Steffy Lou Adkins was here looking for the permits for that Tybee Theater event. Least I found those for her."

Dinky sobbed louder. "Poor Steffy Lou, trying to do this all by herself; poor Mr. Boone; and poor, poor me. He's on the run for his life, Steffy Lou is overworked, and it's payday around here and I'm not getting paid one red cent."

"We need to fix the Boone-on-the-run part, least for a few minutes, and we need to do it fast." I held up the suit.

"I have to fake being Boone so I can sign for an envelope that's to be delivered here any minute now."

Dinky swiped at her tears, a smile breaking through. "Really? If you can sign for an envelope for Mr. Boone, you can surely sign his checks, right? I've got a car payment due."

"I can't sign Boone's checks."

"I can't lose my car."

"Look. Any minute now a courier's going to come trotting in here and you've got to help pass me off as Boone," I said while yanking on the pants to the suit. With my foot caught in one leg, I hobbled over to the window and peered down at the sidewalk. "I figure it'll be a bike courier."

"You mean Donald?" Dinky said. "I think he's got a crush on me."

"Young and muscles and hunky?"

"Seventies, dentures, spindle legs. I can sign for a package, no sweat, I do it all the time for Mr. Boone. The mail guys all know me."

"It's got to be Boone in the flesh or as close as we can get in a pinch." I pulled on the shirt and buttoned it up. "This is Conway Adkins's will and only Boone can sign for it. You need to distract Donald, make him look at you so he doesn't look too hard at me."

Dinky folded her arms. "I can add a little lipstick and toss in some sweet talk with the best of them, but I got to tell you that the only way Donald's going to think you're Boone is if he's got a few double shots of bourbon under his belt. Besides, everyone knows Boone's on the lam and not sitting behind his desk looking forty pounds lighter and shrinking."

I twisted my hair into a bun and slapped on the fedora. "What do you think?"

"You look like a cartoon character."

"Slut yourself up, undo a few buttons, coochie-coo with Donald, and then slip me the papers."

"I'm married, I have a kid, Beau will kill me if he finds out, and it's just plain old sneaky."

I grabbed Dinky by the shoulders and stared her right in the eyes. "Donald's out there parking his bike right this minute." I pointed down to the sidewalk. "Think car payment. Think repossession if we don't clear Boone. Think bye-bye cute SUV that holds all your baby stuff and hello smelly bus."

"Bus?"

"Lugging a stroller, changing poopy diapers, waiting in the rain, germs, sneezing slobbering passengers."

Dinky snagged my comb and flipped up her hair, letting a few sexy tendrils trail around her face, glossed up her lips, and kissed the air to even out the color. She swiped on mascara and undid two, then three, buttons on her blouse as footsteps sounded in the hall. I slid into Boone's wood-paneled office, partially closed the blinds, kept the light off, and parked myself in the big leather chair. Dinky sat on the corner of her desk, legs crossed, skirt hiked up to her behind showing nearly everything she owned. I think "baby on a bus" sent her over the edge.

"Why, Donald, you sexy hunk of mankind," Dinky purred as the courier came into the office. "How are you this very fine afternoon?"

"It's . . . it's Dan and I'm doing okay, I guess, maybe. I need to see Mr. Boone to sign for a package, even though I know he's not around, but I have to try to make the delivery anyway and—"

"Nonsense." Dinky waved her hand in the air and batted her eyes. "Why, Mr. Boone is right in his office working like he always is. He's busy, very busy. That talk about him being on the run is nothing but a nasty rumor."

"I heard it on the police scanner."

Dinky pointed through the half-open door to me, then slinked off the desk. "See, he's right there." She strutted over to Dan and turned his face away from the door to her. "Now tell me what you've been up to, you handsome devil. I'll have Mr. Boone sign these and we can talk."

Dan gripped the envelope tighter. "I can't—"

Dinky flattened herself against Dan and whispered something in his ear as she grabbed the lapel of his blue uniform and led him into the office. I lowered my head and picked up the phone, and with the fedora pulled low my face was pretty well hidden. "Habeas corpus, corpus delicti, Magna Carta, tiramisu," I groused into the phone for good measure.

"I thought he was taller," Dan whispered to Dinky, her hand now on his butt.

"He hasn't been taking his vitamins." Dinky tossed the clipboard and envelope on the desk and slid her arm around Dan, drawing him close to her as I scrawled *Walker H. Boone* on the clipboard beside the date. I'd seen Boone's name scribbled at the bottom of my divorce papers enough times, so I knew his signature.

"How long have you been riding that bike to get all these fine muscles?" Dinky purred.

"Six months. Muscles?"

Dinky slyly ran her other hand though Dan's hair and I handed the clipboard back to her. She waltzed Dan off toward her office area, trapped the clipboard back under his arm, and backed him toward the outer door.

"See you later, handsome." I heard the soft click of the door closing, and I rushed over to the window and peeked through the half-closed blinds. Dan stood by his bike and looked up, and I jumped back, nearly knocking over the little yellow-and-blue lamp on the table. I peered through the blinds again to see Dan pedaling off and smacking flat into a tree. He got back on his bike, shook his head, and wobbled off again.

"You did it," I said to Dinky, standing beside me. "You're amazing."

"What I am is screwed. I've set myself up for more of the same from here on." Dinky pointed out the window. "Now I have to be all Miss Hotsy-Totsy to Dan every time he shows up or he'll suspect something was up, and what the heck was that about tiramisu?"

"I don't speak legal, but I'm pretty good at dessert, and think of it this way: If what's in this envelope helps us find the killer, Boone will be back at this desk real soon and you can keep your car."

Dinky picked up a silver letter opener from Boone's desk that looked a lot more Dinky than Boone, meaning it was probably a Christmas or birthday present. She neatly slit the top of the packet while I clicked on the light.

"It's Conway Adkins's will, all right." Dinky set it on the corner of Boone's desk and flipped through a few pages. "It says here that Walker H. Boone gets the Old Harbor Inn,

the sterling tea service and all jewelry goes to Steffy Lou
Adkins, and the bourbon and cigar collection goes to the
Plantation Club. The cash assets go to St. Mary's Health
Center and Free Clinic over on Drayton."

"The free clinic? Really? I don't think I've ever heard
Conway's name associated with something that would not
benefit him in the long run."

"Well, in my opinion I'd say this was just more of the
same. Not that the money to the clinic won't do a whole lot
of good for a whole lot of people, but it's what we here in
the legal world call bribing the jury. The old boy was making
amends before he croaked. The fear of the Lord is a pretty
powerful motivator when you got the Pearly Gates on the
horizon and the flames of Hades dancing at your feet."

"Here's what I don't get: Boone's Grandma Hilly had to
know that Conway was Boone's dad. Why not hit him up
for money or tell Boone and he could go to him for money?
They were barely getting by, from what I've heard."

"Conway didn't want Walker, ever. Why set up the grand-
son you love for that kind of rejection? I'd say Grandma
Hilly thought she was protecting Walker from a greater evil
than being poor." Dinky waved her hand over the office.
"And I'd say she was right. The guy did okay for himself,
with a little help from his friends."

"Tucker is contesting the will and the big question is: Is
it to just keep Walker from getting the inn, or does he need
the cash? If he needs money, maybe that's motive for the
murder? Even if Conway left him nothing, he had this
contesting-the-will idea up his sleeve."

Dinky sat quiet for a minute, deep in thought, then slowly

DUFFY BROWN

wagged her head. "He just wants the inn. It's a sibling-rivalry thing. Tucker wouldn't go after the free clinic money no matter what. It would ruin his reputation in the community. He owns a big marina out there on Whitemarsh, and no one would support it if he gets a bad reputation. Besides, he's still living large so there's no reason to think he's having money troubles."

"Can I have a copy of the will?"

Dinky rolled her eyes skyward and made the sign of the cross. "I've broken about ten laws in the last twenty minutes. I'm going to hell for sure."

"If we figure this out, at least you won't be headed in that particular direction on a bus."

After I switched back into my regular clothes I picked up the Chevy. I headed for the Fox with a copy of the will tucked in Old Yeller and a promise to say three Hail Marys and three Our Fathers for Dinky's corrupt soul.

The sexmobile and I chalked up more whistles and thumbs-ups and that was terrific, but I also nearly sideswiped an orange trolley coming around a corner and jumped the curb on State Street. The Chevy was a sweet ride, to be sure, but it was big, and Savannah streets were narrow and congested. I'd feel terrible if I dinged Boone's car, mostly because he'd strangle me dead if something happened to it.

When I got to the Fox, KiKi was knee-deep in clothes and three people were waiting in line to get checked out. Anna and Bella were snapping pictures and chatting it up with customers. I didn't have time to ask the dynamic duo what they were up to or even eavesdrop; I was too busy writing up sales and opening new accounts.

"Why did you go over to Boone's?" KiKi wanted to know in a hushed voice when the hubbub died down. She handed me a really cute black-and-white skirt to hang up.

"Have you heard anything about Tucker and his money?" I asked KiKi.

"Only that he spends it like he has his own personal printing press stashed in his attic." KiKi looked over to Anna and Bella. "Why are they still here? We should start charging them rent. Then again, maybe they're trying to see if we have enough space to sell all the great clothes they intend to bring in?"

I slapped a cheery smile on my face just in case KiKi's theory was right, then walked over to Bella. "Can I help you with something?"

She was stooped over holding a tape measure, with Anna at the other end taking measurements. Or maybe it was Anna doing the holding and Bella taking measurements. They both had their hair pulled back today and both wore black slacks.

"You already have helped tons." Anna grinned. "More than you know, but then I suppose you really will know soon enough. With Clive and Crenshaw gone, Bella and I have decided to take care of ourselves the way smart women do. We don't have to be dependent on anyone any longer. We are intelligent and resourceful."

Bella laughed . . . or was it Anna? "We are very resourceful, and it's a terrific idea that we've come up with, almost as good as how we got rid of our husbands."

Anna/Bella pressed the button on the tape measure and it retracted back into the case. "You have a good evening now, you hear," she said, hooking arms with her sister, and together they strolled out the door.

"Got rid of Clive and Crenshaw?" KiKi said on a strangled gasp. "I got a bad feeling the sisters are cooking up something."

"Yeah, and I wonder if it's Clive and Crenshaw?"

KiKi's lips pulled into a sour pucker. "You just had to go say that, didn't you, with me headed off to dinner with Angie and her husband." KiKi swallowed a burp. "Putter and I are meeting up with the two of them at the Green Truck Pub out on Habersham. I am so not a pub grub kind of gal, but it's our good deed for the day. Those two are trying to save their marriage after Conway and the vitamin B encounters. I think her husband stabbed Conway like he did because he was so mad, and at least it proves he cares for Angie, or so she's telling everyone. Putter and I will probably be referees."

"The good part is that the Truck has great burgers," I added while pairing a tan skirt with a cream sweater. "And they have great beer on tap."

"The bad part is that it's going to take more than a slab of meat on a bun and a brew to save the night." KiKi hung up a pink blouse with ruffles down the front. "I never thought I'd say this, but I'm mighty glad Putter carries that golf club with him everywhere. We just might be needing it to keep those two from killing each other."

Hoping to catch some late shoppers, I closed up the Fox at seven, put the cash in the rocky road container, and turned off the lights. BW and I backed the Chevy out of the garage and purred our way up Drayton and past Forsyth Park with dog walkers, joggers, and strollers. A live jazz band played in the pavilion, and magnolias and azaleas scented the air as the fountain caught the last rays of sun sinking below the steeples of St. John's. Spring in Savannah was a bit of heaven on earth, and a convertible was the absolute best way to soak it all in.

By the time we got to Jen's & Friends, the after-work crowd had given way to the before-dinner crowd, and I snagged rock-star parking right across the street. One of the best things about J & F besides the yummy drinks was the outside seating. Little black wrought-iron tables cluttered the sidewalk and noisy traffic on Bull Street made the chances of overhearing conversations slim to none.

I spotted Anna and Bella at a table near the street, their heads together over celebration martinis that had sprinkles around the edge of the glass and were served with a sparkler. KiKi bought me one when I turned twenty-one. I was thirty-three now and twenty-one seemed like a million years ago.

Mamma sat at a back table sipping what looked like a strawberry shortcake martini complete with a big old strawberry. She had another one just like it waiting for me. Drink and dessert together; did I have a good mamma or what? She held up her glass in a salute. "Well, you're alive and breathing and not rotting behind bars for forgery, so that's a good start," she said as I sat down. "What did you find out while visiting the office of our favorite lawyer?"

"That I have no idea what the *H* in Walker H. Boone stands for." I pulled the will and a dog biscuit out of Old Yeller. I fed BW and slid the papers across to Mamma, who had a tinge of red on her cheeks. "Holy cow, you know what the *H* stands for, and it must be a doozie if it made you blush."

"That's just the drink, dear. Besides, I'm sworn to secrecy."

"Just a hint?"

"Judges don't do hints, honey." Mamma winked, then flipped open the will. "Well, we already know who gets the inn, and this says the free clinic gets the cash?"

Mamma's jaw dropped and I added, "That was pretty much my reaction, too. Anything-for-a-buck Conway turns philanthropist? Now that's hard to believe. But the bottom line is that there's no motive for Tucker to knock off his dad; he got nothing out of him being dead and buried. Tucker and Daddy didn't get along, but that's it."

"Or Conway figured Tucker didn't need anything because he had the money from when his mother died. All I know is that Steffy Lou is working on saving the Tybee Post Theater and throwing that big bash. I'm sure she funded the event with a lot of her own money. If Tucker's writing checks for charity he's not hurting financially."

"Steffy Lou and I were in the bathroom chatting and she sang for me."

"Well, there you go: Steffy Lou Adkins, the poster girl for *there's no business like show business*. She's worked really hard to make the dinner and talent show a success."

I twisted my glass around on the tabletop, with a sense of dread settling in my gut. "I'm not getting anywhere on this, Mamma. All I do is eliminate suspects and motives, but somebody knocked off Conway. The killer had to know all along that Boone was Conway's son. That means the killer is somebody close to Conway."

"You're worried, aren't you?"

"I'm running out of suspects and this never happens.

Usually there's a suspect list a mile long and I have to weed through them. I'm thinking about visiting Odilia; maybe she has a potion to help find the killer or at least clear my brain. I think it's fogged over; nothing's adding up."

"While you're at it, light a few candles over at St. John's Church. The way I see it, you can never have too much help in these situations." Mamma reached over and held my hand. "He's going to be okay, you know. He's a survivor."

"He's got Big Joey and Pillsbury."

"There is that."

"Well, Lord be praised and pass the ammunition," Chantilly huffed as she rushed up to the table. She gave Mamma a friendly kiss on the cheek, gulped my martini and chomped the strawberry, then added, "I spotted the Chevy and I need you right quick to do me a favor."

Chantilly swallowed the rest of my drink and smacked her lips together in satisfaction. "The delivery truck went and broke down. What a night it's been for me, and here you are sipping drinks and enjoying yourself."

"What drink?" I stared at the empty glass, and Chantilly pointed across the street to the van with "Cuisine by Rachelle" scripted across the side, and a knife-crossed-with-a-fork logo underneath.

"I have a delivery over at the Old Harbor Inn and the COPS are waiting on me as we speak. You got to help me out."

"I hate to tell you, but the cops and I aren't exactly on the best of terms."

"Collectors of Pewter and Silver COPS; I don't name them, honey, I just feed them, but we need to go now before the mac and cheese starts to separate and the pulled pork goes cold.

We can put it all in the Chevy's big trunk and maybe some on the backseat and run it right over to the inn. With them just doing breakfast, Rachelle and I have been working like dogs to do catering over there, and this is our big chance to do it right. Shake a leg, girl, time's a-wastin'."

"But I have BW." I held up the leash.

"I can take him for you," Mamma offered, all Little Miss Helpful. "I'll drop him off at Cherry House for you. I know where the outside key is. You really should move it, dear."

"I did," I said with a feeling of accomplishment.

"The second flowerpot instead of the first?" Mamma petted BW.

And another accomplishment bites the dust. "Okay, look, here's the real problem: What if we spill something in Boone's car? He's going to kill me. You know that, we all know that."

"We won't spill a drop." Chantilly made a cross over her heart, then grabbed my hand. "We'll be real careful."

She yanked the leash out of my hand, shoved it at Mamma, and then said to me, "Buck up, buttercup, we got to get our fannies in gear. There're hungry people waiting on us."

Chapter Ten

"SEE, I told you this was going to happen," I wailed to Chantilly, with both of us standing over the spilled tray of pulled pork in the trunk of Boone's car, now parked at the Old Harbor Inn. "There's barbecue sauce and meat everywhere. It's a big sloppy mess. Boone really is going to kill me." I cut my eyes to Chantilly. "And I'm not going down alone. You talked me into this."

"Hey, it's all your fault," Chantilly wailed back at me. "You took the turn too fast."

"You said we were late and we had to hurry."

"Not drive like a maniac." Chantilly swiped back her hair and pulled in a deep breath. "Okay, we can fix this. I'm thinking Boone probably never opens the trunk, and to make sure we'll glue it shut and . . . and the car's going to smell amazing and guys love barbecue, right, so that part works and right now we got bigger problems."

"To tell you the truth I can't think of a one," Lamar, our friendly valet, said from behind us. "Sure glad this isn't my ride; that stain's never going to come out."

"You're not helping." I swallowed a whimper and Chantilly said, "But I got an idea." She plucked a bag from the backseat of the car, where the other catering goodies were nestled on the floor, and pulled out three huge plastic serving spoons. She handed one to Lamar and one to me. "Ready, set, scoop."

I held the bag open. "We'll put it in here, and then we can throw it in the trash when we get home."

Chantilly yanked the bag away and held out the serving bowl. "Scoop it right in here."

"Uh, you mean like in someone's going to eat this stuff?" Lamar said, his eyes rounding. "There are leaves in the bottom of the trunk." He looked closer. "And grass, and I see a few little twigs."

"Extra greens free of charge." Chantilly poked her spoon around in the goop. "It's not so bad, I've eaten worse."

Lamar grabbed the spoon out of Chantilly's hand. "You're kidding."

Chantilly snagged the spoon back and furrowed her brows, her lips now thin slits. "Does it look like I'm kidding, buddy boy? I've got thirty people waiting inside for mac and cheese and pulled pork. Now scoop!"

Lamar and I exchanged fearful looks, then did as ordered by Miss Crazy Chef standing next to us. Ten minutes later Chantilly and I laid out a lovely spread of mac and cheese, deviled eggs, and pulled pork with yummy-looking little fresh buns. The COPS filed into the main sitting area flashing big smiles and uttering oohs and aahs as they took in the display.

They piled their plates high and sat on the blue-and-gray couches and matching club chairs as Harper Norton played the baby grand in the corner, filling the room with a fine rendition of "Georgia on My Mind." Harper wasn't kidding when she said she played all over the city for every occasion imaginable. It was a lovely Southern night indeed, even if a bit of unanticipated foliage happened to accompany the pulled pork.

"We did it," Chantilly said in a whisper. We backed out into the hall as one of the COPS members discreetly slid a twig from her sandwich. Bless her heart.

"We halfway did it." I hitched Old Yeller up onto my shoulder, then followed Chantilly down the hall past a meeting room set up with a viewing screen and pictures and pamphlets of pewter.

"I still have the stain in the Chevy to deal with," I added while passing the next room, which was dark and empty. The third room had the door half closed, no one inside but a poker game in progress.

"I hear that Goo Gone stuff works great," Chantilly said. I stopped in the middle of the hallway and Chantilly turned back to me. "It really is good at getting stains out. It'll be okay, I swear."

"Not that." I backed up to the poker room and stood in the doorway, gazing inside. An array of bourbons and beers sat off to the side; a haze of smoke hung over the room, and the "No Smoking" sign had been tossed on the floor.

"Looks like boys' night out to me." Chantilly peered over my shoulder. "And from the piles of chips I'd say they weren't playing for peanuts."

She opened the door wider, walked over to the pinstripe suit jacket hung on the back of a chair, and pointed to the red carnation stuck in the lapel. "Dixon, the little rodent," she said on a quick intake of breath. "I'd recognize that suit and flower anywhere."

"Yeah, me too, that's why I stopped." I held up a red Atlanta Braves hat sitting on the other side of the table. "This is Russell's; he had it on the other day down at the docks." My gaze fused with Chantilly's. "Russell's applying for membership in the Plantation Club, so he and Dixon know each other, but . . . but this little setup is something personal, more than just a club membership get-together."

"Some sort of initiation into the club?" Chantilly grabbed a handful of those orange fish crackers and tossed a few in her mouth.

"That would be at the club, not here at the inn." I studied the piles of chips on the table. "This is gambling, pure and simple, and from the big and little piles I'd say we have our losers and we have our winners."

Chantilly plucked a chip from Dixon's meager pile. "And here we have our loser."

"I picked up a chip from the Atlanta Braves cap pile. "And here we have our winner."

Chantilly gave me the *shh* finger-to-her-lips signal, then pointed to the hall and the sound of voices and footsteps headed our way. I nodded to a closet door and we slipped inside, wedging between housekeeping equipment. The boys' club filed back into the room, chatting about totally boring stuff like drawing to an inside straight, Texas hold 'em, blackjack being the best game on the gambling boats, and how this was small-potatoes gaming and how bigger games and bigger money were coming soon. Okay, if this had been a group of women they'd be discussing the really important stuff of life like spring shoes, the best places for lunch, and that new Milan Day Spa that served wine with their mani-pedis.

The louvers in the door let in slits of light, and Chantilly and I watched the men as they reclaimed their chairs and Russell closed the door to the hallway. I exchanged *uh-oh* looks with Chantilly, tripped over the vacuum between us, and fell against the back shelf. A stack of big trays crashed down on our heads, knocking Chantilly and me to the floor and burying the two of us under a mound of aluminum.

The closet door flew open, and twelve eyes glared. "What the heck?" Russell yelled. "Who are you? What are you doing in there?"

"Taking inventory?" I offered. Chantilly held out her hand. "Care for a cracker?"

"You're the waitresses who brought me coffee over there at the docks yesterday," Russell ground out. His eyes went cold, his jaw set. "Somehow I don't think you're waitresses at all. I think you two are nothing but nosy broads. What are you up to? What are you doing here?"

"I've seen them around the Plantation Club," Dixon chimed in, coming our way. "In fact, the tall one asked about membership, then made a pass at me." Dixon smoothed back his thinning hair with an air of importance. "She said there

was more where that came from if I got her into the club."
A lecherous smile tipped his lips. "She's kind of a cute little
thing if you don't look too close."

"I . . . I made a pass at you?" Chantilly screeched and
scrambled to her feet. "What bunk." With fire in her eyes
she jabbed a finger at Dixon. "You were the one chasing me
around that big old mahogany table. I lost my shoe trying
to keep away from you."

Russell snagged me up by my arm as the other men sat
back in their chairs, enjoying the show. "I don't know what
your game is," he hissed in a low threatening voice that sent
chills up my spine. "Butt out. This is your last warning. This
is business, big business, and you're not screwing it up by
getting in the way."

"Trying to keep it quiet that you're buying the Old Harbor
Inn and the Tybee Theater?"

Russell's fingers dug into my arm and I swung Old Yeller
to make him let go. He caught the purse in midair and I
kicked him in the shins hard, except I had on my favorite
pink flip-flops with the little white daisies to celebrate
spring. Russell's lip curled, and he had a cold sinister look
in his eyes. His fingers tightened, making me wince in pain,
and the men laughed as Russell added, "That's as good as
you got, chickie?"

"What about this, chickie?" Chantilly blurted. This time
she kicked Russell and it wasn't in the shin but several feet
higher, and she was not wearing cute flip-flops but her work
boots.

"Umph!" Russell yelped. He let go of my arm and doubled over. Chantilly pulled free of Dixon. The other men

jumped to their feet, but Chantilly and I were faster and rushed out the open door. "We could have taken them," Chantilly protested as we ran full-tilt down the hall. "I could take three and you could take three and—"

"And then there'd be chaos, somebody would call the cops, and we'd be in a real mess trying to explain to Ross what the heck we were doing in that closet," I wheezed as we bolted outside and sprinted for the Chevy. I cranked the engine, pulled in a deep breath, waved to Lamar, and then merged into the night traffic on Bay Street. "Nice job on opening that door; it made getting out of there a lot easier."

Chantilly finger-combed her hair from her face. "I didn't open that door, you opened the door."

"I didn't open the door."

Chantilly and I exchanged wide-eyed looks. "Lamar," Chantilly offered. "It had to be him. He was probably keeping an eye on us and heard the commotion?"

"Probably," I said with more conviction than I felt. "The good thing is that somebody knew what was going on in that room and that we were in trouble and stepped in, thank you very much, whoever you are. Do you think it means anything that Russell and Dixon are friends?"

Chantilly heaved a weary sigh. "Two sleazebags together is double trouble. I don't know what it means, but I'm betting it means something and it's not good."

I dropped Chantilly off at her van and waited with her till the AAA roadside assistance truck showed up. That the assistance guy was a total hottie kept me around for a little longer to appreciate the beauty of nature, and when Chantilly got the van up and running, I took off.

Savannah was one of those cities that did not roll up the sidewalks at midnight. Fact is, Savannah was more a two A.M. kind of place and maybe a little beyond if there was a private party going on that needed crashing.

I pulled the Chevy around to the back of Cherry House and killed the engine. The car was already starting to smell like roadkill on a hot day, and by tomorrow it would be downright disgusting. I had to at least try to clean up the mess in the trunk. I headed for the house for buckets, detergent, and a scrub brush.

I spotted BW's black nose pressed against the window in the back door and heard his little whines and sounds of welcome. I waved and smiled, and I could picture his tail wagging a mile a minute.

See, that's the thing with dogs, no matter how rotten the day, your best friend greets you with a whine and a wag. Of course it was also time for BW's daily hot dog, the one thing he loved more than life itself. But right now, after my crappy encounter with Russell and who knew how many hours of scrubbing I'd have to put in, I was going with the happy-to-see-Reagan scenario and enjoying the moment.

"GET YOURSELF UP, HONEY, AND DO IT QUICK-LIKE," KiKi said, shaking me awake. "GracieAnn just called and said we need to be getting ourselves over to the Cakery Bakery right away for doughnuts."

I pried one eye open; the clock on my dresser was flashing seven ten. "It's a trick. She wants to pelt me with more doughnuts for badmouthing Boone."

"I don't think so. It sounded downright important. She was all kinds of breathy and excited."

I sat up in bed, finding BW beside me. Guess the cool spot in the hallway wasn't so cool last night. "Why in all that's holy would GracieAnn call you?"

"Now that is a darn good question, and she said to be sure and bring you along. I was up anyway so I'm good to go, and it is doughnuts, so I didn't consider putting up a fuss. Putter has an eight o'clock tee time and last night I promised him blueberry pancakes if he didn't murder Angie and her husband and bury them in the rose garden."

"That bad?"

"I'm sending them to Dr. Phil. Throw on some clothes and brush your teeth. Think glazed, sprinkles, custard filled. That'll get your body up and running for sure. I'll meet you downstairs in five."

Not leaving a doughnut run to chance, BW abandoned me and followed KiKi downstairs. I stumbled out of bed, hunted clean clothes, and met up with KiKi on the front porch. Three and a half minutes later we were all standing in front of Cakery Bakery.

I put my foot on the first step, then stopped, with others hankering for just-out-of-the-oven doughnuts walking around me. "It's too early for a doughnut attack," I whined. "And I bet GracieAnn made some extra-gooey ones for kicks just to aim at me. I got a bad feeling about this."

"Honey, when was the last time you had a good feeling?"

When I danced with Boone, but I wasn't about to say that because there was a big possibility he hadn't been there at all and I'd imagined the whole thing. I took a deep breath, pulled open the door to the bakery, and stepped inside to the smells of America. Yankee Candle should make a Cakery Bakery fragrance. Whatever GracieAnn had in store for me, it was worth it just to enjoy the aroma. GracieAnn started for me, and I waited for the pie in the face or the cream puff in my hair.

"You can sit right over here now." She smiled and took me by the elbow, leading us through a sea of customers, Anna and Bella sat at a table by the window, deep in conversation. They were alone. Clive and Crenshaw weren't early risers? Maybe Clive and Crenshaw didn't rise at all. Where the heck were they? Whenever I saw Anna and Bella it was just the two of them.

GracieAnn nodded to a nice little table in the corner. I looked up to see if one of those pots filled with goop and glue was suspended overhead to dump on me.

"I'll bring you doughnuts," she added. "You just sit tight."

"But we haven't ordered yet," KiKi protested, her gaze fused to a tray of chocolate éclair doughnuts that one of the waitresses had just slipped into the display case.

"I'll bring you the darn doughnuts that I see fit," GracieAnn growled, stamping her foot and adding a *do as I say* sneer for good measure.

"Right." KiKi sat up straight and fluffed a napkin across her lap. "A doughnut . . . any doughnut that you happen to have on hand would be much appreciated."

GracieAnn nodded. "Now that's what I want to hear."

She tromped off and KiKi leaned across the table. "I don't know what we got ourselves into, but I'm thinking it's going to make the rest of the day seem like a piece of cake." The other waitresses wrote up orders and bagged goodies for hungry customers, and in no time GracieAnn was back with a tray. She set down the coffees and then a sprinkle doughnut in front of me, a chocolate éclair doughnut in front of KiKi, and a cake one for BW already broken into little doggie pieces.

"You know," KiKi said to me, "I'm going to give you my chocolate and I'll take the sprinkle one for a change and—"

GracieAnn smacked KiKi's hand and whispered, "You eat what I give you, period. Absolutely no sharing, house rules." She looked around at other patrons sharing. "For you it's house rules. Understand. A mutual friend gave me this doughnut to give to Reagan and to no one else."

GracieAnn headed back to the counter and I stared at the pastry in front of me. "Okay, that's it, it's poisoned. Pelting me with chunks of dough wasn't good enough, now GracieAnn's going to . . . Look at this, there's something stuck in this doughnut."

KiKi gasped. "She really is trying to—"

I poked at the side. "It's an edge of something." I broke off a chunk of doughnut, revealing a rolled-up paper protruding out the end.

"A love note from GracieAnn?" KiKi whispered.

"I'm thinking a warning note from the great beyond."

"I don't think we're talking Bible quotes. You mean . . . Really? Why not just have Gracie tell you whatever it says?" KiKi added in a whisper.

"My guess is she doesn't know what's on the paper. She's doing it as a favor to Boone and he's probably trying to protect her by keeping her out of this as much as possible. The cops must really be tightening the noose to warrant something as crazy as this."

"He could just call me."

"If this all goes south the cops could get a warrant for your phone records. He doesn't want you involved either." I cut my eyes back and forth to make sure no one was looking, then slid out the paper and unrolled it, as little doughnut crumbs floated into my lap.

"Well?" KiKi asked, an impatient edge to her voice.

I slid the paper back into the doughnut to pass to KiKi so she could read it. When I looked up, my gaze landed on Deckard coming toward us. Yikes! The noose was tightening all right; Deckard being here was no accident.

"Starting the day early?" Deckard said, proving my point. How would he know seven was early for me unless he'd been watching me? Ick!

"Guess the police aren't the only ones liking doughnuts." Deckard pulled over another chair and sat down at the table with KiKi and me. He picked up a chunk of KiKi's chocolate doughnut and plopped it in his mouth. "We need to share, right?" he said around a mouthful.

"Sure," I said, my heart pounding.

"But I don't think you really mean that." Deckard took another chunk of KiKi's doughnut. "And I'm not just talking doughnuts. What's going on with Boone? If you don't tell me, that's obstruction of justice; you could go to jail."

"Aren't you going to be late for work? How will the police force function if you're not around? Maybe you should go."

"Don't get smart with me, cookie."

Holy freaking cow, Deckard's big meaty hand was headed for my plate, my sprinkle doughnut! Snapping it out of his reach would look suspicious. *Take the little half, take the little half, take the little half.* I concentrated on the words, hoping mental telepathy really worked.

Except Deckard's fingers headed for the big half of my sprinkle doughnut, the paper-in-the-doughnut half. I grabbed the big half and shoved the whole thing in my mouth at once, my cheeks bulging out chipmunk style.

"I'mnotcookie," I mumbled around the crumbs.

"I'm not cookie," KiKi translated. She stared at me, her eyes huge, not quite believing what I'd done. I couldn't believe it either.

"I think you should go," KiKi said to Deckard.

Deckard flattened his hands on the table and leaned toward me. "Have you seen Walker Boone? And I better get the truth this time."

I shook my head.

"I don't believe you," he said in a chilling tone. "If I find that you're lying to me, that you're in contact with him, I'll lock up you and Grannie Chocolate here, I don't care who her husband is. I'll bury the paperwork so deep no one will ever find either of you. I've had it with Boone on the run and I'm fed up with everyone covering for him. I'm going to find Walker Boone, I'm going to get a conviction, and you better not be in the way. Got it?"

I swallowed down the doughnut plus paper, and Deckard swiped the little chunk of my doughnut still on the plate and headed for the door. KiKi shoved the coffee into my hand. "Drink before you choke."

I gulped from the cup and gasped for air. "Think that's what they mean by eating your words?"

"Oh for crying in a bucket, what did the words say and just who does that man think he is calling me Grannie Chocolate?"

Chapter Eleven

I LEFT a twenty on the table and gave a wave to GracieAnn. Auntie KiKi, BW, and I made for the front door of the Cakery Bakery. When we got outside, Deckard's cruiser was still parked at the curb.

"That man's nothing but trouble," I said to KiKi as I smiled at Deckard. He wasn't the only one who could fake it. The fearsome threesome casually strolled along, the cruiser following us. We turned onto Barnard, where KiKi had left the Batmobile. BW jumped in the back and KiKi and I climbed in the front, just two ladies and a pup out for breakfast. Oh, if only that were true.

KiKi brought the car to life, casually blended into the flow of morning traffic, and then turned to me. "If you don't tell me right now what was in that note, I'm throwing you out at the next stoplight and running you over flat. I'm dying here, honey! What's going on?"

"It said *Follow the money*, and there was a phone number."

"Saints in heaven, tell me you remember the number before you choked it down."

"Of course I remember." Maybe. "I think the three was before the four, or was it after the five?"

KiKi stopped to let a band of happy tourists plus leader cross East Oglethorpe to get to the Colonial Park Cemetery. "You got to be kidding. This is important. James Bond always remembered that kind of stuff."

"Do I look like James Bond? And I was under a lot of stress, and I bet Bond never had to eat the evidence, now did he? Just give me your phone and I'll try some combinations."

"The way things are going, you'll probably get through to China and I'll get nailed with roaming charges." KiKi harrumphed and forked over her iPhone. I punched in the numbers, then hung up.

"Well?" KiKi asked.

"Main menu for the Savannah Chatham County public school system."

"Sweet mother save us all," KiKi muttered under her breath as I punched in another combination. I apologized for having the wrong number, then hung up. "Car Spa over on Jeff . . . Wait a minute." I hit redial and Jimmy at Car Spa answered again. "This is Reagan Summerside and—"

"Bring in the Chevy tomorrow at noon and we'll take care of it." The line went dead.

"What was that all about?" KiKi asked as I stared at the phone in my hand.

"Boone's closer than we think. The number was to have the Chevy cleaned. Chantilly and I sort of spilled barbecue in the trunk when making a delivery and—"

"And Walker knew about it and made plans to have it cleaned up even on a Sunday? That makes sense; a man's gotta take care of his ride, now doesn't he?"

KiKi pulled into her driveway and I didn't get out. Instead I folded my arms. "You're not surprised." I looked KiKi dead in the eyes. "Where is he?"

"I don't know."

"And you wouldn't tell me if you did."

"There is that." KiKi framed my face with her hands. "You saw Deckard; he and everyone in this city knows you got a thing for Walker, and feelings being what they are, you'd be tempted to take off after him."

"Why would I do such a thing?"

"All the TV spots and lies can't hide the way you look when you mention his name. My guess is the only reason he contacted you through the doughnut was he knows you're out there looking and you can get to places he can't right now."

"I thought I was doing pretty good with the dopey-look thing."

"Walker's got to keep on the move. Besides the numbers, what else was in the note?"

"*Follow the money.* What does that mean? There's lots of money floating around. Tucker has tons, Mason Dixon has none, this Grayden Russell guy wants to buy the Old Harbor Inn, and he's after the Tybee Post Theater."

"Anna and Bella married for it," KiKi added.

"And Conway left a bunch of it to the free clinic."

KiKi gasped. "Well my stars, I sure didn't see that one coming. Bet that sent a tremor through the universe."

"I wonder which money Boone's talking about?"

"I'd say he doesn't know, that's why the note. So he doesn't think this is about revenge or love or jealousy, and it's all about the bucks." KiKi checked the clock on the dashboard. "I've got an emergency dance lesson with Bernard at nine. Seems like *Dancing with the Stars* is giving him an audition, probably to get him to back off. I think he calls them every day." She held my hands tight. "If Deckard's keeping an eye on you, my guess is so is the real killer. You need to keep an eye out, honey."

"The problem is I have no idea who the real killer is."

"It's like Cher says, no doesn't mean no forever; you'll figure it out." KiKi was a roadie for Cher back in her college days and never quite left the tour, proven by the fact that Cherisms sprang from her mouth from time to time. "Anyone who can eat a rolled-up note in a doughnut and not gag is capable of most anything," she added.

I appreciated the vote of confidence and all, but what if KiKi and Cher were wrong; what if I didn't figure this out? KiKi pulled the Beemer into her garage and BW and I headed for the Fox. I opened the front door, paused, then closed it and started off for St. John's Church.

The weekday eight o'clock Mass had ended; the smell of snuffed candles, old hymnals, and fresh flowers washed over me as we went inside. BW's nails tapped against the marble floors and we made our way past the stained-glass windows of saints and redeemed sinners. I was sure dogs in church were a no-no, but God loved BW; everybody loved BW.

I was baptized and married in St. John's and frequented it on holidays and when I was in deep doo-doo. I tried to remember to be grateful for the good stuff in my life and not ask for a lot of favors, but this was one of the deep-doo-doo times. I'd gotten nowhere in finding Conway's killer and figured divine intervention was my only hope. Boone would never have sent me the note unless his back was to the wall, and that one factor alone scared the heck out of me.

I dropped money in the little tin box and lit three candles, figuring if this was a three-olive problem, three candles seemed fitting, too. I asked anyone listening to keep an eye on Boone, and BW added two tail wags and a bark. Feeling totally defeated because I had no idea how to fix this mess, I headed out into the sunlight with BW as Steffy Lou Adkins came up the church steps. She had on a yellow sundress that set off her dark hair and dark eyes, and a covered wicker basket hung over her arm.

"Well, I do declare, I do run into you at the strangest places," Steffy Lou said to me. She tried for a smile but failed miserably, meaning I wasn't the only one in a frazzled state this morning. Steffy Lou rolled her eyes toward the church steeple and made the sign of the cross. "It's always a comfort to know the powers above are watching, and right now I need all the help I can get."

"Grieving is a long process," I offered, not really knowing what the heck I was talking about since I was two when Daddy passed. I just felt the need to say something comforting.

"Not that." Steffy Lou let out a sigh. "Well, it's not entirely that, I should say. It's the theater benefit that's got me in a tizzy. There simply cannot be a drop of rain for the fundraiser two days from now or the whole thing's going to fall flat as a pancake, being it's an outside event and all."

Steffy Lou paled and looked unsteady. "I just don't know what I'll do if we can't raise enough money for repairs and the like. That no-good Grayden Russell is just waiting for things to go wrong so he can swoop down like the vulture he is and turn the place into some frivolous resort with canned music and DJs, of all things. If I weren't here on the front steps of God's house I'd tell you exactly what I think of the man and then some."

A spring breeze ruffled through the trees and flipped back the cloth covering Steffy Lou's basket, exposing little angel statues, candles, colored pieces of cloth, an empty green bottle, and a full bottle of rum.

"Odilia?"

Steffy Lou nodded and quickly covered up the basket. "Like I said, I'm in desperate need of all the help I can get."

"I can sure relate to that." I nodded back into the church.

Steffy Lou's eyes brightened, and she put her hand to her chest in a state of relief. "Reagan honey, that's music to my ears." She patted her basket. "I need an East and a West right quick-like."

"As in witches for *The Wizard of Oz*? I have to tell you that I'm not much good at acting. Fact is, it seems I can't even tell a little old lie without all of creation knowing about it and—"

"Not that East and West." Steffy Lou lowered her voice and huddled close, the wicker basket between us. "It's a protection plan for the Tybee Theater. We have to protect the place from all directions. Odilia told me to get these items, and then she also gave me strict instructions on what I needed to do with them. I'd sure appreciate it if you could lend me a hand. Think of the little children who won't get to see *Peter Pan* if Russell gets his grimy hands on our theater."

Steffy Lou cleared her throat and straightened her shoulders, and I could tell she was headed for take two of "I Won't Grow Up" right there on the church steps. How could I say no to a Lost Boy, and truth be told she had me at no-good Grayden Russell. I could still feel his fingers digging into my arms. "What do you need me to do?"

Steffy Lou hugged me with her one free arm. "I so appreciate this, Reagan honey. Be out to the theater around sunset and bring a West with you. I need four participants, you see. Harper Norton's a dear friend of mine and helping me out since Walker's not able to." Steffy Lou bit her bottom lip. "How can this happen to that fine man after all the work he's done for the theater?" She swallowed hard and tilted her chin high. "He'd want us to carry on as best we can. So, Harper's taking the North and I'm the South. That Russell troublemaker isn't going to have his way as long as the Savannah ladies are in charge, I can promise you that. Now, I'm off to light a few candles. Odilia is mighty good at calling in the saints to set things to rights, and in there the Main Man is front and center."

Steffy Lou faded into the cool shadows of St. John's interior, and BW and I rushed off to Cherry House. I went into panic mode to get things ready, and by ten the front door to the Prissy Fox was open and customers were streaming in; I had another busy day ahead. I offered up a prayer of thanks, then started writing sales and taking in clothes.

By four I was dead tired and hadn't even stopped for lunch or had a second to spare in finding a West . . . until my dear Auntie KiKi wandered in. The Lord does provide. "You're limping," I said to KiKi.

"I think my big toe is broken, the others are black and blue, I might have cracked a rib, and Putter has emergency surgery, so he can't even take a look at my ailments. Bernard bought his plane ticket for L.A. He's got an audition lined up and he has to bring a demo tape. We've been dancing for six hours straight to get five minutes of decent footage." There was a little twinkle in her eyes. "The good news is I now have enough to get that new purse I have my eye on."

"I think you should celebrate and take a nice convertible drive out to Tybee Post."

I got the suspicious eye. "Right now celebrating is a long bubble bath and a martini. Besides, there's barbecue shrapnel in the Chevy trunk."

"The top will be down and you won't even smell it." *Much.* "And we can stop off at the Crab Shack for Southern boil, my treat."

"Tybee?"

This was the tricky part. "I met Steffy Lou and she wants you to be a special guest for her event, and tonight is the rehearsal to get things right."

"Yep, you truly are the worst liar ever, but you had me at Southern boil; I can almost taste the shrimp, clams, and crawfish. After a day of Bernard and sore feet, I'm in." KiKi started for the door, then stopped. "So what are we really doing out at Tybee?"

"Odilia sort of plays into it."

"Oh sweet mother, I better not wind up pregnant with triplets."

Chapter Twelve

"WE'RE going to be late," I said to Auntie KiKi as we climbed back into the Chevy, the sun just above the horizon. I handed her my iced tea to-go cup as I backed out of the parking place between two trees.

"How can Boone have a car without cup holders?"

"Maybe it's a hint that we're not supposed to eat or drink here," KiKi said, then slurped her own tea as I slowly motored out of the Crab Shack parking lot. We circled the alligator sanctuary, where dinner guests could buy little pellets of whatever and feed the gators. Some might enjoy the experience, but personally I stayed as far away from snappers as possible. Anything with that many teeth was not to be messed with.

"You just had to go and have apple pie for desert," I said,

taking my cup back. "After all that you ate? Where in the world did you put it?"

KiKi patted her stomach. "Right here and proud of it. I've had a tough day and burned up a ton of calories with Bernard, so the way I figure it, I deserve apple pie and more."

An ocean breeze caught in my hair as I pulled onto Route 80, which ran from Savannah to the island. Marshes stretched off to the right and left, the road like a ribbon of land through the water. It occurred to me that the last time I was out here I had a string of cruisers trailing behind me and was shaking like a leaf.

"Least we know where we're going," KiKi said when we reached the island and passed the first of the T-shirt and gift shops housed in campers and trailers and white clapboard buildings. "Just aim for the lighthouse and the theater's just beyond."

Hilton Head Island was about an hour away and more of a highbrow location. Tybee was a fishing village atmosphere where folks took pride in sitting on the back porch and spitting watermelon seeds. Not that it was poor and destitute by any means, but residents chose not to flaunt their wares and instead lived the simple life of pizza and beer. The sun was starting to dip into the ocean as we pulled into the theater's gravel parking lot, nearly running into Tucker Adkins barreling out of the lot in his big black Escalade.

"Well of all the nerve, did you see that?" KiKi said, her hair standing on end and her eyes bulging. "That jackass nearly ran us down, and he didn't even have the manners to stop and apologize for the experience."

"Tucker's all about Tucker. I wonder if the man even

knows other people live on this planet." I killed the engine, the peace of the island at twilight closing in around us. The main hubbub of tourists, bars, and restaurants sat near the ocean side of the island where the long pier jutted out into the water. The lighthouse and theater were located back here on a natural inlet.

"Lordy, Lordy, here you are at long last," Steffy Lou called out as she and Harper hustled over to the Chevy. "We were getting terrible worried you wouldn't show up. I mentioned to Tucker you were coming to help out, but when you didn't show and I said he'd have to do the chanting and the like, he took off like a shot. He came out here to bring the programs and make sure his name was front and center as a sponsor. Typical Tucker, I do the work and he gets the credit, but that's okay as long as we save the theater."

I did the quick-introduction thing between KiKi and Harper as the four of us walked across the large grassy yard now dotted with white tents, a stage, and stacks of chairs and tables ready to be set up. The redbrick Colonial-style theater was just beyond. It had white-framed doors and windows that could do with a coat of paint, but all things considered it looked pretty sound.

"Isn't it fantastic?" Steffy Lou said with a sigh while staring up at the front facade. "Soon this place will be filled with people having fun and supporting our theater. It's going to be outside because the electricity's not on, but that's all going to change soon, just wait. We simply cannot let anything happen to the place. Live productions are magnificent, a true testimony to culture and civilization and the arts. I think our first show should be *My Fair Lady*, as this theater is truly a lady and at long last we are transforming her from rags to riches."

Steffy Lou stood tall, shoulders back, boobs out. I braced myself for "I Could Have Danced All Night" or "Get Me to the Church on Time" or some other *My Fair Lady* tune till Harper interrupted with, "Uh, the sun is setting quick and we have to get a move on if you think this nonsense we got going on here has any chance of working on this pile of bricks."

"Nonsense?" Steffy Lou's eyes shot wide open. "Hush your mouth, of course this is going to work, it simply has to, and this wonderful theater with so much potential is not a pile of bricks, thank you very much. We got to do everything in our power to protect the place. We are stewards of the arts."

Harper did the good-grief eye roll as Steffy Lou opened the basket she'd had at the church. She handed out the colored pieces of material and angels. "Odilia said we put the cloths on our heads. Orange is East, green is West, yellow is South, and blue is North."

"Our heads?" KiKi asked, staring at the square of material.

"I don't make the rules, I just follow them like the woman told me." Steffy Lou passed out candles. "Let's see now, we need to put angels at each direction, then hold the candles chest high, parade around the theater in a clockwise direction as the sun sets, and chant, *Spirits north, south, east, and west, protect this theater, she is obsessed.*"

I gave Steffy Lou a long look. "Obsessed? Really? You sang 'I Won't Grow Up' for Odilia, didn't you?"

"Well, she had to know I was sincere about saving the place and how much it meant to me and—"

"You all look crazy and stupid," Grayden Russell said, coming around from the back side of the theater accompanied by two of his poker-playing goons from the other night when Chantilly and I were at the inn. "Something tells me this little rite of the ridiculous has to do with stopping me from taking over the theater, which I intend to do in short order, so this is all for nothing."

Steffy Lou jabbed her hands on her hips and tossed her hair. "That's what you think. No one messes with Odilia, and Southern women are a force you don't want to mess with. Walker Boone warned me about the likes of you."

"And look what happened to him," Russell sneered, then laughed deep in his throat, pointing to the tents and chairs and tables. "This fund-raiser you got planned doesn't stand a snowball's chance in Hades of being successful, Miss Steffy Lou Adkins, patron of the arts. No way can you raise enough money to save this dump of a theater. I intend to construct a new one. This heap of bricks will be used for storage at best."

"Over my dead body," Steffy Lou huffed. "And the theater is not a dump or a heap of bricks. The talent show I have lined up is amazing. I alone am doing three lively songs and the cuisine is straight from Sundae Café—their delicious fried chicken, sweet potato fries, fried okra, and key lime pie. I will save the theater and there will be live productions once again."

"Nice speech, except you're running out of time. I have money available, a lot of it, and that's what the island council is going to see, not all your promises that could amount to nothing."

"The council's smarter than you think. They don't want your resort."

"We'll see about that." Russell glared at me. "It figures you'd be here sticking your nose in where it's doesn't belong. Every time I turn around you're there."

"And you're here, too," I said, considering that fact.

"Stay out of my way, Summerside, unless you want to turn that dog of yours into an orphan. A couple of stupid Southern broads aren't going to get in my way and mess things up."

Russell and company strolled off, and Steffy Lou turned to me. "You know him too? Lordy!"

"He's not only interested in buying the theater, he also wants to buy the Old Harbor Inn. There's a connection there somewhere and I can't figure out what it is. Why both places? Why these specific places?"

"Time's a-wastin'," Harper chimed in again, pointing over the water. "Can we play Perry Mason later? The sun's setting, and after seeing Russell here checking the place out, I think the theater needs all the protection it can get. Fact is, I think we do, too." She shivered. "That guy sure does give me the creeps worse than a hairy spider."

Steffy Lou lit the candles and each of us took a side of the building, walking and chanting in a clockwise direction around the place. I caught bits and pieces of the others reciting the words, and truth be told I wasn't sure about the obsessed part, but who was I to argue with someone who could bring on triplets?

By the time we finished chanting and parading, we'd drawn a small crowd of tourists who clearly thought we'd lost our minds, or maybe they considered us a tourist attraction, it was hard to tell which. The last rays of the sun dipped into the sea, leaving behind a panoramic view of stars and a crescent moon suspended in a coal-black sky.

We doused the candles, and the crowd slowly dispersed. Steffy Lou placed the empty green bottle and the full rum bottle on the doorstep along with three oranges and two eggplants as an offering. Someone in need of a free drink might take the rum, but it wouldn't be anyone local. The eggplants and oranges were a dead giveaway that this was a calling from Odilia to the spirit world. Messing with such things resulted in teeth falling out, going instantly bald, and the inability to perform in the sack, something no man or woman wanted to mess with. We bowed three times, then headed for the parking lot.

"Gorgeous, isn't it?" Steffy Lou said with a wistful sigh as she climbed into her Lexus, Harper taking the passenger seat. "It's the magic of the ocean that brings us out here. I thank you kindly for helping out like you did and for being here when Russell showed up. I know I'm one to get my feathers ruffled easy enough, but I have no use for the man. I sure hope the two of you can make it back here for the event. We're needing all the support we can muster, and you can buy the tickets at the door. Local talent is putting on the entertainment, and I'm doing a medley on the old theater stage so everyone can get a feel for the place."

"You can count on us," I assured Steffy Lou.

"Well, bless your heart, you are the best."

Steffy Lou and Harper waved and drove off, and KiKi gave me the *what have you gotten us into now* look as I powered up the Chevy and slurped the last of my watered-down tea from dinner. "If I drag Putter out here for a night of fried and fat, he'll commandeer the microphone and we'll get a lecture on heart and health. He keeps that PowerPoint presentation in his car, you know. He has slides of intestines and clogged arteries. He has a bucket of ten pounds of fat. Do you know what ten pounds of fat looks like up close and personal? It isn't pretty. People will cry and faint dead away. I've seen it happen."

"We have to come to the event. I think Russell might try something. He seemed awfully confident that the fund-raiser wouldn't be successful, and he was here tonight checking out the place. The question is, why? What does he have planned, and you know it's not anything good. Walker's connection to the event has got to be hurting sales; he is a man wanted for murder, after all. If Steffy Lou's hard work tanks, all will be lost for the theater."

"So now what? You're suggesting we dress in camo and bring shotguns?"

"More just follow Russell around and keep an eye out. He can't pull anything if we keep him in sight." I glanced back at the brick building silhouetted in the moonlight. "It would be a crying shame to have the place go to that man and get turned into a resort."

"Fine, fine, fine. I'll be her best off-to-the-gallows voice. I'll get Gloria to arrange for Putter to guest lecture at some legal event and bore the daylights out of those people."

"Buckets of fat on the lawyer community? Are you trying to get Mamma disbarred?"

"We could hit up the county jail; they're supposed to be punished, right?"

"Seems cruel and unusual if you ask me."

We started for home, then got detoured by KiKi's sudden craving for a cherry snow cone at Seaweeds since our iced tea from the Crab Shack was gone. Then it was on to Seaside Sweets for saltwater taffy to sustain life during the long ride home of twenty minutes. By the time we finally got back on the road the clock on the dash was homing in on ten, my head was splitting, and I was tired clear through, but I had to admit the strawberry taffy was really good.

We settled into the comfy leather seats of the sexmobile, with the wide-open asphalt stretched out ahead. The wind was at our backs, the temperature perfect, and the aroma of barbecue barely noticeable if you didn't think about it. KiKi dozed off and I turned on the radio, hoping for a little Adam Levine to keep me awake. I hit the gas a little harder, going faster than I should, but such is the lure of a fancy car with the top down and I just wanted to get home to bed, yes bed with fluffy covers and sleep and sleep and . . .

"Reagan!" KiKi screamed, jarring me awake. KiKi grabbed for the dashboard and I grabbed the steering wheel tight as we careened off the edge of the road, going airborne and then splashing down hard into the marsh.

I jolted forward, smacking my head on the steering wheel and shaking the fog from my brain. "Undo your seatbelt," I yelled to KiKi, as the murky water poured in over the doors and trunk and then over the windshield. "Swim!"

"Honey, we can stand. It's not that deep and where in blazes is my purse?"

"Forget the blasted purse!"

"It's Gucci. I danced my feet off for that purse." Before I could stop her, KiKi took a deep breath and doggie-paddled back down into the water! Dear God in heaven! Doing the only sensible thing, I went in after her. I had to; I was the one who got her and Gucci into this mess. I felt around, connecting with the Chevy's backseat. I snagged Old Yeller but couldn't find KiKi anywhere. Popping back to the surface, I gulped in a lungful of air. "KiKi!"

"Reagan?"

"KiKi!"

"Reagan?"

It was the swamp version of Marco Polo. I turned around and saw KiKi splashing her way toward me, and she wasn't the only one headed in my direction. I pointed beyond her to little white dots appearing just above the water line.

"Holy cow, we got company," I said, as more white dots appeared on the scene like little stars in the sky, except these were not stars and this was not the night sky. This was a creepy swamp of marsh oats and cattails and bugs, and everyone knew that gators slept by day and hunted at night. Right now KiKi and I were a midnight snack.

"It's that blasted barbecue." KiKi pulled up beside me, both of us waist-deep in dark water, the oozy mud below pulling us down. We slogged backward toward the shore. "I'd say we're just like Cakery Bakery to these guys. You know, the lure of things delicious and sublime."

The little dots of white got larger, brighter, and a lot more menacing as they approached. The moonlit surface barely moved as the giant tails swished back and forth, silently propelling the sleek massive bodies our way at an unbelievably fast clip.

"Lord save us, they're coming!" I smacked the lead gator with Old Yeller. He stopped and that was good. Then he hissed just like a snake and opened his big mouth in protest, exposing a whole lot of teeth. I screamed and some white things flew through the air and landed between his jaws.

I looked back to KiKi, who had the Seaside candy bag in her hand. "Okay, who's glad I got the taffy now, huh? A few of those teeth have got to be sweet ones."

"You're kidding!"

"Got a better idea?"

I grabbed a handful of candy and threw the pieces out into the water, then grabbed a fistful of cattail to keep from falling. I pulled myself up onto the muddy bank, snagged KiKi's purse handle, and dragged the all-star pitcher of the taffy world up beside me, the movement in the grass behind us indicating we were not alone.

"They're gaining!" KiKi threw more taffy and we scrambled the rest of the way up the embankment, as car wheels zoomed by right in front of us.

Panting, we belly-flopped onto the berm. "They won't follow up here," KiKi huffed. "The noise and vibrations will keep them away."

"Survival class at the senior center?"

"Three seasons of *Crocodile Hunter*." She pulled in a deep breath and we wobbled to our feet, me stumbling hard against KiKi. "Well, so much for Odilia's protection plan." KiKi wrapped her arm around me, holding me upright as more cars roared by. "It was a waste of good rum, if you ask me."

"Hey, we're alive."

"For the moment. Just wait till Boone finds out about his car."

A dark SUV slowed, then pulled off the road and stopped, the window powering down. Was it Jack the Ripper, the Savannah Strangler, Superman coming to get the car out of the drink?

"There you are," the voice inside said. "I wondered where you went."

"Ross?" I staggered to the car and stuck my head in the window as the aroma of hot pizza washed over me. If the woman didn't get a guy in her life soon, she'd look like a beached whale and she'd get kicked off the force. "What are you doing here?"

"Keeping an eye on you, and right now you don't look so good. Where's the Chevy and why are you all sopping wet and, honey, you smell like wet dog and . . ." Ross's eyes widened as she focused on the wide-open water beyond us. "Oh my dear Lord," she said on a long exhale of breath. "Boone is so going to kill you dead," Ross added as KiKi and I got into the backseat and got the floor mats to sit on.

"What are you doing out here this time of night?" KiKi asked. "Not that we're not grateful. Making a pizza run out to Huca Poos?"

"That, too." Ross pulled onto the road and headed toward Savannah. I settled back against the seat, closing my eyes as she went on. "You don't have a clue what you're doing, Reagan Summerside, but you stir up enough trouble that the way I see it the real killer is bound to come after you sooner or later. Some of us down at the station are taking turns keeping an eye on you. Deckard thinks you'll lead him to Walker."

I pried one eye open. "You're all following me around?"

"*Surveillance* sounds more professional, and like you said, a run out to Tybee for Huca Poos pizza is always a good idea. How'd you come to drive off the road?"

"I think I fell asleep. I was driving along and the next thing I knew KiKi yelled and I woke up."

"Girl, you should know that drinking and driving is serious business."

"Drinking as in a cherry snow cone? I'm just so darn tired."

The next thing I knew Ross was pulling to the curb in front of my house and KiKi was shaking my shoulder. Ross turned back to face me. "Look, I know Boone's innocent, but you should keep in mind that Deckard is a shoot-first-and-ask-questions-later kind of guy, and he's watching you more than any of us. He drives a rusted tan pickup with the right front light busted out, and maybe you're sick, you were snoring like a freight train."

"I don't snore and I think I'm the one who busted out Deckard's light."

"Terrific, another reason for the guy to love you. I'd watch my back, Reagan, and give up snow cones." Ross motored off, and KiKi and I watched the SUV disappear around the corner. "You really don't look good at all; your eyes aren't even focusing." She nodded to Rose Gate. "The light's on in the kitchen; I'm going to get your uncle to give you a quick once-over."

I grabbed KiKi's arm. "I'm fine, I just hit my head and

I'm tired, so darn tired I can hardly stand up, and I am so sorry for . . ." My voice cracked. "I could have killed you. We could have driven into oncoming traffic or hit a pole or tree or . . ."

KiKi took my hand. "But we didn't and you didn't and I think Ross is right, you got a bug or something. Go home, go to bed."

"What are you going to tell Uncle Putter? Right now you sort of look like the Queen of Muck."

"I'm going to tell him the truth, of course."

"That your stupid niece fell asleep at the wheel?" Just saying the words made me sicker still.

"I was thinking more like I dropped my purse in the swamp and went in after it. Putter has his golf clubs and Lord knows the man would dive into a full-blown volcano to save them. I have my purses. It's like Cher says, it's a different stage for every song."

She scrunched up her face. "I don't quite know how that fits into this particular situation." She kissed me on the cheek. "Take in your spare key, honey. From what Ross said, there's too much trouble out there with your name on it to be tempting fate."

KiKi hobbled off and I stumbled my way inside; BW was waiting and wagging for me in the front hall. He got a good whiff of swamp, then backed off and barked. As he followed me at a distance, we paraded into the kitchen. I got him his daily hot dog from the fridge and pulled out food for me— ham, cheese, and bread—but I just didn't feel like eating.

I filled BW's bowl with expensive kibble that he'd eat later when convinced there was nothing delicious coming his way. "You're not going to believe this," I said to BW as he ate. "Our sexmobile is at the bottom of a swamp. No more wolf whistles, no more hot-babe looks, no more cute poodles shaking their pompom tail. It's back to the bus."

BW stopped midway through his hot dog, gave me a pathetic look, and then lay down on the floor. Yeah, that was pretty much how I felt, too.

I ran the shower to hot and took Old Yeller with me to scrub out the swamp smell. The convenience of owning a pleather purse was truly underrated, and it occurred to me that I was now involved in money laundering. I draped the bills over the shower curtain rod, then scrubbed every inch of my poor abused body, hoping to get rid of eau de swamp. I ran the water cold to wake up. I felt as if I'd been walking in a dream since I left Tybee, and the thought of nearly killing KiKi sat like a rock in my gut. How could I do such a thing? I slid into my fluffy terry robe and moped into my dark bedroom to find Walker Boone sitting on my bed. I'd recognize that silhouette anywhere.

Under normal circumstances I'd think this was a good thing, even great. Women would kill to have Walker Boone in their bedroom. Except those women hadn't just nearly killed their favorite auntie and driven Boone's beloved red Chevy into a swamp.

Chapter Thirteen

"WHAT'S going on?" Boone asked as I sat down beside him. Okay, this could be really romantic with Boone, the bed, and the moonlight streaming in through the window. Fact is, it was something I sort of dreamed about on occasion, except in that dream Boone wasn't eating a sandwich like he was now.

"I smell ham and cheese." Not that the sandwich was a deterrent to me, but the way he was going at it, my guess was he'd choose eating over me in a New York minute. "And you'll have to narrow the *going on* part down a little."

"The barbecue? The mess in my car?" He chomped a few more bites.

"How did you find out about the barbecue? Chantilly?"

"Chantilly would never rat you out." Boone swiped his mouth with the back of his hand. "I have my ways. You got the message about taking the Chevy over to Jimmy at Car Spa? And you got rid of the note, right? I don't want Jimmy to have any ties to me or get involved with the cops."

I waved my hand in the air in a dismissive fashion. "If there's one thing I can promise you, it's that no one is ever going to find the note. It's gone where no note has ever gone before." *Or where any note will ever go again, God willing.*

"As far as the Chevy goes," I added, "I took care of the barbecue-in-the-trunk problem on my own. No more worries. Fact is, when you look at the Chevy you'll forget there ever was a barbecue problem at all."

He stopped chewing. "Really?"

"Pinky swear."

"How did you manage that?"

"I have my ways." I winked. Actually it was a nervous tic from telling such a whopper of a lie. "So, why are you here?" I added, in a hurry to get away from the Chevy topic of conversation.

"I was hungry." Boone finished off the sandwich, with BW right beside him begging bits and pieces. "So, what do you have?"

"There might be some Fig Newtons left, and there's an apple or two and the vegetables are mostly all there and—"

"I mean information." Boone smiled, his teeth white against the dark. He was relaxed now, more Boone than worry.

"For openers, you should know that Ross and some cop named Deckard are watching me, hoping to land their hooks into you. That Russell guy you warned me about is after the Old Harbor Inn as well as the theater, and he and Mason

Dixon are poker-playing friendly, though Russell is the better player. I think Tucker's tied up in this some way."

"He hates my guts, and truth be told he's got a right. Seems Conway told him I was the successful bastard son and proceeded to throw it in Tucker's face for the next four years. Conway saw Tucker as the spoiled mamma's-boy offspring who would never amount to much, and Conway liked rubbing it in his face."

Walker yawned, then stretched as only a guy can, and I nearly melted into a blob on the floor. He fluffed a pillow against the headboard and settled back against it, shoes off, denim-clad legs stretched out in front.

"Best I can tell," Boone went on, "is that all roads lead to Conway. Tucker's his kid, I'm his kid, Grayden Russell wanted to buy his inn, and Mason Dixon wanted his job."

"And Dixon was blackmailing Conway because he knew about you." I started to pace. "I need to get into Conway's house. There's got to be records of Conway paying Dixon. There might even be a proposal from Russell to buy the inn and Conway refusing the offer. Those are good motives for murder, and maybe we can figure out how you tie into it. I still have the signed agreement between Conway and me about consigning his furniture. I'll sneak into his house and look around, and if I get caught I can say I need to get measurements. I'll bring along my business cards, a tape measure, and a notebook to look official. I'll bring doughnuts in case I get caught. This is a great plan, right? Boone?"

I turned back to the bed. Boone's head drooped to one side, his breathing deep and even, his eyes closed. BW was in pretty much the same condition and sprawled across Boone's chest. Some dogs had all the luck.

"Right," I said in a whisper, in answer to my own question. "And I nearly killed KiKi," I added, needing to confess to someone. "How could I do such a thing?" A tear slid down my cheek, and then more and more. I swiped them away but still felt sick to my soul. I pulled on my Hello Kitty nightshirt because it was out and I didn't have to open drawers and risk waking Boone and dog.

Every time I saw Boone he looked a little worse for wear, a little more unkempt, a little more street guy than successful-lawyer guy. His face was leaner and thinner than even a few days ago. Worry did that to a person, and I hated that it was happening to Boone.

I slid in beside him. I closed my eyes, the heat of Boone's body warming mine, BW's snoring a comfort. Not exactly the sort of night in bed with Boone that I dreamed of, but he was here and fed and safe. I closed my eyes, and a second later I opened them to someone pounding on my front door.

Okay, it was more than a second because now sunlight blasted through my window. BW had reclaimed his spot in the hallway, Boone was gone, and I had a note taped to my forehead that read, *Cute jammies, you snore like a buzz saw.*

"That's not me," I said aloud, pushing myself up and shoving tangled hair off my face. "It's the dog." I glared at BW. "You need to fess up about these things. You're ruining my love life. Right, I have no love life."

BW cocked a brow and snickered. More pounding echoed through the house; the clock read seven ten. Did no one in this city sleep? I pulled on jeans and hobbled down the steps, my poor body sore and achy from a night of fun and games with gators.

I yanked open the door. "Sweet mother above, what have you gone and done with that there hidden key of yours?" Mercedes wanted to know as she bustled inside. "I looked my eyeballs out for the thing. It's under the flowerpot. Everyone knows it's under the flowerpot, until today. It's stuff like this that upsets the balance of nature."

"I brought it in. Seemed like a good idea with my enemy list getting longer than my friend list." Mercedes had on black-and-white maid attire, and her hair and makeup were perfect as always. She took my hand and dropped the Chevy keys in my palm. They were dirty and encrusted in sea grass.

"How did you . . . where did you . . . ?"

"Ross made a late-night run to Cakery Bakery and I was in need of a glazed fix myself. She told me about gators and the Chevy and falling asleep." Mercedes gave me a long look. "That's not like you. You'd never put KiKi in jeopardy like that and you look terrible, like you've been on a bender."

"It's the look of guilt and shame. Nobody else was driving that car, it was me, all me. I think I'm taking to walking for a while."

"I don't think you have a choice on that one. But accidents happen, that's why they call them accidents. Don't beat yourself up over this and besides, Ross and I both agreed that if anyone can fix the Chevy, its Jimmy over at the Car Spa. A few weeks ago a garbage truck sideswiped my pink Caddy, and Jimmy made things good as new. Mr. Boone's going to have an aneurysm if he hears about this, so we need to fix it right quick; the man's got enough to deal with. How is he holding up?"

"I haven't seen him."

"Worst liar ever."

"Dopey look on my face?"

"Yellow Post-it stuck to your shirt." Mercedes peeled off the note and tsked. "You snore? Honey, how on earth do you expect to catch that fine man if you snore?"

"It's the dog."

"Uh-huh."

"Waitaminute. If I brought in my spare key, how did Boone get in last night?"

"It's Boone, he has his ways."

"So he keeps telling me. I got a favor to ask. Ever since you found Conway dead as Lincoln in that tub of his, everything's gone haywire. What about going with me to his house? You were his maid; you know his secrets. And somehow all the mess with Boone started with Conway's murder. We need to find something concrete to save Boone's butt."

"And such a mighty fine butt it is, too. On behalf of ogling women citywide, count me in, but it'll have to be before the five o'clock viewing. Yvonne Ledbetter's layout is tonight and I have to keep watch. The woman had a big family, and that means lots of tears and kisses good-bye. I need to be making sure Yvonne doesn't streak. Meet you at Conway's at three?"

"And if we get caught I got an excuse why we're there. I can say I'm measuring the furniture Conway's consigning to me here at the Fox."

"Considering that there's yellow crime scene tape across the front door, your explanation might be a hard sell."

"Better than nothing."

"Uh-huh."

Mercedes hustled out the door, and I left it open in case an early shopper was in need of some retail therapy at a good price. The Fox was one of those season-based businesses. Business was best when the seasons changed. Christmas was beyond slow, with everyone out at the mall. Summer was the same, with it being just too darn hot to think about trying on clothes. Holidays were bursts of splurge, with women needing a party dress or new going-to-church attire. With that in mind and knowing slow days were ahead, I had to make money now. Today should be busy again like the last few weeks, but it wasn't at eleven, and by three things were still dead.

"Where is everyone?" Elsie Abbott wanted to know when she and AnnieFritz strolled into the shop, gazing around at the emptiness. "Sister and I were all primed up for a day of shopping madness." Elsie held up a straw basket covered with a yellow napkin and placed it on the counter. "We made lemon scones to keep everyone shopping happy and to celebrate our good news."

Elsie hooked her arm through her sister's and beamed. "Sleepy Pines retirement home is offering us as an incentive to spending their autumn years at their facility."

"You're going to be a welcoming committee? Play bingo? Shuffleboard? Help plan bus trips to Vegas and Mall of America?"

"We're more like a good-bye committee," Elsie said. "You see, anyone staying at the center who kicks the bucket while in residence gets a four-by-six spray of white roses for their casket, and they get us to mourn at their funeral for two hours solid."

Elsie fluffed her silver hair, done up in big curls. "We get paid by the body."

"Don't think I ever heard of Sleepy Pines."

"That's just the point. They needed enticement for people to come stay, and everyone's always looking for a good deal. You know how Savannah loves a big funeral with lots of splash."

Elsie handed me a brochure, and sure enough there on the back was a picture of the sisters in their mourning best standing in front of a casket draped in roses.

"Kind of morbid."

"Depends on how you look at it. If there's one thing old folks save for here in Savannah, it's their final big bash. None of this *family only* wake and funeral stuff around here, you know that. It's the bigger the funeral the better, and now with sound effects, that being Sister and yours truly here to do things up right and sorrowful. We even made up a demo CD of our greatest hits send-off for the dearly departed."

It seemed a little off the wall, but why not? Who was I to criticize advertising practices when my business was so in the toilet? I gazed at my still-vacant shop. "I cannot believe I've sold a few sweaters and skirts and that's it. I wonder where everyone is? What is going on?" I asked the sisters.

"Now, now, don't you be fretting none," Elsie said, putting a scone in my hand, knowing that baked goods were the South's answer to a bad day. "My guess is folks are just catching up on errands. Tomorrow will be better and the good Lord knows it has to be with Boone's nice car in need of serious repairs and you being responsible and all. That's bound to cost you a pretty penny."

"You know about Boone's car?"

"The Chevy in the swamp was beetweet all last night; that means *hot tweet* in Twitter talk. For old broads, Elsie and I are pretty with it."

"Everyone knows about the Chevy?"

"Unless they live on Mars."

My only hope was that Boone's phone had died and he was so far underground he didn't have a clue what was going on aboveground.

"Where are you headed off to?" AnnieFritz asked, taking up roost behind the desk.

"Checking out Conway Adkins's furniture to consign here. He promised it to me before his . . ."

"Unfortunate tub experience?" Elsie volunteered.

"That's one way of putting it. I'll try to hurry."

Elsie waved her hand over the shop. "No need to be doing that."

With the sexmobile in the repair shop I was back to walking to get where I needed to go, and truth be told that was okay. It would take a while for me to get behind the wheel of a car again, or maybe I never would. I hitched up BW and together we headed for Abercorn. I spotted Old Gray the bus for us, growling its way in a cloud of exhaust and hydrocarbons.

BW and I were too far from the bus stop, and there was the possibility that if the driver spotted BW he or she would just drive on by. Taking my chances, I jumped out into the street and waved my arms over my head as if landing a 747. The bus stopped right in front of us, Earlene glaring down from her perch on high.

"Girl," she said to me as BW and I climbed aboard. "The only reason I'm letting you on here is that I figured you've done lost your ever-lovin' mind standing in front of a bus that way, and I couldn't see myself running over a poor defenseless pup."

"I'm desperate. I need a ride to Chippewa Square."

Earlene folded her arms across her ample chest, the buttons of her navy-and-gold uniform straining under the expansion underneath. "You said some mighty bad things about Walker Boone that I didn't much care for."

"Look," I said standing closer. "I said all that to try to lure the real killer. If he or she knew I was on Boone's side they'd run from me. If I act the part of not being a Boone fan, then I can find others who have it in for him and maybe find the killer."

"I get what's going on here." Earlene looked down her nose at me. "That big fancy Chevy you've been strutting your stuff around in is now keeping company with swamp gators, and you're back to slumming with the likes of us here on public transportation."

Earlene's lower lip formed a pout, and she ignored the honking cars trying to get somewhere and the evil looks from the passengers on board. My guess was that the driver of the bus was like the captain of the ship; she ruled all, no questions asked.

"I do believe you're just too all high and mighty, Miss

Summerside, to be sitting yourself on a bus like this," Earlene added.

"There is no high and mighty. The Chevy isn't my car, you know it's Boone's, and I'll be lucky if he doesn't throw me in that swamp after what I did to it and . . . and besides I did fix you up with Big Joey so you sort of owe me."

Mentioning fix-ups was always a little chancy. If the two lovebirds were still dating, all was well; if they'd broken up I'd be kicked off the bus in a heartbeat. I held my breath and Earlene grinned. Thank the Lord.

"There is that," Earlene said, the grin widening. "Big Joey is some kind of man." She glared at BW. "And just what am I supposed to do with the likes of him? No dogs allowed unless they're service dogs."

"He just helped me stop the bus; that's pretty good service, right?"

"Good thing I'm still dating Big Joey." Earlene closed the double doors behind me, and Old Gray motored off to a round of applause from the other passengers. I took the front seat across from Earlene, with BW right next to me.

"What's so important over on Chippewa?" Earlene wanted to know.

Murder, mayhem. "Furniture for my shop. Does Big Joey say anything about Boone?" I lowered my voice. "Any suspects in mind?"

Earlene's bit her bottom lip as she pulled up to a bus stop to collect another passenger. "He's worried, I can tell you that," Earlene said as we took off again. "There's this new guy in town that Big Joey met when he was with Walker. Seems the guy has his eye on the Old Harbor Inn, and he wants to buy the Tybee Theater. Both places involve Boone, and now Boone's on the run. Too much of a coincidence in Big Joey's book."

"Does he say anything about Tucker?"

Earlene guided Old Gray to the curb to let someone off, and after we started up again she said, "Walker's brother is some piece of work, and Big Joey doesn't think he's worth the powder to blow the man up." Earlene stopped in front of Chippewa Square, and BW and I made for the door. "Good luck with that there furniture." Earlene's eyes twinkled. "Big Joey seems to think that you and Walker need to be keeping the name Joseph Jefferson in mind."

"Why?"

"I think that's something you should be asking Walker when this is all over."

I had no idea what was with Joseph Jefferson, I didn't even know the guy, but obviously Big Joey thought I did. I thanked Earlene for the ride, BW added a bark, and then we got off Old Gray and cut across the square. We dodged a group of tourists gathered at the base of the big James Edward Oglethorpe statue, our illustrious leader and founder of the great city of Savannah. The fact that there was an Oglethorpe Square a few blocks down and that James Edward was not standing tall and pompous in that particular square named after him was just one of those little mysteries of Savannah.

We crossed Hull Street to Conway Adkins's house, the yellow tape across the front doorway proclaiming this a crime scene. "Breaking and entering in broad daylight with tourists looking on isn't a great idea," I explained to BW as we headed for the rear entrance. Except the rear entrance

wasn't nearly as secluded as I'd hoped. Conway's fine Colonial Revival had a garden to the back with hidden nooks
and crannies and no alley to sneak around in. The back door,
which was also crisscrossed with yellow tape, stood out like
a neon sign.

"Now what should we do?" I asked BW, as if expecting
him to answer. I stared at the door for a minute till a *pssst*
came from a pink azalea bush across the yard. A hand
reached up through the flowers, two fingers pinching a key.
Well dang, this was so much better than the last time Mercedes and I did a B&E, when we had nearly got eaten alive
by the guard dog.

I gave the place a quick once-over to see if anyone was
watching. Hugging the bushes, BW and I made our way
toward the house, cutting behind a stand of magnolias and
then on to the back door. Mercedes pulled up beside us.
"You're late," she said.

"I had to sweet-talk the bus driver to get here or we would
have been really late. How'd you come up with a key?"

"I cleaned house for Conway for three years. He gave me
a key. I'm a very trustworthy person." She studied the crime
scene tape in front of us. "Well, usually I'm a trustworthy
person." She shoved the key in the lock, gave it a turn, and
the door opened.

"Piece of cak—" Mercedes started to say, till a big hand
landed on her left shoulder and another one on my right shoulder, followed by, "What do you two think you're doing?"

Chapter Fourteen

MERCEDES, BW, and I turned around to face a man, a really super hunky Italian man in jeans and a white shirt rolled up to the elbows, with a superb tan and raven-black hair. I felt a little dizzy just looking at him. "Raimondo Baldassaro?"

"Reagan Summerside and dog. The dog I can handle," Raimondo said, giving BW a good pat-down. "The Summerside part I hoped I'd never run into again. You accused me of murder, broke into my house, went through my mail, and hid in my tanning bed."

Raimondo was the gardener everybody wanted. Not only did he possess his own brand of patented rosebushes that were to die for, but having the Italian stallion digging around in your petunia patch was worth any price the man wanted to charge.

"We're here on a mission of mercy," Mercedes chimed in. "It just so happens that we're trying to find out who went and did in Conway. I was his housekeeper and we're looking for something to get Walker Boone off the hook for murdering the guy. He didn't do it, that much we know for sure, but someone's setting him up for the fall."

"You're right about Walker," Raimondo said. "He gave me some really good advice on getting a patent for my roses, and he's helped some other friends of mine. I seriously doubt if he plugged Conway, but there's a list of people who would." Raimondo let out a long sigh and rubbed his neck. He cut his eyes my way. "The fact that Walker's innocence is resting in your hands should scare the heck out of the guy."

"That list you mentioned, do you happen to know any of the names on it?"

"For starters, Conway's son is a mooch. I've done the gardens here for a while now and heard father and son arguing more than once, and it was usually about money. The daughter-in-law tried to make peace between them, but it was a lost cause. I felt sorry for her; she was caught in the middle of a battle royale on more than one occasion. This guy with a bow tie and thinning hair showed up a few times and there was more yelling. Conway actually tossed him out of the house. Two hot-looking babes came around and were crabbing at Conway about their husbands, and Conway told them to get lost. That man was no saint, but he didn't deserve to get plugged in his own tub."

Raimondo headed for the rose garden in the back and Mercedes and I slipped inside Conway's house, our footsteps being the only sound. "The place feels different somehow,"

Mercedes said in a hushed voice. "It's like when the person dies, so does the house till someone fills it full of life again."

"Raimondo said someone with a bow tie was here, and my first guess is Mason Dixon from over at the Plantation Club. And I'm willing to bet the two hot babes were Anna and Bella."

"Talking about hot babes, old Raimondo sure fits the bill. Did you really accuse him of murder?"

"It seemed like the right idea at the time." We entered what was obviously Conway's office, with a blue Oriental rug across the polished hardwood floors. A mahogany desk sat in the middle of the room, with a yellow-and-blue lamp parked on the corner that sort of reminded me of the lamp in Boone's office. My guess was that maybe on some level Boone knew or at least suspected that Conway was his dad. Bookcases lined three walls, a fireplace graced the fourth, with a gilded mirror above.

The three of us made a beeline for the desk; Mercedes pulled open the bottom drawer, I took the top one, and BW stretched out on the carpet and went to sleep. Mercedes hauled out a ledger. "Conway was old school, he wrote checks." She flipped some pages. "Checks for the utilities, water, phone, me, American Express." She flipped a few more pages. "Wow, I bet he chalked up some serious Sky-Miles on that credit card of his."

I dropped three photos beside the ledger. "This is Conway, mamma, and baby Boone."

"How do you know?" Mercedes gasped, picking up one of the photos to get a closer look.

"These are just like the ones I found over at Boone's

house and in Mason Dixon's office. Dixon could have stolen the pictures when he came here to see Conway, or maybe he lifted them right out of Conway's office at the Plantation Club. Dixon blackmailed Conway, knowing that if Conway's wife found out about Walker she'd divorce Conway without a dime. After she died, Conway obviously didn't care who found out."

"And this Dixon guy then lost his meal ticket? I see where he might be ticked off enough to kill Conway, especially if Conway threatened to expose him as a big fat blackmailer, but why frame Walker for the deed?"

Mercedes flipped through the checkbook. "Here's a check to Tucker but it's over a year ago, nothing more recent. That explains the fights Raimondo overheard."

"Why hit up his dad? Tucker has money, lots of it."

"Wanna bet?" Mercedes put the ledger back in the drawer. "I'd say Tucker's up against it and Daddy wouldn't bail him out. Why else would Conway be writing checks to Tucker, then suddenly quit?"

I shuffled through more papers. "Here's Conway's will. It's his old will where he actually crossed out Tucker's name and wrote in Walker's name to inherit the Old Harbor Inn. The free clinic got his monetary assets and the proceeds from the sale of this house."

"Okay," Mercedes said as I dropped the pictures and will back in the drawer. "So Tucker knew Walker was his brother, that he was inheriting some mighty fine real estate, and that he got nothing. That had to rattle Tucker's cage big-time, especially in light of his financial situation. That makes

Tucker furious at Conway *and* Walker. I'd say Tucker's our prime—"

Mercedes didn't finish her sentence. Instead she pointed to the kitchen and the sound of the door opening and footsteps. It was Deckard. I could feel his presence seeping into my bones. I grabbed a fancy pen set off Conway's desk, crept to the doorway, and threw it down the hall, where it bounced off the front door with a loud thud, the sound echoing like a gunshot though the quiet house.

Deckard ran past the office doorway, his footsteps thundering down the hall. Mercedes, BW, and I hurried into the kitchen and out the back door. We dropped down behind the azaleas, with Raimondo watching from his rose garden. Deckard came to the door and signaled to Raimondo. "Hey you, see anyone come out here?"

"Nothing but me and the neighbor's dog." Raimondo clapped his hands and I unleashed BW, letting him take off to help convince Deckard all was well.

"Sec," Raimondo called back to Deckard, with BW drawing up beside him. "Nothing but a dog."

Deckard slammed the door shut, rattling the panes of glass, and headed for the street. Mercedes and I waited a beat, then joined Raimondo and BW in the rose garden.

"Thanks," I said to Raimondo. "You saved us. Uh, *why* did you save us?"

"Deckard gave me a ticket for double-parking my truck the other day when I was dropping off some plants. I wasn't parking for all afternoon, mind you, just to make a delivery. How'd he know you two were in the house?"

I slapped my palm to my forehead. "I told the gals at the Fox where I was going. Deckard thinks Walker killed Conway and that by following me around he'll find him. And it doesn't look like he's giving up."

"I got to get going," Mercedes said to me as we headed off. "Yvonne Ledbetter is probably in the pastoral room right now with her family gathered around." She took my hand. "Watch out for Deckard. My guess is if he can bring in Conway's killer it's a real feather in his cap, and the man won't care two figs if you happen to be in the way."

Mercedes headed for the Slumber and I headed for the Car Spa, located in a back alley off Jefferson Street. I needed to see the damage and check out payments with Jimmy. Business was good at the Fox, or at least it was good until today. I could pay for the car repairs, though it would eat my reserve for the rest of the slow summer months ahead.

Well, that was just too bad for me. I was the one who fell asleep. I could have killed KiKi, and all I had to do was fork over money to make this all right; it was a small price to pay. Besides, I was done with cars, so I didn't have to sock money away to buy one of my own. And I had my new pink scooter . . . somewhere.

I turned onto Lincoln past Gifts To Go, Flowers by Wanda, and a new shop that had "Anna and Bella's Boutique" scripted in cream and gold across the display window. Anna and Bella were opening a boutique? With curtains over the windows, I couldn't see inside, but the sisters had excellent taste, so I knew the shop would be nice and I'd eventually get their clothes in my shop.

I turned down an alley, where the Car Spa was on the

right. It was a blue clapboard building with the office in the front, the working area to the back, and minimal parking to the side. "Is Jimmy available?" I asked the woman standing behind the counter. "I'm here about the red Chevy you fished out of the swamp."

"I'm Jimmy." She twitched her hips and batted her eyes. "I got my mamma's red hair and my daddy's deep voice and Grandma's skinny behind, so I look good in these here jeans. And you're Reagan Summerside. Honey, I gotta say, you're lucky to be alive, girl. Do you know how many gators we had to fight off to get that car out of the drink?"

"How's the Chevy? Can you save it?" I heaved a sigh. "You see, what happened is that I fell asleep behind the wheel and drove the car right off the road and landed in the swamp and it's all my fault and I nearly murdered my own auntie and if Boone kills me he has every right." I bit my lip to keep from crying.

Jimmy came around the counter. "Look, you're alive, so quit being so hard on yourself. We can put this here car back together good as new, and you need to know that you didn't just fall asleep. It doesn't work like that. When you fall asleep, you relax and your foot slides off the accelerator. You flop over into a ditch somewhere or just run off the road. Best I can tell, you were going at a good clip to get that car propelled so far out in the swamp like it was. You didn't fall asleep all by yourself; you had some help in that particular direction. What were you drinking?"

"Cherry snow cone."

"And?"

"Taffy." I stared at Jimmy. "I don't get it, you lost me."

"Girl, you were drugged sure as I'm standing here. Somebody gave you something to send you off into la-la land a lot faster than just slowly dozing off like normal. Your body crashed and then your car crashed. Make any enemies lately?"

"Oh, boy."

Jimmy took my hand. "Like I said, you're lucky to be alive."

BW and I left Jimmy with a check, then caught a bus back to the Fox; BW got his very own seat on the bus thanks to a Zunzi's Conquistador extra-sauce sandwich bribe.

"Well, did you get Conway's furniture measured?" Elsie Abbott asked as BW and I came into the shop. "I sure hope you had some success because we didn't do much here today, I can tell you that." Elsie waved her hand in the air. "I can't imagine what's going on to keep people from shopping the Fox. It's like there's a new thing coming along that we don't know about."

"Did a policeman come in looking for me?" I unleashed BW, and he headed for AnnieFritz to beg a scone.

AnnieFritz broke off a chunk of pastry for the resident mooch. "He was as nice as can be. We told him where you were off to. Did he catch up with you?"

"Almost."

By six, business still sucked and I'd changed into a sundress and cute flip-flops. I even managed to put on makeup and eyeliner and curl my hair, which made me look more Shirley Temple than Beyoncé.

"I do declare," Auntie KiKi said to me as I parked myself in the passenger side of the Beemer. "If you aren't pretty

as a Georgia peach, a curly Georgia peach but a peach all
the same."

THE SUN HOVERED WHERE OCEAN MET SKY AS KIKI
parked the Beemer. "Well, we're in the overflow lot, so that's
got to be a good sign," she said as we headed for the theater
surrounded by big white tents of food and drink. The round
tables were filled to capacity, with theater patrons milling
about and torchlight casting a soft romantic glow over the
lawn. Harper Norton was at the piano on the large makeshift
stage, and strains of "Sweet Georgia Brown" wafted over the
crowd.

"Sure wish Walker could see how well the event turned
out," I said as we paid for our tickets. "He donated a lot of
time and probably money to make this a success."

"Never figured Boone for a theater buff," KiKi said as
we headed for our latecomers' table in back.

"Boone has a house out here. I think it was more of a
keep-the-developers-off-the-island situation than 'I can't
wait to see *Oklahoma* for the tenth time.' We need to keep
an eye out for Russell. You know he's out here somewhere.
This event being a success is the last thing he wants."

"That means we need to fit in, and that means we need
to wander around with a plate of food and a glass of wine.
Sweet Lord in heaven, I can smell fried chicken and okra
and biscuits. Let's get a move on before it's all gone."

I followed KiKi to the main tent, where the buffet table
was piled high with Southern cuisine. "Look there," I stage-
whispered to KiKi, and nodded to the head of the line. "It's

Anna and Bella, and they're alone once again. Where do you suppose Clive and Crenshaw are?"

"Honey, can you give this sleuthing thing a rest for just a bit? Look at all this here food. Putter never lets me eat like this. I intend to enjoy the moment and forget cholesterol even exists." KiKi loaded her plate with fried chicken, fried okra, three biscuits, and green beans seasoned with ham hocks and salt pork.

"I'm plumb out of hands," KiKi said, a euphoric glint in her eyes, a hint of awe in her voice. "It's going to take both of mine to hold this here plate and get it back to the table without spilling. How about you get the wine since you've only got one puny drumstick and a little dab of okra."

KiKi wobbled off under the weight of all things unhealthy, and I headed for the wine tent with Anna and Bella just ahead of me in line. Getting the evil eye, I elbowed my way past two old ladies and drew up behind Anna and Bella. There was something going on with Clive and Crenshaw not being around, and the whole thing was even stickier in that the gold-digger sisters had it in for Conway and Boone. Men who came in contact with the sisters did not live a long carefree existence. Conway advised Clive and Crenshaw to redo their wills, Boone agreed, and the husbands were nowhere to be found. Four men involved; four men gone.

"We did it," Anna said to Bella, keeping her voice low. "We pulled it off. No more sneaking around."

I advanced with the line and tried to stay close. "We're all set," Bella said. "And if we do this right, nothing can stop us now and . . ."

Dang, I lost the rest of the conversation. I inched closer and dropped my napkin on purpose. I bent to get it and heard, "Who needs husbands around to keep them, we can do this on our own now that we got the money and . . ." I lost the rest of what Anna said. I scooted close, then closer still, till Anna spun around and hit my plate of food, sending chicken and greasy okra down the front of my dress.

Our eyes locked and Anna said, "Were you spying on us?"

"Hey, you're the one who just knocked food all over me."

"Why were you so close to us?"

"It's crowded."

"There's no one behind you." Bella glared, her voice low and menacing to not attract attention. It was okay to be nasty and downright rude at a Southern event if you just did it quietly and with a pleasant smile so as not to make a scene. The one exception to the scene rule was catching your spouse in the arms or bed of another. Then scenes were encouraged and applauded.

"So you're here with your husbands tonight?" I asked with my own smile in place, my voice equally low.

Anna's eyes turned to bits of ice. "You should be enjoying the night, because tomorrow things aren't going to be very nice for you at all, Reagan Summerside. It's time for you to go, and Anna and I are just the ones to make it happen. Seems like people who get in our way don't fare so well." She cocked her perfect brow at my destroyed dress. "If you know what I mean . . . honey."

Anna and Bella got their wine and headed for one of the front-row tables. I kicked my upended plate under the wine table, knocked off the okra clinging to my dress, and got a

glass of pinot-something for KiKi and one for me. I headed
for our table in the back, trying to ignore stares of *your dress
is a mess.* I spotted a few of my good customers and they
looked the other direction, acting like they didn't know me.
It could be because of my appearance, but it felt like something more, something personal.

A standup comedian took the stage as I parked down next
to KiKi. "Mason Dixon's here," she said around a mouthful,
her eyes fixed on her food. "He tried for the slice of key lime
pie I had my eye on, and I stabbed his hand with a fork."

"You didn't."

KiKi cackled.

"Lord have mercy, you did."

"I think I need another biscuit and the line's kind of long,
and I still have chicken sitting here waiting for me to enjoy
and it would be a sin to let it get cold." She gave me the *I
am your dear auntie who you dragged all the way out here*
look. That I hadn't eaten one bite didn't bother dear Auntie
KiKi at all. Then again, I knew I didn't stand a chance
against fried chicken and okra.

"Right, I'll get you a biscuit." I hitched Old Yeller up
onto my shoulder.

"And some mac and cheese would be mighty nice too,
now that I think about it."

"You're going to explode."

A little smile tipped the corner of KiKi's full mouth. "But
until then I'm going to be enjoying myself, and don't you go
wandering off. Our tour of the theater is at eight and Steffy
Lou is doing *The Music Man* on the old stage lit up with oil
lamps like from back in the day, all very nostalgic. I hear

she's dressed up like Marian the Librarian. Broadway comes to Tybee."

I got into the mac-and-cheese line and spotted Mason Dixon heading off toward the back of the theater. All the activities for the evening were in the front of the theater, and there was nothing in the rear except open field and crumbling docks down by the water. Moonlight silhouetted the Tybee Lighthouse, tall and graceful and sending its powerful beacon far out to sea. I gave Dixon a head start, then followed, the music and event chatter fading behind me, replaced by night sounds of crickets and other many-legged things I didn't get along with jumping around in the tall grass. I could see Dixon up ahead, then lost him in the shadows of the trees down by the water.

Either he was headed for the old docks to relieve himself because the bathrooms were too crowded, or he was meeting someone. I broke into a run to get to the trees before Dixon knew I was following. Moonlight dappled through the leaves and branches, and I kept to the edge of the shadows to find my way. I spotted Dixon by the rotting docks, and well looky there, Grayden Russell was right next to him. Those two were in cahoots, and it involved the theater and my guess was it involved the Old Harbor Inn, too. I knew it! They were up to no good. A branch snapped behind me and I spun around, catching a glint of moonlight reflecting off metal. A gun? A gun! Holy cow! I ran, not knowing where I was going but needing to get away. Ground gave way to wood, rotting wood that collapsed under me, sending me down into the black water.

Chapter Fifteen

I SWORE that if I got out of this in one piece I was moving to the desert. I popped back to the surface, but it took a few seconds; the water was deeper than I thought. Part of a dock was suspended over my head, there were three men on shore, and only God in heaven knew where the gators were hiding out. I doggie-paddled between rotting planks, but there were no cattails to hide in; the water wasn't shallow enough. I was between the devil and the deep blue sea . . . literally. I froze in place not only so the men above wouldn't see me but to keep from attracting the gators if this was indeed a freshwater inlet. Being still was good; arms and legs flailing about was *come and get it, it's dinnertime*.

"Where is she?" Russell yelled. "All the docks are busted, where did she go through?"

"There she is," Dixon said.

"That's a log, stupid. We got to find her, and you, put that blasted gun away. One shot and everybody and their grandmother's heading out here wondering what's going on."

"She's in the water somewhere," Dixon said, as the beam of a flashlight darted back and forth over the surface. "I bet there're some big gators out there. I bet they got her by now and are stashing her under a log to eat on later. Gators like their meat nice and tender."

"There're no gators, it's too deep; that's the whole point of being here, and anything you're willing to bet on is a sure loser," Russell added in his oh-so-charming way.

"You know," Dixon said, "I'm tired of your crap."

"Yeah, well you're into me for a ton, so you'll take what I dish out and like it."

"We got to go," someone else said, but I didn't recognize the voice or maybe I just couldn't tell because I was so freaking scared. "If you want to pull off this great plan of yours, we got to get a move on now."

A cone of light bounced over the water again. "I bet she drowned. Maybe the snakes got her."

Snakes! My eyes shot wide open. If I wasn't running from gators, I was running from snakes! I heard some rustling, then retreating footsteps, and the sounds of night and marsh took over, my heart still pounding in my ears. I peeked over the edge of the bank as something slithered around my legs. My heart stopped, I couldn't breathe, and terror shot up my spine.

The bank was steep, really steep, and I was out of the blasted water in two seconds flat. I ran for all I was worth in bare feet as my soaking dress slapped against my legs. I didn't think snakes were fast, but I wasn't taking any chances. Nature hated me, that was it. If there was something gross lurking in bushes or water, I was in the middle of it and they were licking their chops.

I tore across the yard and headed for the merrymakers till I tripped and fell, landing flat on my face with a solid *whoomph*. I figured I'd put enough distance between me and snakeland, and I lay there for a second catching my breath and thanking the dear Lord above for once again getting me out of a mess. The fact that a cricket jumped on my hand and something was crawling in my hair didn't even faze me.

Someone screamed off in the distance, and it seemed to come from the direction of the theater. Sweet Lord, now what? More screaming filled the air, and I bolted up to see lights on the theater. The lights were moving, dancing up into the sky. Fire! This was the big plan? Burn the theater to the ground? But why burn it if you wanted to buy it?

I ran toward the flames, feeling somewhat relieved knowing KiKi was devouring more heart-attack-on-a-plate and nowhere near danger. People were running and yelling as thick black smoke billowing upward. A wailing fire truck, then another, pulled up to the theater and then around to the back, their strobing red lights reflecting off the flames and the building. Firemen yanked fat hoses from the pumper truck and headed to the back, where the flames seemed to be. I headed for our out-of-the-way latecomers' table and stopped dead. No KiKi. Her chair was empty; the piece of key lime pie she'd fought for was sitting right there on the table.

The eight o'clock tour! The one time I wanted KiKi to

choose food over all, she didn't. I looked back at the angry flames and thick clouds of black smoke and took off for the theater door.

"You can't go in there," a fireman said, snagging me around the waist as I tore past him.

"My auntie—"

"We'll find her." He gave me a hard look. "Stay. Got it?"

"Look, I almost killed her yesterday by running the car off the road, and I can't let that happen two days in a row."

He studied my dress and hair. "What happened to you?"

"I fell in the water 'cause bad guys were chasing me and there were snakes and—"

"And here I thought I was married to the craziest woman in Savannah."

I darted past the fireman and ran through the door into the theater. It was smoky, but there was no fire and there was no KiKi. I turned around and was suddenly tossed over the fireman's shoulder, hauled back outside, and dumped none too gently onto the grass. "Move from that spot and your butt's in jail."

"What's going on?" Auntie KiKi asked, coming up beside me sitting on the ground. She had a drumstick in her hand and two more on a plate. People were still running around, but the scene wasn't as frantic as it had been two minutes ago.

"Where in the name of all that's holy have you been?" I screeched. I jabbed my finger back at our table. "You had pie. Why aren't you with your pie? You fought for it, remember?"

"I wanted more chicken before it was all gone." KiKi sat down beside me. "What happened to you? You're a mess."

"Bad guys, snakes, guns, the usual." KiKi didn't skip a bite, underlining the fact that general chaos of some variety truly was the usual, at least lately. "How in the heck did we get to this point?" I sighed.

KiKi took another bite and said around a mouthful, "We drove, honey. Then we walked a little ways."

"I mean . . ." I puffed out a weary breath. "Never mind. I'm really glad you're okay. Poor Steffy Lou."

"You don't have any shoes."

"They didn't really match the dress that well."

"How'd you get all wet? Helping the firemen? That's mighty nice of you, dear." KiKi took a drumstick off her plate and handed it to me. "It wasn't much of a fire, you know. A bunch of boxes and pallets behind the theater, is all. Lots of smoke and drama is about it. Steffy Lou thinks those rotten developers set the blaze, trying to scare everyone away so they could get the theater for cheap. Let me tell you, all this commotion is having the exact opposite effect of running scared. Folks are mad as hornets and so ticked off that the theater has more supporters now than ever. Just wait till news of this hits the papers in the morning."

A smoky haze hung over the theater as the firemen packed up their trucks. Most of the rescue work to put out the fire was around back, so the grass in front of the theater wasn't too soupy from the fire hoses. Even the tents looked unscathed. Steffy Lou got up on stage and commandeered the microphone. "I want to thank you all kindly for helping out during this frightful time, and we owe a debt of gratitude to the wonderful and brave Tybee Island firefighters who saved our beloved theater."

Everyone applauded and Steffy Lou added, "Now you all know there is an abundance of food and wine that needs your attention, so there's no need to be heading home just yet. We have a lot to be thankful for tonight."

Steffy Lou then cleared her throat and launched into "The Sun'll Come Out Tomorrow." Harper accompanied her on the piano and everyone joined in. Even KiKi took a chicken break to add her voice to the chorus. It wasn't exactly the *1812 Overture*, but it wasn't half bad.

It was after midnight when, moaning and groaning, in desperate need of Alka-Seltzer due to chicken gluttony, KiKi pulled the Beemer into the driveway. I headed for home sweet home, my bare feet sinking into the cool spring grass. I took my front steps, careful not to get a splinter and thinking how nice it was to be concerned about a splinter and not snakes and guns. I turned the doorknob and stopped. There was a note taped to the door. *Forget what you saw or next time the snakes win.*

It was all too much. Everything got black, little dots danced in front of my eyes, my legs went to jelly, and I waited to faint like any decent Southern woman worth her lace hankie should. Nothing happened. I just stood there staring at the note like one of those stoic Yankee women who run corporations and have stock options. I ran a little old consignment shop and the only option I had was what to put in the display window. I had a right to faint.

Instead I opened the door to let BW out, then plopped down on the top step. My dress was ruined, I'd lost my shoes, some guy with a gun had chased me into the water, and I didn't even meet up with a hunky fireman who wanted my phone number. Nothing was going right. And I was darn tired of getting pushed around.

I yanked down the note, crumpled it up, and tossed it into the bushes. Dixon and Russell and the guy with the gun were not getting to me!

BW and I went inside the house, *our* house. I locked the doors, stomped my way upstairs with new determination to overcome all, and turned on my bedroom light to find a knife stuck through my flip-flops and into my pillow. I blinked once and dropped to the floor like a rock.

"REAGAN? WAKE UP. REAGAN?"

There was something cold on my face and someone was licking my bare feet.

"Come on, blondie, get up. Rise and shine."

I opened my eyes and looked into darkness. Maybe I'd died? Except there was a streetlight streaming in through a window and my guess was the Pearly Gates had better facilities than fluorescent tubing. "I don't want to get up. Stick me with a fork and call me done."

"We don't have time for done." An arm slid around my back and I sat up. "Drink this, all one gulp."

A glass was shoved into my hand and raised to my lips and I drank, gagged, spluttered, and coughed as the liquid burned a path to my toes. "Boone?"

He sat down beside me on the floor. "Are you okay?"

"There's a knife in my pillow."

He put his arm around me and held me tight. He smelled tired and worn, but it was the safest I'd felt in days. His scruff was morphing into a beard, his eyes weary. "You have hair."

"I've always had hair."

"Quarter-inch buzz is not hair."

"I'm sorry," he said in a quiet voice. "I'm sorry about all this. You wouldn't be getting knives in your pillow if it weren't for me."

"You mean if it weren't for Conway, and that started when you were a baby so I think you're off the hook."

Boone took my glass and replaced it with a sandwich. "Meat loaf? Parkers? How'd you do that?"

"Lucky for me Parkers delivers to felons. Eat up. So, what's with the midnight message?"

If I told Boone everything that was going on, he'd lock me in a closet for sure. I had to pick and choose what to say and what not to say, and sinking the Chevy was definitely off the table. I took a bite of sandwich. "This Grayden Russell guy is after the Tybee Theater, and Mason Dixon is tied in with him. They started a fire out at the theater tonight during the fund-raiser to scare off the supporters, but all it did was get everyone more on board. Russell and Dixon know I'm onto them and this is a warning to butt out."

"And Russell's after the Old Harbor Inn. Why those two places and just those two places?"

"Nice real estate?"

"There's lots of nice real estate in Savannah. Why not just buy another hotel here in town or another place on Tybee or maybe out at Whitemarsh?"

"Well, let's see, the inn and the theater are good locations, easy to get to and close to shopping, restaurants, and action. They're both on water. The Savannah River's a deepwater port and the water by the theater is a deep inlet, deeper than you'd think. Both are places where people can dock their boats when they come in off the ocean? Russell wants a place for fishing boats and taking people out for deep-sea fishing? Fishing's big around here."

"Big Joey made some calls. Russell's a money man and tied to some serious cash back in Charleston. There's no money in fishing trips or docking boats, and what's in this for Dixon? He's a stuffy little old man who likes hobnobbing and feeling important."

"Dixon's a gambler and in debt to Russell; I overheard them talking." Not a complete lie. "So the one thing that ties Dixon to Russell is gambling." I stopped my sandwich in midair. "They said something about how bigger games and bigger money was coming their way. That gives us boat docks, hotels, and gambling?"

Boone and I exchanged looks and we said together, "Gambling boats!" Boone added, "Savannah is one of the few Southern ports that doesn't have one. Go beyond the three-mile limit and out into international waters and people gamble. Russell needs docks to pick people up, and he needs hotels to draw people in and a nice place to stay. There's big money in this, really big money."

"And Conway wouldn't sell the inn because he left it to you in his will. Least he held true to that. But how does any of this figure into killing Conway and framing you for it?" I looked up at the clock on my dresser. "I hate for you to eat and run, but Deckard's all over me trying to find you. He could break in here any minute, and he doesn't seem the sort of cop to give a flying fig about search warrants."

"I'm going to grab a fast shower."

I took a bite of sandwich. "You could get caught in your birthday suit."

That brought a devil smile. "You wish."

I did wish, but saying so would lead to someplace we didn't have time for. "If Deckard storms the citadel, I'll keep him busy."

Boone kissed me on the forehead and levered himself off the floor. He grabbed a towel from my hall closet as if he lived here, then headed for the bathroom.

"Boone?"

"What?"

"I drove your Chevy into the swamp."

"I know."

I listened to the water running as BW and I ate my sandwich. Least the bathroom was decent; I redid it myself four years ago when Hollis and I first moved into Cherry House. I took it from broken tiles and rust to cream and willow green with a totally cute claw-foot tub. I could wash Boone's clothes for him, but that would take about an hour and a half and Boone didn't have that long. Deckard was too close, too often, and—

"Let me guess," Deckard's voice said from behind me, as every hair on my body stood straight up. "Parkers meat loaf sandwich."

"With extra provolone," I added in a steady voice that surprised the heck out of me, since my heart was in my throat and I had no idea how to get Deckard away from the bathroom door. I swiped my hand across my mouth, my brain spinning. I turned to face Deckard as he ripped open the bathroom door to . . . nothing? "Where is he?"

"Who?"

In two steps Deckard was beside me, yanking me to my feet as my sandwich flew out of my hand. He jabbed his hot, ugly face to mine, his onion breath making me gag. "Boone, that's who. What did you do with him?"

I didn't say a word, and Deckard dropped me back on the floor like a rag doll. A voice came from below my bedroom window. "He's not down here, Sarge."

"I'm going to find him," Deckard hissed, his big grossness looming over me. "And I'm going to shoot him dead. You tell him that when you see him again."

Then he kicked BW, making him yelp, and stomped out into the hallway and down the steps. I raced over to BW and held him in my lap. I heard a car drive off and figured it was the police cruiser. I didn't have a phone to call the vet. I didn't have a car. I didn't have a grenade to blow up Deckard.

"My poor baby." BW licked my face, then went over to my sandwich and finished it off. Maybe BW was okay, but nothing else was, and where the heck was Boone? Where did he go, and how in the world did he get out of that bathroom? Houdini lives. There was a window in the bathroom and a downspout, so that had to be it, except the downspout looked like it would collapse if a grasshopper landed on it.

I hoisted BW up onto my bed and put my pillow under his big head. "You just rest."

BW jumped off the bed and went back into the hallway

and lay there. I did what any good doggie mommy would do. I got my blanket and pillow off my bed and curled up beside my pup to make sure he was okay. I kissed his snout, he licked my face, I pulled up our blanket, and we went to sleep.

"You really think BW is okay?" I asked Auntie KiKi the next morning as we stood in her kitchen watching the coffeepot do its thing.

"He's eaten two bowls of Cheerios, a biscuit, and two hot dogs, and Putter checked him over teeth to tail. I think he's good to go. What happened to get you to worrying like this?"

"A shoe got in his way. Can you just watch him for me for an hour to make sure?"

"Where are you off to at eight in the morning that we can't go with you?"

"I need to see a man about my flip-flops."

"Well I'll be, someone found them?"

"Yeah, that's exactly what happened. Someone found them."

I turned to leave, and KiKi grabbed my hand. "I know you're not telling me everything. Be careful, honey."

I gave KiKi a kiss on the cheek and headed for the bus stop till AnnieFritz pulled up to the curb in her old white Caddy, with pink plastic tulips taped to the antenna and "WWJD" on the bumper. "Hi there, sugar. Now where you headed to this fine morning?"

"Orleans Square?"

DEMISE IN DENIM

"Well, climb on in. Sister and I are headed over to Sleepy Pines, but we don't mind making a little detour. We need to be acquainting ourselves with the establishment so we can talk it up and get them some business."

I opened the back door and got in. "Did you have any late-night visitors?" I asked as we headed up Whittaker.

"Now that you mention it," AnnieFritz said. "That there nice Officer Deckard came calling. Said he was looking for a fugitive in the neighborhood. Can you imagine such a thing, right here in the Victorian district, of all places? Mercy me, what's this world coming to?"

"What did you tell him? Did you see anyone walking around, hiding in your bushes?"

The sisters exchanged looks and Elsie said, "Quiet as a graveyard. Why? Did you hear something going on?"

"Me? Nope, nothing at all, just like you said, quiet as a graveyard." I thanked Elsie and AnnieFritz for the lift, then crossed the street to the Plantation Club. Dixon and Russell were bringing in a gambling boat and wanted the Old Harbor Inn and the theater to make it happen. Somehow this played into killing Conway and framing Boone, but I had no idea how. If I pushed them they might let something slip. And there was the fact that the knife-through-the-shoe thing totally pissed me off.

I headed for the front door of the club, then changed direction, figuring the back door where I'd run into Dixon was a better bet. I wouldn't have to try to get past the guard dog at the front desk, and I'd look like another employee going to work. One of the maids came out, hauling trash to the Dumpster, and I caught the door before it closed and slipped inside. Dixon might be in his office, but it was breakfast time, and that translated into free food for Mr. VP. I headed for the restaurant and there was Dixon, eating bacon and eggs and sipping coffee.

I plopped into a chair at his table and slapped the knife on the white tablecloth. "Hi there, sweet pea."

Chapter Sixteen

"WE need to talk," I said to Dixon as he grabbed the knife off the table.

"What do you think you're doing?" he hissed under his breath.

"The firefighters from last night send their regards."

Dixon cut his eyes back and forth and lowered his voice. "I didn't set that fire," he said, his thin lips barely moving. "Neither did Russell. We were going to do it and someone beat us to it; it's the truth. Think about it. There wasn't enough time from when we left you to get a blaze like that going that fast. Somebody else wanted that that place to burn besides us."

"You left me in the water."

"Quit your complaining; you made it out, that's more than I can do."

"Meaning?"

Dixon heaved a weary sigh, his shoulders sagging. "Russell's got me by the short hairs. I'm supposed to help him get some property because I know the people here and how to play them."

"Gambling debts? As long as you could blackmail Conway, you were ahead of the game. Then when he quit paying you off, you knocked him off. Plus everyone knows you've had your eye on being president around here. What was Conway going to do, blab that you were blackmailing him all this time? You'd never get to be president if that got out, would you? Pretty good motive for getting rid of someone, if you ask me."

One of the waitresses started to come over to fill Dixon's coffee cup, and he waved her away. "Look, I might be under Russell's thumb and have to play his game, but I didn't do anything to Conway. We didn't get along, but I didn't kill him; I'm not a murderer."

"Somebody beat you to that, too? You got a lot of people doing your dirty work. So you're paying off Russell by helping him set up the hotels and gambling boats?"

Dixon's eyes shot wide open. Bingo! Boone and I were right on with that one. I got up and started to walk away, then turned back. "Have you seen Clive and Crenshaw lately here at the club? Two older men, friends, they're married to Anna and Bella the—

"Sisters. C and C, as we call them here, always came in for lunch, but I haven't seen them in days, maybe a week now. Their wives come in for lunch now, but not C and C."

I headed down the hall and out of the building. The

Clive-and-Crenshaw disappearing act was strange and getting stranger, but right now Russell and Dixon had my full attention. I knew as soon as I left, Dixon would call Russell. He'd tell him I knew about the gambling boats, and Russell would make himself scarce or send one of his goons to shut me up.

The thing was, I just happened to have my very own bodyguard, and my guess was that after last night that particular bodyguard would be extra attentive. Deckard was a lot of things . . . big, ugly, mean, corrupt, and a jerk of the first order . . . but he wasn't stupid. He knew Boone was in that bathroom, though where he'd disappeared to I have no idea. As much as I hated being on Deckard's radar and that he might connect with Boone again, Deckard offered me a certain amount of protection. Keeping me alive was his best hope of finding Boone, or at least I hoped that was Deckard's plan because I intended to use Deckard just like he was using me.

Since Russell knew I was headed his way, I started for home. Russell would stonewall me, make excuses, and lie, and the conversation would go nowhere. I could take the bus back to the Victorian district, but spring in Savannah was for walking as much as it was for convertibles. The colors, the smells, the perfect temperature, the food . . . always the food . . . made Savannah a little piece of paradise.

Forsyth Fountain played in the morning sunlight, and there wasn't a cloud in the sky. Why would anyone live someplace else? I turned onto Gwinnett and spotted Mamma's black Caddy parked at the curb, and Mamma and a mannequin sitting on the front porch.

"You're dating?"

I got the *give me strength* Mamma eye roll. "This is Gwendolyn. She was a part of the crime lab for ten years and even made appearances in court from time to time to illustrate evidence and crime scenes. Poor thing got kicked to the curb for Sebastian, a newer model with a computer chip that determines the exact direction of the shooter, but Gwen's not the main reason I'm here."

Mamma whipped Conway's will out of her purse. "There's something you need to see."

"BW's over at KiKi's and I should go get him before she feeds him all the pound cake and he has intestinal distress for a week."

"Well, she better have saved some of that cake for me."

Mamma and I trooped across the grass to KiKi's, the land of good coffee and cake and probably fruit to keep Uncle Putter happy.

"I brought company," I sang out to KiKi as Mamma and I came in the back door, with BW doing his wagging-tail howdy routine.

KiKi looked at Mamma and made the sign of the cross. "Sweet Jesus, somebody died? Why else would you be here at this hour?"

Mamma set Conway's will in the middle of the round oak table that had been in the Vanderpool family since cotton was king. "I was reading this over and there's an interesting wrinkle."

"Interesting good or interesting bad?" KiKi wanted to know as she set the table. I got the coffee, cream, and sugar, and Mamma headed for the pie safe taking out the delish pound cake inside. The Summerside girls were a study in perfection when it came to arranging food.

We sat down and spread our napkins, and KiKi cut the cake. "We all know that Conway left the Old Harbor Inn to Walker," Mamma said while pouring the coffee. "But there was a codicil that said if the clinic could not manage the money and if Walker could not manage the inn for whatever reason, they passed on to the next heir."

KiKi stopped cutting and stared at Mamma. "Tucker? Why would Conway do such a thing? They didn't get along, and that's putting it mildly."

Mamma sipped her coffee. "It's a legal item. Clinics come and go like everything else. They aren't forever and there's a chance Conway could have outlived the free clinic. He could have been in a coma when it closed or whatever, and then what happens to the money? Provisions had to be made for such an occurrence; that's what wills do, and the inn was included in that provision."

KiKi took a bite of cake. "But the clinic is around and Walker is alive and kicking, so what difference does this codicil make to anything?"

"The clinic is up and operating, that's true enough, but what about Boone? What if he were out of the picture? What if he were dead—"

"Or in jail," I said on a quick intake of breath, as the pieces of the puzzle finally fell into place. "Holy cow, this makes a huge difference. Think about it, Tucker kills Conway and the inn passes to Boone. Tucker frames Boone for the murder, Boone goes to prison, and the inn passes to Tucker. If Tucker is indeed in a hurt for money, he sells the inn to Russell or whoever and all is well. It's like a freaking ballet, all perfectly orchestrated."

KiKi drummed her fingers on the table. "I have to say, a son killing off his own father is still a stretch for me."

I wagged my fork at KiKi. "Conway was giving Tucker money, and he stopped about a year ago and Conway wrote him out of the will probably about the same time. Father and son probably never got along, and things got a lot worse after the mother died. After that happened, Conway didn't have to behave himself or risk a divorce and wind up with nothing."

"Or," Mamma chimed in, "what if it's Russell who engineered the whole thing? He kills Conway and frames Walker, knowing Tucker will sell him the inn. Tucker doesn't have to do anything, he just sits back and gets rich."

"But how would Russell know about the will and the rest of it?" KiKi asked, pouring another cup of coffee.

"Tucker could have told him. They travel in the same circles, like at the Plantation Club," I said. "Tucker knew the contents of the will; a copy was in Conway's house along with pictures of Conway and baby Boone and his mother. Everyone knew Boone had a gun in his office, and getting in his office isn't that hard. Dinky's his only secretary and she can't be everywhere. There are spare keys."

Mamma cut a second piece of cake. "Either Tucker as the killer or Russell as the killer, it all hinges on Tucker needing money and selling the inn. We have no proof that Tucker needs money. In fact, rumor is just the opposite, that he inherited money when his mother died, and by all accounts the man's rich. He lives in a historic house, drives nice cars, has a love affair with boats, and owns that expensive marina out on Whitemarsh."

Mamma checked her watch. "I have to be in court." She looked at me. "If Tucker or Russell is our killer, they will kill again. Let me talk to Ross. You can't get involved in this, Reagan. It's just too dangerous. Promise me you'll stay away from these men. No telling me *Yes, I'll be good, Mamma*, and crossing your fingers behind your back. I want the truth." And she didn't move or blink or back down one inch.

"I promise."

"Good girl. Now I have to go. I'll talk to Ross this afternoon and see what she can do." Mamma walked out the door, and KiKi turned to me.

"So what are we going to do?"

"I just promised. Daughters rot in hell for breaking promises to their mothers, everyone knows that."

KiKi grinned. "But I didn't promise, and you only promised to not confront Tucker and Russell. We'll just do what we do best. We'll sneak."

"I'm not sure about the heavenly legalities of saying one thing to Mamma and going off and doing another, but the Tucker/Russell explanation opens a really big door."

"And it all hinges on Tucker being desperate for money. That's it." KiKi slapped the table and grinned. "We don't need to be facing that Russell person or Dixon, we need to find out what's going on with Tucker. We need financial information. That marina cost a bundle, and so do those boats he sails around in. If Tucker's on the ropes, he's not going to keep his problems at his house where Steffy Lou might find out. If things were bad financially, she'd divorce his sorry butt. She likes being the woman about town and the focus of attention, and that means money." KiKi held up her hands in surrender. "See, we're not confronting Russell or Dixon, we're going after Tucker."

"Mamma always said to follow the money, and so does Boone."

"Well, there you go; we're doing exactly what she told us to do, and we have Walker's blessing."

"She may not see it that way."

"Then let's not worry her with these little old details; your mamma has enough on her mind. I hear the sunset at Whitemarsh is lovely this time of year. I'll have the Batmobile ready to fly at eight after the sun goes down. Snooping always goes better when the sun goes down."

BW and I trudged back to the Fox—trudging mostly because whereas I wasn't breaking my exact verbal promise to Mamma, I sure as heck was breaking that promise in spirit. She'd have a canary if she knew KiKi and I were headed to the marina, and I couldn't very well keep KiKi out of it since it was her idea.

I OPENED THE FOX AT TEN SHARP, THE FOX BEING A seven-days-a-week kind of business. I was now ready for a great rebound day of many customers, and spring shopping, but by noon I hadn't had one, not one customer till Harper came charging into the shop all out of breath. "Do you happen to have that pair of wedding shoes I brought in with my wedding dress to sell? I think I left them here."

DEMISE IN DENIM

I fished around under the counter, then held up the satin heels minus Boone's business card. "Did you want to open an account and sell them? They're really nice shoes."

"Perfect." Harper beamed, studying the shoes. "You held on to them. I just know they can sell these; they're selling everything and I need the money. It's crazy over there."

Little spasms of alarm crossed my shoulders and I swallowed hard. "Them? Over where?"

"Anna and Bella's Boutique. It's a new consignment shop that those girls I was talking to here the other day opened up." She glanced at my shop. "The boutique is a really nice upscale consignment shop. They have all designer items for dirt-cheap prices. They connected with this group of got-rocks women over there in Atlanta. Seems they like to turn over their wardrobe every season, and they consign their barely worn items, sometimes even their unworn items, with Anna and Bella. It's amazing how they lucked into this, how we lucked into having the boutique in Savannah. What a deal."

Harper held up a Louis Vuitton wristlet. "I got this little gem for thirty bucks; it's on the Louis website for eight hundred."

She grabbed the shoes. "You should go take a look at the boutique, and Anna and Bella promised more to come. They said they're getting in shipments every week. Don't say anything to Anna and Bella, but you know, I was thinking of contacting the Atlanta ladies myself and see if they had some gowns. I have a wedding I'm playing for and a few anniversaries, and I need fancy clothes. Anna and Bella are cheap, but buying direct from the source would be even cheaper and I am so strapped for money these days. Maybe I'll undercut Anna and Bella and open a place of my own, wouldn't that be something? Beat them at their own game."

Harper gave one more look around. "I hate to say it, but you should just lock this place up and throw away the key. Maybe you can get a job with them. They sure could use the help; they're swamped. The Prissy Fox is bust."

Harper snatched up her shoes and dashed out the door, leaving me in a state of sheer panic. "This can't be happening," I said to BW, who was sleeping under my checkout counter. "This is my busy time. Spring and fall are my Black Fridays, the time the Prissy Fox is in the black and not the red and . . . What am I going to do?"

"Do about what?" Chantilly wanted to know as she strolled into the shop. She plopped a white bag on the counter.

"Look at this." I waved my hand over the empty shop. "I'm doomed."

"I brought you mac and cheese."

"Even mac and cheese won't help."

Chantilly shoved the bag into my hand and snarled, "It might if you just take a look."

I pulled out the take-out container of deliciousness and fluffed the napkin to read *No Tucker*. "How does he know these things?"

"Do you see a crystal ball in that bag? I'm just the delivery girl."

"How busy are you?"

"Soup's on, pulled pork is simmering, and Rachelle's got the buns in the oven. I got a minute."

"What about going shopping, a little retail therapy? Anna and Bella have—"

"Their boutique, right! I hear it's amazing. It's been in all the papers; everyone has been waiting for this and they were interviewed on two morning talk shows and on the radio and . . ." Chantilly's voice dropped off as she gazed around the empty and very quiet Prissy Fox. "I'm sure there's room in Savannah for more than one consignment shop." But the look in Chantilly's eyes said she wasn't so sure.

"Can you check it out for me? Just run down and see if it's as good as the hype?"

"You look mighty stressed. You know, I bet this is one of those opening-day things where everyone is excited, and then the hoopla falls off and everyone will be right back here at the Fox."

"Will you go?"

"I'll do a quick run through. You just sit here and enjoy the mac and cheese."

"I think I've gained ten pounds since all this started."

"Five pounds tops. You look great; full-figured women are in."

"I'm full figured?"

"Just from the boobs down." Chantilly turned and headed for her Jeep.

I was a pear! I shredded the napkin into a million pieces and dropped the mac and cheese back in the bag. No mac and cheese for me; I'd give it to KiKi. Okay, so how come she didn't gain five pounds? She had the worst eating habits on the planet and she'd just pigged out at the theater event.

Because, I realized, Auntie KiKi was next door dancing while I was here standing in one place looking at an empty store.

I needed to get with the health program. That meant I had to put on gym shoes instead of flip-flops and workout pants instead of denim shorts and move my derriere now instead of parking it at Cakery Bakery! I could do this. I was not destined for peardom. An hour later I was dripping wet, out of breath, and I was still a pear, just a wet pear.

"What in the world are you doing?" Chantilly asked as she hustled up the walk. "You're all sweaty and you're limping and you look like something the cat dragged in."

"Running . . . around . . . the . . . house . . . for exercise."

"Why didn't you at least run around the block?"

"Afraid I'd miss a customer." I dropped down onto the porch and flopped onto my back, staring up at the sky through the hole in my roof.

"Your dog's laughing at you."

"Still? You'd think the humor would wear thin."

Chantilly grinned and shook her head. "You're wearing red-and-white striped stretch pants. I'm guessing they're a leftover from Christmas, least I hope so. Honey, there's a lot to laugh at."

"And you're wearing an absolutely adorable scarf and earrings." I levered myself up on one elbow. "And you have a new purse. I love that purse." I bolted upright. "You shopped!"

Chantilly blushed. "Maybe a little."

I cut my eyes to her Jeep parked at the cub, with bags

piled in the front and back seats and spilling out the windows. "You shopped a lot!"

"But I didn't enjoy it, I swear." She made a cross over her heart. "It was too crowded and too much to choose from and way too many designer items crowding the racks. It's all designer items for really cheap!" She cleared her throat and slapped a frown on her face. "I mean for sort of cheap."

"My best friend's a turncoat." I stood, parked my hands on my hips, and scowled. "If Anna and Bella had one of those kinds of coats on sale I bet you would have bought it, too."

"But—"

"Go. I can't take any more." I pointed to the Jeep, and Chantilly headed off.

"It can't last," she called back over her shoulder, "Nothing that good can last."

"Wait. Did you see any men there, old men maybe with canes or walkers or something?

"This was so not an old-men-with-canes event. This was *women just want to have fun.*"

Chantilly ran for her car, and I started running around the house again. Least my present financial situation would make it easier to lose weight 'cause I wouldn't be able to afford food! The only positive of all this was that I had something else on my mind besides who murdered Conway. I'd rather that something else be where to take a vacation.

By six I'd managed to slash the prices on most of the clothes in the Fox, put a "Sale—30 Percent Off" sign in the display window, and dress Gwendolyn in a cute denim skirt, tan blouse, and rust accent scarf. Business picked up marginally, but I needed to combat this Anna-and-Bella situation with more advertising. That would cost more money, and the 30 percent cut in my prices was killing me.

It would also kill my consigners. Since I did a fifty-fifty split with them, they wouldn't get as much money either, and they might stop bringing clothes in to me and take them to the boutique where all the shoppers were. They might not get as much as for their clothes, but it was better than nothing. If that happened, I was out of business.

I fed BW his daily hot dog and told him to savor the moment, as there wouldn't be many more. I kept the gym shoes and pulled on B&E black, then stepped outside to find Auntie KiKi in black Zumba pants and Uncle Putter's lucky nylon black golf jacket. She looked like a garbage bag with red hair and really cute black-and-white sneakers. The Batmobile was in the drive, but KiKi wasn't alone. Big Joey was with her, dressed in raggedy jeans, ripped shirt, and beat-up leather jacket and riding one really sweet Harley.

Two women walking their dogs caught sight of Big Joey and ran into each other, a car with a female driver ran up onto the sidewalk, and Elsie Abbott parked her Caddy, got out, and stared openmouthed. Then she applauded. When it came to the bad boy all women were the same . . . they wanted one! They especially wanted one who looked like Vin Diesel with hair. Lord have mercy.

"You're not smiling," I said to Big Joey as I walked over to him. Not that Big Joey was a smiley kind of guy, but this seemed different, serious different.

"There be a development," Big Joey said, sitting back on his bike. "Tucker giving ten Gs for Boone's arrest."

My blood ran cold, and for a minute I couldn't breathe as KiKi asked, "He can do that? I tell you that man is ten miles of bad road. Now he'll have every crackpot in the city after Boone. Isn't there a law or something? People can't just go around shooting people, can they?"

"T-man say this be a missing-person situation and he's putting up a reward for Brother Dear."

"Brother Dear, my old tomato," KiKi fumed. "What are we going to do now?"

"End this." Big Joey's eyes went dead cold and his hands clenched the handlebars of his bike. He kissed me on the forehead. "Thought you should know. Later, babe."

Big Joey nodded to KiKi, powered up his machine, and purred off into the sunset.

Chapter Seventeen

I CRACKED my knuckles and took a deep breath. "I can't believe this. It's like right out of the Old West. Next thing there'll be posters with Boone's face and 'Wanted' splashed across the top." I stared at Auntie KiKi. "Is this ten grand alive or . . . ?" I couldn't say the D-word.

KiKi bit at her bottom lip. "But we know folks around here don't shy away from firepower much, do they? Putting a price on Boone's head is like declaring hunting season. How can Tucker do this financially? If the man's hard up for cash, how's he going to get his hands on that kind of money as a reward?"

"Because when Boone's in jail, Tucker gets the inn and he'll sell it," I said, trying to see things from Tucker's demented point of view. "He'll be in the chips again. I'd say this all makes Tucker look more broke than ever. He's desperate for money right now, and he's getting tired of the police not being able to bring Boone in and put him behind bars."

"Everything's got to do with Tucker's money situation, meaning we need to be getting ourselves to that marina and see once and for all what's going on with that guy."

KiKi headed for the driver's side of the car, and I snagged her arm. "There's another problem and I swear this one isn't my fault. Deckard's following me around, and he pops up at the worst times. What if he follows us to the marina? We can't snoop around with a cop on our tail."

"Then we'll give him the slip."

I patted the car hood. "You got a navy Beemer here with the deluxe trim package, you have red hair, and your license plate is 'FOXTROT.' I think the jig's up."

KiKi pursed her lips. "It's like Cher says, we'll have to pull up our big-girl panties and follow the path. So are you going to hang around here and be Debbie Downer or get a move on?"

"Lord save me," I muttered as I got in the car.

"I heard that," KiKi said as she took the driver's side. She set the GPS to Whitemarsh Marina, then hit the gas and barreled down Gwinnett to Abercorn. She hung a right onto Victory Parkway. "Wrong way." I pointed in the other direction. "Whitemarsh is a left. Look there on the GPS. Google Maps knows all."

"And you can be telling that to that beat-up truck that's been following since we turned out of the drive and don't look back, just act natural."

"Does it have the front light out? That's Deckard."

"Well, that little pipsqueak."

"Actually he's a big fat—"

I swallowed the rest of the description as KiKi turned off Victory Parkway, zoomed down Montgomery, and hung a sharp right.

"We're going to McDonald's? Uh, you're in the drive-through."

KiKi checked her rearview mirror and grinned. "Yep, he's still there. Sucker! Hold on to your French fries, honey, KiKi's got the wheel."

"I don't have any—" The *fries* part died in my throat because KiKi tromped the gas pedal and laid rubber as we squealed around the other cars in the drive-through line. The Beemer ripped across three lanes of traffic on Montgomery and swerved between cars; the railroad crossing up ahead was flashing its red light and making that cute ding-ding noise . . . except it wasn't so cute right now!

"The crossing gate's dropping!" I yelped. "I hear the train whistle! Stop!"

KiKi floored the Beemer and all gazillion horses under the hood went off in a full gallop as we zipped around the other cars, with KiKi yelling "Yeee haaaaa" as we went airborne across the tracks, landing with a bouncy thud on the other side, then sped away.

"Well buy me a hound dog and call me Elvis!" KiKi thumped the steering wheel and laughed.

"We could have died!"

"Nope, not our time. I figure if it was our time, the gators in that swamp we were in the other day would have had us for dinner. Plus this here situation is just the reason Putter, the wonderful man that he is, sprang for the BMW 5 Series instead of the lowly 3 Series."

"Uncle Putter thought you'd need a getaway car?"

KiKi smiled lovingly. "Guess he figured it would happen sooner or later. We haven't been married all these years for nothing, now have we?" KiKi looked in the rearview mirror. "Well, now I do think we lost him."

"I think I lost five years of my life." I braved a peek in the mirror on the back of the sun visor to check for gray hair.

"Gotta keep the juices flowing. Good for the complexion and important bodily functions that you need to keep primed. You should keep in mind that Walker Boone isn't going to be on the run forever, and that there primed part of yours might finally get put to good use, least I'm hoping so."

KiKi followed Route 80 out onto the island, the quiet night of sea and sky surrounding us like a warm blanket. We pulled off at the white-and-blue Whitemarsh Marina sign. "Take that narrow gravel road," I said, pointing to the side. "We don't need anyone knowing we're here."

KiKi killed her high beams, using only her parking lights, and slowed the Beemer to a crawl, rocks crunching under the tires, with the sounds of lapping water close by. Lit docks sat to the right as boats rocked in the gentle current. Larger buildings loomed toward the back, smaller ones to the front. Picnic tables, grills, and two horseshoe courts dotted a grassy section under low-hanging trees.

KiKi killed the engine; the car was hidden behind a cluster of heavenly oleander bushes. We got out of the car and didn't close the doors, to preserve the silence. "I'm thinking that pole barn thing is for boat repairs and storage. Wonder if it has an alarm?" she whispered.

"An alarm to who and what? The marina is out here in the boonies; who's going to come?"

"I am," came a man's voice behind us. KiKi screamed, I jumped a foot, and the man aimed a high-powered flashlight in our faces. "What are you doing out here this time of night?" he asked in a not-too-friendly way.

"Wait," he added, looking at me. "I know you. You're that gal on TV who's getting even with that attorney guy who messed you over in a divorce. Tucker, the guy who owns this place, says you're a pain in the butt."

"You work for Tucker?" I asked. "I hear he's another pain in the butt."

"For the moment I work for him. He hasn't paid me in three weeks, but I get free rent on a house back there in the woods. I got a feeling that's coming to an end, too. Fact is, I think he might be moving in there himself. I hear stuff like the guy's overextended. This place costs a bundle to keep up, and old Tucker has expensive hobbies." The guard pointed to a sleek white sailboat two slips down. "So, what are you two doing out here?"

"We got lost," KiKi said. "But I think we know our way now. You sure have been a big help." KiKi opened the door and climbed in, and I did the same.

"Hope you get even with that attorney guy," the guard said to me as he stood aside. "I just went through a divorce myself, so I know what it's like. I heard there's a ten-thousand-dollar price on that attorney's head. If you find him it would be one way of getting your money back. Heck, I might go looking for him myself for that kind of payday."

"So, what do you think?" KiKi asked once we got back on the road.

"That Boone's in one sorry state of affairs with everyone out gunning for him, and that Tucker's burned through a ton of money. I'm sure our friendly night guard is bound to tell Tucker we were out here looking around. Tucker's going to know we're onto him needing money, and that sets him up as killing Conway and framing Boone."

"I suppose we've still got Anna and Bella to consider, but do you really believe they'd do in Conway and frame Boone because of some advice over wills and inheritance?" KiKi said as the Batmobile motored through the night.

"All I know is Anna and Bella opened that consignment boutique; where'd that money come from, huh? If they buried C and C somewhere or tossed them overboard, the girls could draw on the bank accounts no questions asked. Kind of the best of all worlds, and where'd you get those cute sneakers?"

"What cute sneakers?"

"The ones on your feet." Even in the dark I could see patches of guilty red on KiKi's cheeks. "I don't believe it, you shopped at Anna and Bella's? How could you? They're ruining me."

"It's not my fault, I swear." KiKi held up her hand as if taking an oath. "The shoes were sitting there in the front window of that cute little shop they have and calling . . . *buy me, KiKi, buy me.* What's a woman to do?"

"What else called out to you?"

"My lips are sealed." KiKi housed the Beemer and I cut across to my humble abode that I loved with all my heart. I loved the paint-chipped door, the original glass in the display window that now showcased the adorable Gwendolyn. I even loved the hole in the porch roof and the weeds in the front yard. I'd rescued it from Hollis, opened a business, and it was all mine . . . but for how long? How was I going to compete against an all-designer consignment shop at such cheap prices?

Feeling lower than a flat frog in a dry well, as Auntie KiKi would say, I went inside to puppy whines of *yippee, you're home*. That should make me feel better, right? Except if things didn't improve in the very near future, BW and I were homeless.

"What kind of dog mommy am I?" I asked BW as we headed for the fridge. "I have two, just two, hot dogs left in there and the electric bill's due and there's the hole in the porch roof to contend with. I think I have an apple and orange from *care package by Mamma* and somehow we gobbled through all that food quick. Okay, *I* did the gobbling and I swear I don't remember eating half of it."

I opened the fridge, and BW and I gasped. "It's full." BW barked.

"We have cottage cheese, tomatoes, some other veggies in the veggie drawer. I forgot we had a veggie drawer. We have grapes and apples and sliced turkey and whole-wheat bread, and Lord be praised, we have hot dogs. They're organic beef uncured hot dogs, and I have no idea how such things can taste any good, but they're the right shape."

I slid one from the package, popped it in the nuker, and

blasted it for a minute in case that uncured part meant uncooked.

I chopped the hot dog, which smelled pretty darn good, into bite-size pieces and tasted one to make sure I wasn't poisoning my BFF, not to mention I was starving. "Not bad," I assured BW, and resisted taking another chunk of hot dog for myself.

I put the plate on the floor and dished out cottage cheese and tomato for me and made a turkey sandwich. I hoisted myself up onto my chipped yellow Formica counter. I dug into my dinner feeling sadder by the bite, thinking how few of these dinners I had left. It was always good to have a plan B in life for when plan A failed. The consignment shop was my plan B. Now what was I going to do?

By two A.M. and after a lot of tossing and turning and even an apple and peanut butter snack that was nowhere as good as a doughnut, I still couldn't sleep. Maybe a run would help me feel better. Deep down I knew it wouldn't help at all; I'd just be sore and achy and probably pull something, but at least I'd be skinnier, I hoped.

I yanked on shorts, T-shirt, and gym shoes as fast as I could so I wouldn't have time to change my mind, and then BW and I took off. If I had to run, he had to run. We were in this together. Plus it was two A.M. and I was lonely. We headed up Habersham, as the soft glow of the old wrought-iron lights cast the city in creams and gold. "We need to do this more often," I said to BW. "I don't feel so bad. Exercise is terrific."

We passed Whitfield Square with the gazebo lovely in the moonlight, and I slowed down a bit, well maybe more than a bit, but I was only limping a little. When we got to Troup Square, I let BW get a long, long drink at the doggie fountain while trying to convince myself this really was great and I wasn't really dying.

I hobbled past the police station. Deckard's truck was in the back parking lot. I doubted the man had a home; if he did, it was probably under a rock. Huffing, puffing, and sweating like a roasted pig, I hobbled into Madison Square and dropped down onto a bench. I was having a near-death experience, I was sure of it. I saw the tunnel with the light at the end. Actually it was headlights coming down Habersham, but close enough. BW looked fit and ready for more. "You have four legs," I explained to him between gulps for air. "I only have two."

I sat up, my heart settling back into my chest at the slower-than-jackhammer rate it was before. The illuminated fountain in the center of the square bubbled over, cascading into the basin below, adding to a sense of peace and contentment. Two late-night lovers ambled past holding hands. They stopped and kissed and she snuggled into his shoulder, and I wondered if I'd ever be with Boone again.

"Do you think Boone got his hair cut?" I asked BW. "Do you think he has clean clothes, and where do you think he's been sleeping, and it better be alone if he knows what's good for him, and do you think he misses us as much as we miss him?"

BW yawned and lay down at my feet. "You know, no one else calls me *cookie* or *blondie* or *shop girl*. Not exactly terms of endearment, I'll give you that, but Boone's usually trying to tick me off so I stay away from a case and get out of harm's way. Not that it ever works, but he does try. That's kind of sweet even if he does drive me crazy, and truth be told maybe I drive him a little crazy, too."

I sighed and gazed over at Boone's office, feeling lonely and depressed. "Things aren't as dire as before," I said, trying to reassure BW. "Russell and/or Tucker had motives to kill Conway and frame Walker, so that's good, but I need something to tie them to the scene of the crime or even stealing Boone's gun and . . . and . . . That little yellow-and-blue light in Boone's office window isn't on, and neither is his porch light."

BW looked up at me. "I know," I answered. "They're always on, probably even connected to a timer. You think I'm being paranoid?"

BW put his big doggie head on my leg. "Yeah, I'm worried too, so here's what we'll do," I said as I petted his silky snout. There might be trouble and BW needed to know what was going on. "If the door's locked and we don't hear any commotion inside, we'll know all's well and we can head for home and maybe stop at Parkers for one oatmeal-and-raisin cookie. One can't hurt, plus we get grain and fruit, and I think that's part of that food pyramid thing. But you need to cowboy up a bit in case there is someone in there, okay? You're my only backup and Old Yeller's back at the ranch."

BW sat, hiked his leg, and licked himself. We all prepare for battle in our own way. We crossed East President Street, nearly deserted this time of night, and took the stone steps up to the office, BW's nails tapping on the hard surface.

"*Please don't open, please don't open, please don't*

open," I chanted as I turned the brass doorknob. The white door with frosted panes swung wide, not a sound inside. Faint rays of moonlight drifted in from Boone's office and spilled across Dinky's desk.

I fumbled for the light and switched it on to find papers, Dinky's flowered stapler, and her computer on the floor, and chairs overturned. Gazing at the mess, I let go of BW's leash, and he beelined straight into Boone's office, stopping by his desk. "He's not here, but I really wish he were," I said to BW as I went into the office and switched on Boone's desk light.

"Watch what you wish for, blondie," Boone said, hunkered down on the floor. And that would have been just fine except for the fact that Harper Norton was on the floor in front of him facedown with Boone's silver letter opener in her back.

I gasped and jumped backward.

"I saw you in the square," Boone said to me. "I hoped you wouldn't come over."

"What the . . . How did you . . . Holy crap!"

"Someone let me know that the lights were out here, and I knew something was up," Boone said.

"And they were right," Deckard said from the doorway, his gun drawn. He came inside, his hulking profile silhouetted in the dimly lit office. "Put your hands behind your head," he said to Boone. "I've been waiting a long time for this. Now you got two murders to answer for."

"Waitaminute," I said, my brain starting to function beyond *yikes, there's a dead person in the room!* "You can't believe Boone did this."

"His office, his letter opener, and I'm guessing his fingerprints. Yeah, I'd say he's the killer all right. This woman probably had proof Boone here killed Conway, and he had to shut her up."

"In his own office?" I tried to reason. "How did he get her here? Why would he get her here? This makes no sense, Deckard, think about it."

"A desperate man doing desperate things, it happens all the time and I don't have to think about anything, I just need to bring this killer in."

"But he's innocent."

A smile pulled at Boone's lips. "I appreciate the support, blondie, but I really can talk for myself."

I parked my hands on my hips. "This is not your fight, it's my fight, and I'm fed up with this . . . this lunatic following me around."

Deckard sneered as sirens headed our way. "I knew if I tailed you long enough you'd lead me to Boone, and I'll be darned, it looks like I was right on the money. Nice work, blondie."

Red flashed in front of my eyes, I swear it really did.

"Get him," I yelled at BW.

Deckard laughed deep in his throat. "That dumb dog doesn't do anything but eat and poop, everybody knows that."

In a flash all four paws left the ground and big growling dog plus big shiny snarling teeth sprang for Deckard, the moral being never ever kick a dog and think you'll get away with it.

I lunged for Deckard along with BW, both of us sending

Deckard flat on his back and his gun skittering across the floor.

"Run!" I yelled to Boone.

He hesitated for a split second, our gazes locking. "Good God, go!"

Boone jumped up and gave Deckard a solid right hook to the jaw along with, "Never call her *blondie*." Then he tore out the door.

Chapter Eighteen

"**Y**ou're going to pay for this," Deckard bellowed, shoving me to the side and struggling to his feet, as sirens approached. "That dog bit me! I'm having him put down. He's history, you're history."

"What dog?" I panted, amazed I was so calm. Then again, after gators, snakes, a fire, and being on the road with NAS-CAR KiKi, I was a seasoned veteran of chaos and crazy.

I sat up and tried to catch my breath. "I didn't see any dog. I was here, you were here, you tripped over poor Harper Norton who is unfortunately also here, and you knocked me to the ground. You hit your jaw and I bet the forensic people are going to be totally pissed you screwed up their crime scene by falling all over it; at least they would be ticked off if this happened on a TV show."

Ross bolted into the room, two uniforms behind her. She

had on jeans and a sweatshirt, and a shirttail of Mickey Mouse jammies stuck out from under the sweatshirt. "What in the world is going on that can't wait till morning?"

I pointed to Harper, and Deckard bellowed, "Boone was here, right in this room, and Reagan Summerside and her stupid dog attacked me and Boone got away."

"What dog?" I held out my hands and did the crazy-man eye roll. "I went for a run and noticed the lights were off in Boone's office and they are never off, and I came to investigate because I'm a good Savannah citizen doing my duty. I found Harper Norton on the floor." I made the sign of the cross and meant it. I didn't know what Harper was involved in, but she sure didn't deserve a knife in the back.

"Then the concerned and ever-vigilant Officer Deckard rushed in to save the day," I continued. "He tripped over the body and hit his chin." I stared at his face. "You're going to have a dandy bruise there, buddy. Knock any teeth loose?"

Ross looked me in the eyes, then let out a long sigh. "You can really say all that with a straight face and not be freaking out?"

"It's been a rough week; I think I used up all my freak." I wobbled to my feet and stood beside Deckard. "How could little old me possibly overpower this guy? He's got six inches and about a hundred pounds on me."

"I keep telling you, there was a dog who went at me," Deckard roared. He held out his shredded jacket sleeve. "How do you explain this?"

"Must have been some other dog." I did crazy-man eye roll part two.

"I want her locked up for obstruction of justice," Deckard

roared again. "And I want her dog locked up and I want Walker Boone."

"What dog?" And maybe I should have left out that last *what dog* comment because ten minutes later I was sitting in the Bull Street police station and was back in the way-too-familiar putrid-green interrogation room. The only upside was that this time after jogging my guts out I smelled even worse than my surroundings.

Ross came in and sat down across from me. "You just had to poke the bear, didn't you?" She put her hand over the microphone sitting on the table. "Not that he doesn't deserve poking, but do you have to do it at three A.M.? You're not the only one who's had a rough week."

"Are you going to arrest me?"

"Only if being a smartass is a crime or if one more of the cops on duty here trips over himself ogling you. Short-shorts in the middle of the night?"

"I was exercising and people laugh when I wear red-and-white stripes."

"You're off the hook this time. Boone's fingerprints are on that letter opener, not yours, and you overpowering Deckard is a little tough to swallow, and the only thing I've ever seen BW attack is a hot dog, so Deckard is lying his heart out to save face. But we need to talk."

"Got a doughnut sitting around?"

"Does the wild bear . . . ?" Ross winked; I followed her to her desk and took a seat, and she opened a desk drawer that looked like the Cakery Bakery's annex. "A cop's got to do what a cop's got to do."

I told Ross my great Tucker/Russell theory involving

Conway, Boone, and the inn. And the best part was I only ate half the doughnut. "Those two have motive and opportunity," I told Ross. "But I don't have any actual proof that ties either of those guys to Conway's murder."

"Contrary to popular belief and the evidence in front of you, the police do more than eat unhealthy food and write parking tickets. We think we have enough to indict Dixon on blackmail. We matched up his deposits and Conway's withdrawals, and he had pictures of Conway and Walker Boone and his mom taped to the bottom of his desk drawer. He also had a .38, but it's registered and who around here doesn't have a .38? Grayden Russell has applied for large-boat docking privileges down on River Street and a gambling permit, so we know why he's after the Old Harbor Inn and the Tybee Theater. He's in the gaming business. What do you know about Harper Norton?"

"She's friends with Steffy Lou, they went to school together, and they worked on saving the Tybee Theater. She's in a big hurt for money. I have no idea why she was at Boone's office. She didn't like the guy at all, but he's wanted for murder, so what more can she do to him?"

"They found her phone under her. 9-1 was punched in; she never got to the other 1."

"So what do you think she was she doing at Boone's office?"

"You're not going to like it."

"Boone's accused of murdering her; what more isn't there to like?"

"We think Walker and Harper Norton were lovers. He has to be staying somewhere, and he was staying with her on and off. She probably did her best to convince everyone they were enemies, like you did with the reporters and on the TV show thing. There was no evidence of breaking and entering into Walker's office, meaning he let her in for another little rendezvous but she decided that ten grand was better than Walker in the sack and tried to turn him in, and he killed her. You just happened in on him before he could get rid of the body."

"They're lovers?"

"Got a better idea? Why else was she there with Boone? How did she get in? Who else would kill her?"

"They're lovers?"

"We all like Walker, but his dad screwed him over big-time, and revenge is a powerful reason for murder. We got Boone's gun killing Conway and now a dead woman ready to call 911 and Boone standing over her, his letter opener in her back. You do the math."

"Tucker knew Harper," I said, trying to get beyond the lover idea. "Maybe she had the goods on him for killing Conway. And there are two sisters, Anna and Bella, who married rich old guys. Conway and Boone both advised the husbands to change their wills, and Harper planned on screwing their business. Any of them wanted to get rid of her."

"Except Harper was in Boone's office with Boone, there was no forced entry, and she was killed with his letter opener. It's a slam dunk."

"Can I go?"

"Keep me in the loop, and if you can talk Boone into surrendering, it might be in his best interest. A lot of people behind rifle sights are looking for the guy."

The sun was just peeking over the spire of St. John's as I came out of the police station and saw Mamma pulling to the curb in her black Caddy. She rolled down the window. "Some people put on PJs and go to sleep at night, dear."

"You should have seen BW, he was magnificent." I took shotgun and we headed down Bull.

"What in the world happened?" Mamma asked. "And you smell like the bottom of a garbage can."

"I went out for a run, and then I went to jail. See, this is why exercise is really a bad idea, least for me. There was a dead body and getting picked up by the police in the middle there somewhere."

"Did Boone get away?"

"He flattened Deckard."

"Well there you go, all's well that ends well." Mamma parked the Caddy in front of Cherry House and we hoofed it up the sidewalk to Auntie KiKi sitting on the steps in yellow curlers, yellow housecoat, and matching bunny slippers. BW was sprawled out across the porch doing his buzz-saw routine. I sat downwind on one side of KiKi, and Mamma took the other. "You're wearing jeans," I said to Mamma.

"If they didn't let you out of that jail, I figured there might be some serious butt-kicking in order." She patted her thigh. "Plus I just got these new shaper jeans and wanted to take them out for a run."

KiKi handed me a steaming mug of coffee and gave Mamma hers. "Harper Norton's dead?" she asked.

"As a mink hat." I took a sip of coffee. "How'd BW get here?"

"Chantilly, our friendly doggie delivery service."

I took a deep breath. "They think Boone was having an affair with Harper Norton and she tried to turn him in for the reward money and he killed her. I got to his office before he could ditch the body, and BW is more Bruce Willis than we give him credit for."

Mamma stared wide-eyed, and KiKi sat perfectly still for a second. "An affair?" KiKi asked.

"So they say."

"Don't move." KiKi got up and scurried off to Rose Gate, her robe flowing out behind her like Batman. "What do you think she's doing?" I asked Mamma.

"It's either Putter's golf club to beat up Walker the next time she sees him or it's booze."

KiKi was back in one minute flat with three glasses and a bottle of vodka. "Screw the vermouth." She filled the shot glasses; we toasted, then chugged, then did a repeat performance.

"Better?" Mamma asked.

I touched my nose. "I don't feel anything."

"Good, now we can figure this out. It's a known legal fact that a relaxed brain is better functioning."

"Right now I think I could pass for a rocket scientist." I reached over and patted BW. "Best I can come up with is that someone lured Harper to Boone's office, then stabbed her, and Boone just happened to show up, but why did he do that?"

I sat a little straighter. "Because of the lights. They were out in the office. I knew something was up and came in to check, and so did Boone. He showed up at the wrong time, and then Deckard followed me in."

Mamma and KiKi exchanged looks and Mamma asked, "So you're not buying the Walker/Harper lover idea?"

"I suck at men, I truly do. Look at Hollis, could I have made a worse choice than getting involved with that man? Probably not . . . but . . . but I know Boone, and the scary part is he knows me. He calls me *blondie*. Bet he never called Harper Norton that."

"I believe she was a brunette, dear."

"Now you're just getting picky."

Auntie KiKi kissed me on the forehead; well, she tried and it landed on my ear. Such was the power of early-morning vodka, but the thought was there. "If you ask me"—she hiccupped—"it still stands that Tucker and Russell have the most to gain by getting rid of Walker. They're both dirty as bathwater on a Saturday night. Harper could have had something on them and they suspected as much."

"Harper planned to cut into Anna and Bella's boutique business," I added. "The sisters wouldn't let her get away with that."

I ran my hand through my hair, still feeling nothing as Mamma said, "The problem with all these great ideas is, how did the guilty person, whoever it is, lure Harper into Boone's office? We know they had the key because they broke in to get Boone's gun to frame him. Now we need to figure out who had it in for Harper."

"Okay," I said, trying to put things together. "So Anna and Bella had a connection to Harper, but who else did?"

"Probably a lot of people came into contact with Harper," Auntie KiKi said. "She was working all over the place. I first saw her over at the Slumber playing at Conway's farewell bash."

"When I helped Chantilly with the barbecue fiasco over at the Old Harbor Inn, she was playing there, and that brings her into contact with Russell and his dealing to get the inn."

"And she helped Steffy Lou with the theater project," Mamma chimed in. "That brings her into contact with Tucker, and he's always been tops on my who-framed-Walker list."

"We went and talked to the guard out at that marina that Tucker owns and found out the old boy's bust," KiKi told Mamma. "If Harper found that out, Tucker would not have been a happy camper. He sure didn't want Steffy Lou or anyone else to know what a really bad businessman he is."

"We're back to the big three suspects," I sighed. "Nothing new."

"But whoever's behind this is getting desperate," Mamma said in her *I am the judge and know all* voice. "We're going to find him or her, it's just a matter of time." Mamma put her arm around me. "I'm glad you're safe. What can I do to help?"

"You filled my fridge."

Mamma gave me a long steady look, a little smile tripping across her face. "Always nice to have someone watching out for you, dear."

Mamma headed off to court, KiKi had morning twinkle-toes time with Bernard Thayer, and I woke BW the wonder puppy and we went inside Cherry House. I fed BW his morning kibble along with a peanut butter apple for saving my butt last night. I grabbed a shower to try to sober up, maybe wake up, and for sure wash away interrogation-room grime. With my hair still wet I dabbed on some eyeliner and slid into a black cotton skirt. Not exactly a fashion statement of the season but the best I could do with no sleep and two shots of vodka under my belt on an empty stomach.

The boutique wouldn't be open for shopping at this hour, but I knew firsthand what went into getting things ready for a busy day . . . when I used to have a busy day. I told BW to hold down the fort, snagged a protein bar, then flagged down Earlene for a lift on Old Gray. Mamma was right in that Harper dead in Boone's office held the key . . . literally. So, who needed to get rid of Harper and why, and the last time I talked to Harper, and Anna and Bella's Boutique were our topics of conversation.

"Did you hear what happened over at Walker Boone's place?" Earlene said to me as I sat down behind her. "That poor man keeps getting in deeper and deeper; someone's sure out to set him up, even put a price on the man's head, and I don't believe for one minute he had a little something going on the side with that Harper Norton woman." Earlene gave me a sideways glance. "Do you? So, honey, where can I drop you this fine morning?"

"Everyone knows about Harper and Boone?" I asked.

"Got five tweets this morning discussing the situation, as much as you can discuss on Twitter, that is. But we all know that there is no Harper and Boone, and you shouldn't concern yourself with such talk." She added another sideways glance. "Right?"

I got off the bus two stops early so I didn't have to listen to the rest of the Harper and Boone scenario. I crossed the street, where a line was already forming in front of Anna and Bella's Boutique. I spotted Mercedes sitting on a bench behind Colonial Park Cemetery, sipping coffee and checking her e-mail. See, that was what I wanted to be doing, coffee and e-mail, not hunting a killer.

"You're looking none too happy," I said to Mercedes as I sat down beside her. "Bad news?"

"That's all it is these days, with dead bodies piling up like pancakes on Sunday morning. First it's Conway in the tub and now it's that girl in Mr. Boone's office and him standing right over her, least that's what the gossips are saying and they usually get it right."

She gave me a hard look. "Well I'll be, I heard you were there, too. You should know that nothing was going on between that Harper woman and Mr. Boone. I keep the man's house and I know wrinkled sheets when I see 'em and if there be more than one doing the wrinkling, if you know what I mean. There hasn't been any wrinkling for quite some time now. He likes you."

"Why?"

Mercedes laughed, her whole face happy. "Now that you have to be asking him. So, are you here to check out the competition?" She nodded to the boutique.

"Hope they're giving you a discount because you're working for them."

Mercedes fluffed her hair and looked ticked. "I *used* to work for them; then they up and fired me after only one time cleaning."

"But what about the bonus of doing up their dear old

husbands for the big meet-their-maker party? That was the whole purpose of getting you to clean their houses, right?"

"See, that's the thing, it's like the boys just dropped off the face of the earth and my excellent Slumber services aren't needed. I stopped by here to see if they showed up. You'd think they'd be at their wives' new business venture, now don't you, but I didn't see them today or yesterday."

"We could just ask Anna and Bella where Clive and Crenshaw are."

"I did, and they told me to mind my own blankety-blank business and went back to unpacking all their fancy New York clothes."

"Atlanta, aren't these rich ladies from Atlanta?"

"New York, I saw the boxes being delivered myself when doing the cleaning that one time." Mercedes checked her watch. "I need to be getting myself over to the Slumber. Junior Lambert enjoyed Walls' barbecue one too many times and thumbed his nose at Lipitor once too often. Let me know if you run into C and C. They're always nice to me. I hope nothing's happened to them, I truly do."

Mercedes headed for her pink Caddy parked across the street and I studied the line of customers, a lot of whom used to be *my* customers. But the strangest part was the Clive and Crenshaw disappearing act. If I'd picked up on the two of them gone and so had Mercedes, there was something to it. Going in the front door of the boutique was for shopping; going in the back door was for snooping. I crossed the street, then cut down an alley off Lincoln used for local deliveries. A panel van sat parked at the end, the back door to the boutique propped wide. A man tore boxes open and ripped plastic bags off clothes, really nice-looking clothes.

"What are you doing back here?" Bella said to me from the doorway. "This here is private property."

"Actually it's an alley."

"Too bad about your pathetic little business going belly up like I'm sure it is, not that I've had time to check it out. Come here to see what success really looks like!"

"Where're Clive and Crenshaw? Thought they'd be here to support your success."

Bella's eyes went to bits of ice. "Clive and Crenshaw are none of your business."

"Thought your rich consigners were from Atlanta, that's what everyone's saying." I picked up the side of a box with an address on the side. "New York? Why New York? Did Harper Norton wonder the same thing? She told me you have a sweet scheme going on here and she wanted in on it."

Bella's hands fisted at her side.

"Is that why you killed her?" I asked.

"I didn't kill anyone, you annoying person. Now get out of here before I call the cops and they put you behind bars where you belong."

"Let me see if I got this right, you obviously don't care about your husband, but just mentioning Harper Norton sends you into a tizzy? What did she have on you? Enough to want to shut her up permanently?"

Bella took her phone from her pocket. "You'll be sorry you got involved in this, Reagan Summerside. My sister and I know how to get what we want and keep it, and get rid of people we don't want around. You are not messing things up for us."

I didn't need another run-in with the police in less than twelve hours, so I turned and left. I still didn't know about C and C, but I'd hit a nerve with Harper. Least I wasn't the only one starting off the day with a bang; now Anna had a little something to think about, too.

I started for home. If I could just catch a few hours' sleep before I opened the Fox, that would be terrific, not that there'd be any customers, but I had to figure out what to do to improve my plight and . . .

I lost my train of thought as a red SUV pulled up beside me; Dinky stuck her head out the window, crying and sniveling.

"Please don't tell me there's another body." I leaned against her car, feeling weak in the knees.

Chapter Nineteen

"I've been looking for you," Dinky said between sniffs and nose blowing. "I'm desperate for a place to stay and I didn't want to just show up at your place, and you really need to get a phone."

"Oh, honey, your husband kicked you out?"

"No, he didn't kick me out," she sobbed. "He wouldn't know what to do with baby Boomer; the man can't change a diaper to save his life and the only bottle he knows is the kind with Budweiser on the front. Boone's office is a crime scene, of all things. There's blood on the carpet, the new Oriental."

She cried louder. "This keeps getting worse and worse. Will you take me in? Can I set up the office at your place? I've got paperwork that Mr. Boone started before all this murder stuff started up, and I need to be filing legal documents with the courts and the like and keep the office going.

With that new boutique in town going gangbusters you probably don't have any business so I figured you wouldn't mind."

I heaved a sigh. "Sure, why not." I opened the passenger-side door to get in; files spilled out onto the street, and the morning commuters were less than thrilled with the show making them late for work. I scooped up the files and set them on my lap as we motored across Congress. "Don't you use computers for this file stuff?" I asked Dinky.

"We use both, and paper files can't be hacked. This will be fun," Dinky said, swiping at her tears. "It's been so lonely sitting at the office all by myself and I'm getting depressed. I heard that the police think Mr. Boone was carrying on with that Harper Norton woman, and that's just not true at all. She went and sent him her dead wedding bouquet, and that really kills the mood, if you get what I mean."

Dinky pulled up in front of the Fox. I hooked my arm around a stack of files and hauled them up the walk.

"Nice display window," Dinky said, trailing behind me with a box. "The mannequin with BW sitting next to it looks like a magazine cover. Maybe you should go with a vintage shop; that Anna and Bella boutique isn't competing against that."

"Not enough money in vintage clothes." I balanced the files on my hip and unlocked the door. I nudged it open and BW barreled out onto the porch, jumping and whining as if I'd been gone a year; the files slid out of my hands and scattered across the floor.

Dinky looked at the mess. "I think you were missed."

I picked up a file labeled *Clive and Crenshaw.* "Boone gave them some advice on their wills, right?"

"I can't say."

"They were clients, right?"

"I can't say."

I sat cross-legged on the porch while BW inspected the landscape. I flipped open the file and Dinky snapped it out of my hand. "Lawyer-client privilege is sacred. You can't just read this stuff 'cause you're nosy."

"Both these guys are missing; no one's seen them for days. They're old and rich and their wives just opened a store in the historic district. Smell a little fishy?"

Dinky sat down beside me. "I'll look. I'm like an attorney . . . sort of. It's just notes saying Clive and Crenshaw told Mr. Boone to butt out of their affairs, and he tried to point out the error of their ways in setting up their wills making their wives sole beneficiaries." She closed the file. "That's it, just that one meeting. Fact is, it's the last meeting Mr. Boone had that night before he took off."

"The night he found out Conway was his dad?"

Dinky nodded. "Yeah. I remember setting it up. It was late and I left at six, and they didn't come in till around seven."

"That means Boone didn't give Clive and Crenshaw this will advice till after Conway was dead. Anna and Bella, the dear wives, had no reason to swipe Boone's gun, kill Conway, and frame Boone for the deed. They had no reason to be pissed at Boone at the time of Conway's demise."

"You mean Anna and Bella were suspects in all this?

Why, I had no idea, and that surely is mighty fine news. I'd hate to see that boutique of theirs close. I love that place." Dinky pressed her lips together tight. "You sure you don't want to go vintage?"

I helped Dinky unload more files, file cabinets, and a leather chair that a passerby tried to buy right out of the back of the SUV. Another lady tried to buy the Tiffany-style lamp that I hauled in, and AnnieFritz offered fifty bucks for the little petit point footstool Dinky used to keep her feet elevated to avoid the much dreaded varicose veins.

I went to the car to retrieve the espresso maker, amazed how much stuff Dinky had crammed into the car. When I came back in, Dinky's red leather chair was parked behind my green door checkout counter. She'd plugged in the Tiffany lamp, giving a soft glow to the hallway; the antique floral desk blotter with matching pen holder sat on top along with her flower stapler, laptop, printer, and two framed pictures of baby Boomer.

"Ta-da." Dinky spread her arms wide over her new home. "The red and the green look great together, and the antique desk set fits the vintage décor of the house." She slid into her chair looking like she owned the place. "I'll piggyback onto Miss KiKi's Wi-Fi—we'll have to get her password—and once I get a landline in here for faxing, this will be a really great office."

"You know that other dead body I mentioned when you stopped me, there might be one after all."

"Really?"

"You never know. This is my checkout area."

"Checkout what?" Dinky glanced around the empty shop.

"When I had customers this was where I checked them out."

"And when that happens we'll talk relocation. Now let's charge up the espresso machine and get to work."

I muscled the espresso machine into the kitchen, then did what every woman did when she got herself into a mess she didn't know how to get out of: whined to a friend. I slipped out my back door and right into KiKi's back door.

"Save me." I plopped down into a chair at the oak table and banged my head on top.

KiKi turned off the mixer where she was undoubtedly making something totally delish and sat down across from me. "You'll have to be more specific, dear. Save you from murderers, Deckard, no business, Walker when he finds out about the Chevy?"

"All of them except the Chevy one. Boone already knows. Dinky's commandeered my checkout counter as her office, and I can't stop her because I have no reason to. I don't have any business and the only potential business I've had all morning was people trying to buy her really nice office stuff. I can't compete with Anna and Bella's Boutique."

"It's just like Cher used to say to us when we were on the road in that big tour bus of hers eating salt and vinegar chips, all of us need to invent ourselves."

"I did that, I invented the Prissy Fox."

"Well, Prissy something else. You said people tried to buy Dinky's furniture, and you have the furniture at Conway's house lined up, and I have an attic full of Lord-knows-what and I bet your mamma does, too."

"I'm not selling the family wares because I'm in a funk, but . . . but the furniture angle might work." I grabbed an oatmeal cookie from the golf ball cookie jar. "I can sell my bed frame and dresser and maybe Boone's leather couch."

"Honey, we've got enough dead bodies around here, we don't need to be adding yours to the heap. Men got a thing about their golf clubs, their couches, and their remotes. Best to leave them be."

"Mind if I use your computer to make up flyers and pass them out?" I asked around a mouthful of crumbs.

KiKi gave me a toothy grin as a shiver of doom slid down my spine. "The Shakin' Seniors are on their way here as we speak, and Melvin Pettigrew's been asking about my cute little niece. I can do those flyers in lemon yellow or electric green, what do you think?"

An hour and fifteen minutes later BW and I hobbled our way—actually I was doing the hobbling; BW was in the pink of health—down Abercorn. I put lemon-yellow flyers about the joys of consigning furniture on billboards, on phone poles, and in shop windows if I begged and pleaded with the proprietor and offered him or her a 10 percent discount.

I tried to hit places where the locals congregated, like Jen's and Friends, Pinky Masters, Blue Moon Brewers, and the CVS. By the time I got to Bay Street I was almost out of flyers and pretty much in tourist territory, but there were hotels and inns here updating on a regular basis that might be looking for a place to sell that slightly worn club chair or nightstand. And besides, I was a breath away from the Old Harbor Inn and Grayden Russell. He and Harper must have run into each other. He hadn't had any qualms about me in the water; he would knock off Harper without batting an eye if she had some juicy dirt on him.

BW and I cut through Emmet Park, the Spanish moss floating lazily in the breeze. We took Factor's Walk down to the inn. Grayden Russell was getting into his sports car, top down, luggage in the back. "Going somewhere?" *To blazes, if I had any say in the matter.*

"You're like a bad penny," Russell sneered. "You keep showing up, and this time you have your mutt. Hear you were at Boone's office with that dead girl. Too bad you lived to tell about it."

"Harper Norton—she worked here. Did you knock her off because she found out you torched the Tybee Theater?"

"Prove it."

"Maybe Harper could, and that's why she's dead. Or maybe she knew about your gambling and that you cheated Mason Dixon so he'd be in debt to you and do your dirty work. You seem awfully lucky and Dixon seems awfully unlucky."

"It's the way the cards fall, and you better watch your mouth. You saw Harper; you know what happens to people who don't."

Russell took a step closer. "I've just about got the Tybee Theater in my pocket. That Steffy Lou gal can't come up with the cash and I can. Do anything to jeopardize that and it'll be the last thing you do, got it?"

"What about the inn? Got your grimy hands on that, too?"

"The inn's history. I'm done with this place. Between murders and wills the place will never be free. It looks like Tucker Adkins will wind up with it, but how long will it be tied up in courts? They still don't have Boone and I need to move now. Cheers, chickie."

Russell got in his car and cranked the engine. I pulled BW to the side to get out of the way as Russell roared off. Lamar strolled over, the three of us now staring as Russell squealed around the bend.

"Well, good riddance," Lamar said while patting BW. "Though I got to admit I did get one decent tip out of that guy."

"He really is leaving?"

"Checked out fifteen minutes ago. I pity the staff at the Savannah River Inn. That's where he said to forward his mail and contacts; he just up and left without any warning. We're having a little celebration dinner in the breakfast room tonight. Chantilly's doing the catering. Darn shame about Harper. She sure could play the piano, and she and Mrs. Adkins were trying to save the theater out there on Tybee. They said if it worked out I could valet for them when they had productions. Now it looks like Russell's going to get the place after all the work those two put into it."

"Did you ever see Harper with anyone else here? Were she and Russell friends?"

"Never saw them together, but I'm outside mostly. I don't believe Mr. Boone killed her like they say, and I don't believe the two of them were getting it on. Mr. Boone wouldn't do you that way. He's a righteous dude." Lamar hurried off to help a guest pulling up to the inn, and BW and I headed for home. Russell was no longer interested in buying the inn? Where did that come from? And if he and Tucker were in cahoots, Tucker had to be spitting nails this very minute. The man was desperate for money, and his salvation had just hightailed it over to the Savannah River Inn.

"There you are," Dinky said as BW and I ambled inside. She nodded at a chest of drawers, two wingback chairs, and two white floor lamps in the hall. "A lady dropped them off and I took her information and wrote her a receipt and said you would be in touch. Wouldn't be legal to take her things without a receipt. What's this all about?"

"Having running water and electricity, thank you, Jesus, and . . ." I looked at the info sheet "Thank you, Daphne Weeks." I kissed the lamps. "I never expected such a fast turnaround. I can't compete with the new boutique."

"Girl, no one can compete with that place," Dinky tossed in.

"So I'm trying furniture, decent, usable, gently worn. Not antiques, I know nothing about antiques, but I know a rickety chair from a sound one and oak from cherry."

Dinky slapped me on the back. "Well, there you go, and I'll take those two chairs for my family room. Got to do something to spruce up that place and get the attention off my husband's leather couch that he won't get rid of."

Dinky helped me stage the furniture in the dining room, putting the floor lamps on either side to light up the place. We pulled the clothes that weren't very stylish and tossed them into the hall to donate, then shoved the nicer clothes to one side so it looked like a cute closet.

After Dinky left at five to go to her own home of baby Boomer plus husband, I dismantled my bed. I put the mattress on the floor and slid the four-poster that Hollis had left behind down the steps. I did the same with the dresser: dumped all my clothes on the floor, then pushed the dresser to the steps. I angled it down like a giant sled. The fact that I didn't get squashed at the bottom was a freaking miracle.

I took the curtains from my bedroom too, and put them at the dining room window and tied them back with a yellow scarf, making the room look homey. I turned on the chandelier that had been with the house forever, and the light danced on the ceiling and walls. It was late and I was beat, especially after no sleep the night before followed by two shots of vodka, but the fear of being broke and living in one of Anna and Bella's cardboard boxes on the banks of the Savannah River spurred me on.

"So, what do you think?" I asked BW, as the two of us sat on the steps eating a granola bar. He barked and wagged his tail, and "Not bad" came from the top of the steps. I jerked around to see Boone smiling down at us.

"Holy Christmas, are you trying to wind up in jail?" I asked in a loud whisper as Boone trotted down the steps.

"Your bedroom is trashed."

I turned off the chandelier to offer a bit of privacy; the only lights left on were the two floor lamps just brought in. "Anna and Bella's Boutique ran me out of the clothing business," I explained to Boone. "Least temporarily, so now I'm in the used-furniture business. Wanna donate your couch?"

"Hands off the couch, blondie." Boone added a weak smile, but his eyes were sunk deep, his face lined with fatigue, his sweatshirt filthy, jeans ripped and torn. He draped an arm around me and I snuggled close as we sat back on the steps. "Sorry about leaving you with a dead body and Deckard," he said. "I had no idea he'd show up."

"How are you doing?"

"I've been worse," Boone said, but somehow I doubted it.

"Why are you here? Look," I said, coming to my senses.

"You have to leave. Deckard could show up any minute. He's like the Black Plague infecting our lives."

Boone still didn't budge, his eyes serious as he looked into mine. "I know what the cops say about me and Harper, and I wanted you to know it's not true."

"Did you ever call her *blondie*?"

"Of course not."

"There, case closed. Now go."

"You believe me, right?"

"Of course. I know you. I know you as an enemy and as a friend and a fugitive on the run and . . ." I swallowed. "And whatever we are now. You're a righteous dude, Walker Boone." Then I kissed him, his mouth hot and hungry against mine. His fingers wound into my hair, his hand firm against my back. I could feel him breathe and it felt wonderful having him here with me even if it was just for a few minutes.

"You have to go," I whispered against his lips. Using every ounce of willpower I possessed, I pushed myself away and stood gazing down at him, my heart tight in my chest. "Take care of yourself, okay?"

"You too, blondie." He gave me another smile, this one coming all the way from his heart. Then I took Boone's arm, pulled him up, shoved him toward the back door, and froze. I did the *shh* sign across my lips. I swear if someone hadn't invented that sign we'd all be dead.

"Deckard," I whispered, pointing to a shadowy figure passing by the rear dining room window.

"Is the back door locked?"

"I was busy."

Think, Reagan, think! I snatched a coat from the donate pile that Dinky and I had assembled and tossed it around Boone because no way would it fit him. He stared at me wide-eyed as I wrapped three scarves around his neck, covering his chin and draping down his front. I added a floppy hat, then shoved a big pink purse that I had no idea why I took to consign in the first place at him. Boone's pants and shoes wouldn't fool a woman, but Deckard was no woman, he was just a slimy creep.

"This worked before," I whispered to Boone, then shoved him into the display window next to Gwendolyn, positioned his arms mannequin-like, tossed a scarf around his shoes to hide them, and then sat back on the steps, heart pounding, as Deckard strolled into the hallway.

"You're not allowed to come into my house like this, you know," I said to Deckard, my voice wobbly and my legs shaking.

Deckard's teeth flashed against the dim light and he flipped on the dining room chandelier, the brightness stretching out into the hall. "I am if I think there's illegal activity going on."

Deckard prowled his way around the furniture I'd just assembled. He paused in front of the closet Dinky and I had arranged and yanked the clothes apart, hangers flying out into the air.

"Running a consignment shop isn't exactly illegal," I said as Deckard ambled my way. "My permits are up to date, I have insurance, and I pay my taxes."

Deckard stopped by Dinky's desk, which was way too close to the display window. I needed a distraction; I needed to keep Deckard focused on me and not looking around. Maybe if I acted a little crazy or maybe afraid, anything to keep his attention away from the blasted display window.

"Your office?" Deckard asked.

"Maybe."

"It's that chick's who works for Boone, I recognize that flower stapler piece of crap. You're just one big happy family here, aren't you?" Deckard's eyes went to thin slits, his jaw set. "So where is he?"

"Where's who?"

Deckard started toward me and BW's back arched, his tail stiff, eyes glowing, and he growled deep in his doggie throat.

Deckard stopped. "I should shoot that dog."

My back arched, my eyes glowed, and I growled, and it was not acting at all, just pure gut reaction. "Bad things happen to people who shoot dogs, Officer Deckard."

His lip curled. "You're threatening me, blondie?"

"Bad things happen to people who shoot dogs. They can be walking along and just keel over, and lo and behold if someone didn't poison their doughnut or their coffee or put a rattlesnake in their car, a scorpion in their bed. Maybe someone just throws the jackass in the river and no one ever finds him again. Bad things happen to people who kill dogs."

Deckard didn't move a muscle for a full minute, my eyes not leaving his. "You're a scary person, Reagan Summerside."

"No one messes with my family."

"Does Boone know what he's getting himself into?"

"Get out of my house."

Deckard turned and headed for the kitchen. He disappeared around the corner and I heard the door click shut, and then Deckard's shadow passed by the dining room window. "Well done, Reagan Summerside," Boone said from the display window, not daring to move a hair just yet.

"The bastard threatened our dog."

Chapter Twenty

I TURNED off the chandelier, then peeked around Boone and gazed out into the dark. Cones of streetlight dotted the sidewalks; porch lights were like a string of pearls running down Gwinnett. "Think he'll be back?" I asked Boone, still in the display window.

"Not tonight, but the next time he shows up he'll be playing for keeps and it won't be pretty. You pissed him off."

"The feeling's mutual."

Boone slowly backed up, then hopped out of the window and flattened himself against the wall. "In case you have nosy neighbors."

"In case?" That brought a smile. "All I have are nosy neighbors; the good part is they like you better than they like me. I'm the one who lets BW get away and poop in their flower beds."

Boone snagged me around the waist and brought me to him hard, his dark mysterious eyes gazing down at me. He smoothed back my hair and planted a kiss on my forehead.

"That's the best you got?"

His eyes went coal black. "What I got we can't start now."

"You're not going to jail."

"It's not looking too good right now and . . . and if things don't get better . . . like you said, I'm not going to jail."

"Take me with you."

He smiled the way only Boone can, with a soft gleam in his eyes that bordered on devilment. "And then I'd have to take your mamma, Auntie KiKi, BW, and probably even the Abbott sisters."

"No Chantilly or Mercedes?"

"Yeah, Chantilly and Mercedes, too." Then he kissed me again, hard and fast and a bit desperate. He took my hand and headed for the kitchen, not exactly the room of the house I was hoping for.

"What are we doing?"

"Eating. I'm starved and you have ham and cheese and whole-wheat bread and an avocado. I love avocados when they're perfectly ripe and—"

"Waitaminute." I yanked Boone to a stop right there in the hallway. "You know what's in my fridge? You're the one who filled my fridge, and you're the one who ate most of the food Mamma dropped off."

I parked my hands on my hips, bits and pieces falling together. "How did you get out of my bathroom when Deckard came calling, and why is BW always sleeping in the hallway? You're . . . you're living here!"

"Sometimes." I gave him the *bite me* look. "Most of the time."

"And you never told me, and I was worried where you were and—"

"You were worried?" He tried to kiss me.

"That's not going to work this time, lawyer boy. Yes, I was worried and all the time you were . . . Where were you?" I glanced around. "Where the heck were you?"

"You have an attic; actually it's more like a third floor that a lot of older houses have and got blocked off over the years. There's an access panel in the hallway that you can crawl through, and in the bathroom there's—"

"I didn't finish off under the sink in case I needed to get to the plumbing again, an old house hazard. It leads to the attic." I punched Boone in the arm. "Why didn't you tell me you were here?"

"Well, you see, you sort of get this dopey look when you talk about me," Boone said, looking a little smug.

"You rat."

"You're the one who looks dopey and it's cute, actually it's adorable, but if you knew I was right over your head, well, everybody would know I was here."

"Mamma knew, didn't she? That's why I got the care package and why it all disappeared so fast. You're the one who got rid of that stalker guy, and you're the one who pulled that fire alarm at the Plantation Club and pulled me away from getting run over by that truck. And you ate all my Fig Newtons. How'd you know about the third-floor attic? I didn't even know how to get up there. You know more about my house than I do?"

Boone ran his hand over his rough chin and studied the hardwood floor. "I sort of had your house appraised. Look," he rushed on. "When you were divorcing Hollis, he wanted to sell the place and I talked him out of it."

"And I got the house. All along I thought it was because Hollis didn't want people to think he was a complete ass, except Hollis is a complete ass and no way would he not sell the house and kiss off all that money." My eyes shot wide open. "You paid him for my house?"

"No, of course not. I waived my attorney fees and we called it even, so can we eat now or what?"

It was after midnight; BW was in my bed and Boone wasn't. Deckard knew something was going on when he showed up tonight, and like Boone said, the next time he came calling it would be with a warrant and half the Savannah police department. They'd find the attic.

I stared at the ceiling from my mattress on the floor and watched shadows dance across the cracks that needed plastering and painting. I'd told Boone about Russell not buying the Old Harbor Inn, and we agreed that if he did knock off Conway and frame Boone for it, Russell wouldn't have walked away from the deal. We also agreed Tucker had to be spitting mad and that he was suspect number one. The problem was still how to prove it.

DINKY WAS AT THE FOX AT NINE SHARP WITH A fresh fruit salad and mini muffins and a little bit of baby puke down her back that we got cleaned up. The phone guys said they'd come tomorrow to work their magic and set

Dinky up with a fax. I got in a platform rocker, twin beds, a nice yellow rug, and two desk lamps. A moving truck pulled to the curb and unloaded a dining room set, a step stool, and four bar stools and said the consigner would come around later to fill out the papers.

"This is never going to work," Dinky said to me as I dragged furniture around to arrange things. "You're too busy; it's like a three-ring circus here."

I swiped hair from my face and massaged my achy arms. "Yeah, now I got a house full of furniture but I need customers. The customer part is the whole point."

"I know," Dinky said with a clever look on her face. "I'll move my desk into the kitchen. That way I'll be out of the traffic area and closer to the coffee. Great idea, huh?"

Now I had no bed, no money, no customers, and no kitchen, but Dinky did bring fruit salad and muffins. "Sure, I'll help you. We can lift the door off the back of the two chairs and take it into the kitchen, then come back and get the chairs and just reassemble the—"

"There you are!" Tucker Adkins yelped as he staggered through the door and into the hall. His eyes looked like Google Maps, his breath at about eighty proof and counting, his suit wrinkled and dirty, no shower, no shave, lots of odor.

"You've ruined my life." He waved his hand in the air. "Everything was going to work out and then you had to start poking around, make Russell nervous, and now he's gone."

"Actually I think he's just down at the Savannah River Inn."

Eyes huge, Dinky inched closer to me and held my hand. Tucker picked up the flowered stapler from her desk and threw it across the room, breaking one of the lamps that had just arrived.

"The Old Harbor Inn should be mine," Tucker slurred. Dinky squeezed my hand hard as Tucker added, "I shouldn't have to wait for Boone to get out of the way to get it. It's mine! Conway bought it with my mother's money."

"Pisses you off, does it?"

Dinky gave me a *shut the heck up* look and Tucker pushed the fax machine off the desk; the machine crashed, pieces scattered everywhere. I took that as a yes, he was ticked.

"Wish Boone never showed up?" I said, trying for more information as Dinky kicked me in the shins.

Tucker hurled the lamp on Dinky's desk across the room.

"Wish Boone were dead? Glad Conway is? How did you get Boone's gun from his desk? Swipe a key? Get a locksmith?"

"Key?" Tucker blinked, trying to fight through the alcohol fog. "Gun?" He wobbled. "I didn't kill Conway. Russell came to me, said he'd take care of everything."

Tucker stumbled, then tumbled onto the desk; the door listed to one side, then flipped up and smacked Tucker on the forehead, sending him backward onto the floor, completely knocked out.

"Dear Lord above!" Dinky shrieked, her hair standing straight up. She took a closer look. "Is he dead?"

Dinky nudged Tucker's arm with her toe, and I bent down and felt his neck like they do in the movies. "He's alive . . . I think."

"Too bad. What do we do now, call the police?"

"Freaking no, not the cops. Let's call his wife. Poor Steffy Lou, she's got to live with this . . . thing. I don't know her phone number."

"I do. She and Mr. Boone were on that theater project together." Dinky retrieved her computer off the floor and pried it open, and the screen came to life. Dinky folded her hands and gazed skyward. "And God bless Apple." She scurried over to her iPhone, which had skittered into the corner, and punched in the numbers.

"Uh, Mrs. Adkins," Dinky started. "Your husband is out cold over here at the Prissy Fox on Gwinnett, and I hate to be the bearer of bad news but he's still alive, he's just sort of a big blob in the hallway. So if you could come get him we'd be mighty grateful." Dinky disconnected.

"Bad news? A big blob on the floor?"

"I was nervous."

I looked back to Tucker, and Dinky did the same; then she jumped back. "He's making noises!" She picked up her flowered stapler and stood over Tucker in battle mode. "I'll protect us."

I leaned closer. "I think he's snoring."

A car squealed to a stop at the curb and I caught sight of Steffy Lou hustling up the walk. She threw open the front door. "Land of Goshen, can anything else happen in my life?"

She nudged Tucker with the toe of her shoe, and her nudge was a lot harder than Dinky's. "Get up, you drunken sot, you're embarrassing yourself to no end and me right along with it. I do declare, sometimes I wonder what in the world I got myself into marrying you like I did. I could have been on Broadway."

For a second I thought Steffy Lou might burst into song, but instead she pulled Tucker's big beefy arm to get him up. Not wanting Tucker in our hallway, Dinky and I each grabbed a leg.

"To the car," Steffy directed, dragging Tucker out onto the porch, and Dinky and I followed. Pushing and pulling, we manhandled Tucker Adkins to the white Lexus SUV. Steffy Lou opened the back hatch, and it took all three of us to hoist the two-hundred-plus pounds of inebriated fat into the back.

Dinky ran back inside to answer her phone, which was ringing like no tomorrow, and Steffy Lou said to me, "My housekeeper will help once I get him home." She leaned heavily against the car. "First I lose Harper; now Tucker's off the deep end, and if something doesn't happen right fast the Tybee Theater will go to Grayden Russell." Steffy Lou swiped away a tear. "I just can't let that happen. I'll have to figure something out. She looked back to me. "I hate to ask, but I'd be mighty grateful if you'd lend a hand."

"Steffy Lou, if I had a spare dime, you'd be the first person I'd give it to."

She smiled oh-so-sweetly, just like a true Southern belle. "Not that, honey. I just need to sit with somebody and chat a spell. I know you're tied up with trying to find Walker innocent, but maybe together we can come up with a way to save the theater. You were so helpful with the Odilia chant. I'll have Blanch make us up a batch of her shortbread cookies. They are truly divine."

"Does eight work for you?" How could I say no to Steffy Lou after all she'd been through, and of course there were shortbread cookies to consider and seeing the Hampton Lillibridge House up close and personal.

"Why, that will be perfect." Steffy Lou brightened and started for the driver's side, then turned back. "Tucker's a lot of things, you know, but he's no killer. He didn't do in his own daddy. He simply doesn't have it in him. Tucker's all show and bluster, and a bit of a drunk at times. If we put our heads together, maybe we can figure out who's responsible for these terrible murders. I never did like that Russell person, maybe because he's after my theater, but there's just something about him you can't trust."

Steffy Lou drove off, and I caught up with Dinky cleaning her desk off the floor. "And here I thought working at a law office was drama. Lordy, honey, if I worked here I'd be on Prozac in no time at all."

Except for the busted fax machine and broken lamp, we got Dinky back in business in the kitchen. Auntie KiKi buzzed in for a second to say she and Uncle Putter were doing a charity golf outing at Sweet Marsh Country Club and not to have fun while she was gone. By four Dinky declared her nerves totally shot, that she couldn't put two intelligent thoughts together if her life depended on it, and she was headed for home with a good bottle of wine.

I gussied up Gwendolyn in chic business attire and set her behind a desk in the display window, then added a "Furniture for Sale" banner that I ran off on Dinky's printer. I missed selling cute clothes, I really did, but there was no use in taking them in if all my customers were at the boutique shopping their little ol' hearts out.

Hoping for a little more business, I stayed open till seven

before closing up. I headed for a shower and peeked under the vanity to the gaping hole I'd left in back and nearly forgotten about. I wondered where Boone was now. I doubted he was in the attic, but he wasn't far away, I just knew it, I could feel it.

I pulled on white capris and a navy top and pilfered a bouquet of roses and hydrangeas from KiKi's garden. No Southern woman would show up to tea and cookies empty handed, but expensive florist flowers were out of the question.

"Well, aren't you the sweetest thing to be bringing me flowers," Steffy Lou said when she answered the door. "I do declare, after the day I've had, they surely are a lovely sight."

"This is an amazing home," I said to Steffy Lou as we headed to the back of the house. The place wasn't all that big, but every nook and cranny was done to perfection with just the right antique, painting, or expensive acquisition. "Is the house really as haunted as they say?"

"Oh my, yes, shadows and noises all the time; it certainly is haunted and probably going to get worse before it gets better." Steffy Lou put the flowers on the tea table, then turned around with a lovely Southern belle smile on her face and a gun in her hand. "Now why don't you take a seat over there by Tucker. He's a little drunk and he's passed out at the moment, but that's all part of the plan. The fact that he overindulged and had a hissy at your place was just an extra bonus I hadn't counted on."

I didn't move, I couldn't. I just stared at Tucker Adkins slumped over in a gorgeous peach brocade wingback chair next to a piecrust cherry table set with a silver tea service and cookies. Steffy Lou gave me a hard shove. "Move along now, ya hear?" She waved her gun toward a matching peach chair. "These were my dear grandmother's. She left them to me in her will. They were owned by Robert E. Lee himself, and Tucker intended to sell them to pay off his marina. Fact is, he intended to sell my house here and move me out to the wilds of some godforsaken marsh so he could afford his boats. I gave up everything for him. I gave up Broadway, I gave up the theater, until I get one of my own on Tybee."

"You . . . you killed Conway!" I sat in the peach chair mostly because I couldn't stand.

"I had to, dear, you can understand that. Mr. Financial Wizard is in hock up to his eyeballs. Conway cut us off and then left the cash in his estate to that clinic place and the inn to Walker. I had to fix things. I even had Harper helping me out by planting those pictures in Boone's house and setting that fire at the theater to drum up support."

"And she spiked my drink? I could have killed my own auntie!"

"That was the plan. Then Harper got greedy and planned to blackmail me. She had to go."

I took a deep breath. "You killed Conway, framed Walker, so Tucker will inherit the inn?"

"And now dear Tucker has to go. If he gets the inn he'll sell it to save his marina. If I get the inn, I sell it and the money goes to save the theater, a true philanthropic endeavor. And the bonus is that I can sell his marina to pay the mortgage on my lovely home here. It's a perfect plan, you see."

"You just can't kill Tucker. People will know, and why am I part of this?"

"You just don't get it, do you? You're the worm on the hook. Where you go, Walker goes, and of course he has to die. Conway, Walker, Tucker, then me, that's how the inn gets passed on. It has to wind up with me."

Steffy Lou looked at the hall clock as it bonged out the half hour. "And it's just a matter of time now before Walker shows up. I left a little note taped to your door that says Tucker's the killer, like you figured it out all by yourself. Walker the wonder boy is going to come looking for Tucker, thinking you've gotten in over your head like you always do and not suspect a thing when he sees me."

"Hey, I do not always get in over my head."

"Look where you're sitting, dear. I'll simply shoot Walker with Tucker's gun and make it look as if Tucker did the deed, then had brother's remorse and took his own life. Messy, but all good drama is terribly messy. After it's all over I'll go retrieve my note."

"Why would anyone think Boone would come here? He's a wanted man, there's a price on his head."

"And Tucker put that price on his head to try to get Walker in jail quick so he could get the inn. The way people will see this is that Walker is a distraught individual. He's already killed the father who abandoned him, so it makes perfect sense that he'd go after the brother who cheated him out of everything. You're collateral damage. You came to keep Boone, the man you love, from making a terrible mistake and got caught in the crossfire."

"What crossfire?"

"Honey, he's coming to save you; he'll have a gun."

"And you'll be the witness to all this."

"I'm a performer; I could have been on the New York stage. *I am magnificent!*" Steffy Lou squared her shoulders and tipped her chin, and if she burst forth with "Give My Regards to Broadway" I'd strangle her with my own two hands, the consequences be damned.

A weapon, I needed a weapon. There were tea and cookies, a fire poker just beyond, and a quick shadow in the mirror over the mantel. Here's the thing, it could be Boone, meaning I'd have backup if I tried something. Or it could be one of the infamous Hampton Lillibridge ghosts. Never in all my born days did I think my life would depend on ghost or no ghost.

"I think I'd like some tea," I said to Steffy Lou, my heart pinballing around in my chest.

"Last meal and all, help yourself."

I picked up the teapot. Steffy Lou looked back to the clock, and I took the lid off the pot and threw it in Tucker's face. He jumped awake, blubbering and drooling. Steffy Lou looked to him and I jumped on her as Boone tore in the back door. The gun went off; a vase of immaculate white magnolia blooms blasted into the air as we wrestled Steffy Lou to the floor.

"Let me go," she yelled. "I have to save the theater, it's my destiny."

I handed Boone a gold tasseled window tieback for Steffy Lou's wrists and laughed. "You're not a ghost."

"I think I've come close a few times this week." Boone laughed back, fatigue melting from his face.

I leaned back against the blue love seat, with Boone beside me. Tucker staggered awake, rubbed his eyes, and tried to focus. "Walker. What are you doing in my house? I've had enough of this. I'm calling the cops."

"Tucker, for once in your life do something," Steffy Lou bellowed as Deckard barged through the front door, with Ross right beside him.

Arms spread, I jumped up in front of Boone in full defensive mode yelling, "He's innocent, He's innocent! Don't shoot! Don't shoot!"

All smiles, Boone stood up next to me. "They know, blondie." He put his arm around me. "It's okay. They know it's a setup just like I knew."

I watched the uniformed cops haul the arguing Steffy Lou and Tucker out the door, and I looked from Ross to Deckard to Boone. "I don't get it. Why didn't I know it was a setup?"

"That's because you didn't see the note on the front door," Deckard shrugged. "*Walker, it's Tucker.* Steffy Lou might just as well have written *I did it.*"

"Because?"

"Because you never ever call me Walker."

"Boone," I said on a breath.

"The note said *Tucker*," Boone added. "So it wasn't Tucker, and the only other person living here who would want us to get here is Steffy Lou. Once I had the name it all made sense. I figured it was just a matter of time before Deckard got that search warrant, and he saw the note, too."

"And you," Ross said to Boone with a big grin on her face, "can go home."

Boone stood there for a second taking it all in. Then he smiled and took my hand, and we walked outside into the perfect spring night.

"Now what do we do for fun?" I asked as we ambled along.

Boone picked up a corner of his frayed hoodie, sniffed, and made a face. "For starters I need a shower, and the next thing I'm going to do is burn these jeans."

"Well, Mr. Walker Boone." I took hold of his sweatshirt and gazed up into his oh-so-handsome face. "You just happen to own a really nice inn about two blocks away. Bet there's a vacancy." I kissed him, savoring the feel of his lips on mine. "I have to tell you, I could do with a vacancy right now, maybe longer than now? A week?"

Boone kissed me this time, as my toes curled against my flip-flops, my heart dancing. "I want more."

"Okay, a month." My mouth laughed against his. "It's a really nice inn with a terrific view, wonderful breakfast, the valet's a super guy. You're going to like this inn, I promise."

"I want you." Boone smoothed back my hair, starlight in his eyes. "I can't imagine life without you. My life would be a bore without you in it. You're the one, Reagan Lee Summerside, the only one, and I want us to be together forever. Marry me?"